LAST TENKO

This novel is based on the
BBC-TV series created by
Lavinia Warner
and written by
Jill Hyem
and **Anne Valery**

Produced by Ken Riddington
and Vere Lorrimer
Directed by David Tucker,
Jeremy Summers
and Michael Owen Morris

LAST TENKO
Michael Hardwick

British Broadcasting Corporation

Published by the
British Broadcasting Corporation
35 Marylebone High Street
London W1M 4AA

ISBN 0 563 20324 2

First printed 1984

Printed in England by
Cox & Wyman Ltd,
Cardiff Road, Reading, Berkshire

Contents

Cast·List

Marion Jefferson	ANN BELL
Rose Millar	STEPHANIE BEACHAM
Sister Ulrica	PATRICIA LAWRENCE
Dr Beatrice Mason	STEPHANIE COLE
Mrs Van Meyer	ELIZABETH CHAMBERS
Dorothy Bennett	VERONICA ROBERTS
Christina Campbell	EMILY BOLTON
Kate Norris	CLAIRE OBERMAN
Sally Markham	JOANNA HOLE
Jocelyn Holbrook	JEAN ANDERSON
Blanche Simmons	LOUISE JAMESON
Verna Johnson	ROSEMARY MARTIN
Miss Hasan	JOSEPHINE WELCOME
Dr Natalie Trier	CAROLLE ROUSSEAU
Lillian Cartland	PHILIPPA URQUHART
Major Yamauchi	BURT KWOUK
Captain Sato	EIJI KUSUHARA
Shinya	TAKASHI KAWAHARA
Kasaki	TAKAHIRO OBA
Lieutenant Nakamura	SABU KIMURA
General Shimojo	KRISTOPHER KUM
Clifford Jefferson	JONATHAN NEWTH
Maggie Thorpe	ELIZABETH MICKERY
Phyllis Bristow	ELSPET GRAY
Stephen Wentworth	PRESTON LOCKWOOD
Jake Haulter	DAMIEN THOMAS
Script Editors	EVGENY GRIDNEFF
	and DEVORA POPE

1 Home

For some reason, which eluded her, Marion did not turn off the tree-shaded pavement of Alexandra Road into the driveway of the house. She stopped and stood there in the humid heat, and surveyed her home.

As always, she admired its almost prim colonial neatness: a benevolent colonel's lady of a house, dignified without being forbidding, impeccably turned out in white, down to where the slope of the verandah roof marked the hipline's outward curve; feminine also in its trim but colourful flower borders, the razored lawns and constantly raked gravel pathways and drive as immaculately groomed as Marion herself; and she was a colonel's lady, too.

From first sight she had thought it a delightful house, by far the best she and Clifford Jefferson had been allocated in fifteen years. When she had married him as a subaltern at Aldershot it had been in the knowledge that 'home', throughout his career in the Service, would be no fixed point in a world of movement and change. Only shallow roots would be possible, when each two or three years in a place would end in yet another move to another, half a world away perhaps, with a different climate, a different race and tongue, different smells, a different pace and style of life, different acquaintances of one's own sort, in the usual proportions of friendly, agreeable, aloof, and obnoxious.

England, India, Hong Kong, England again, Hong Kong again: the sequence had progressed predictably as the British Army moved its pieces about the chessboard of the Empire, sometimes purposefully, as often merely a move for movement's sake. Step by step, in slow peacetime sequence, Clifford Jefferson had moved in rank also. It had been an anxious progress for him and Marion both: captain had been a worrying sticking point for several years, the barrier between it and field rank looking more impenetrable as Clifford's fair hair began to fade from more than tropical influences, and his forties approached.

Suddenly, though, there came a war, and with one mighty bound he was over the hurdle, and wearing a major's crowns. The whole outlook was changed. Instead of having to worry that if one hadn't made half-colonel by a certain age, one had, like the unwanted spinster, set one's cap in vain, the possibilities were now limitless. Full colonel, brigadier, general even – all was possible to the sound career officer who chanced to find himself in the right place at the right time. A friend of theirs had gone home one night a lieutenant and issued forth next morning an acting-brigadier, to the awe of his friends and the confusion of his enemies.

Like him, they would all get cut down to size again when the war was over and the temporary appointments disappeared.

'You can get too far too fast, darling,' Clifford had said without envy as they discussed their friend's meteoric preferment. 'Can you see Toby climbing down from those rarefied heights?'

'Certainly not Angela,' Marion had said, referring to the new brigadier's wife, who was rumoured to have spent hundreds on accoutring herself for her new role.

'There's only one cure for lasting altitude sickness,' said Clifford, 'and that's a bowler hat. Go on calling yourself Brigadier and grab a good civvy job on the strength of it. But you're finished with the army, unless you can get a taste back for humbler pie.'

'*Definitely* not Angela.' Marion was sure, and knew that in the same circumstances she would feel the same way about it as the brigadier's wife.

'Here we go,' Clifford told her one day some months later, holding out a closed fist for her to open. In his palm lay four shining, crested stars, two for each epaulette, to place above the crowns. He had been made a full colonel.

Marion did not spend a penny on new outfits. Not a dollar, rather, for the posting which had carried the promotion with it was to Singapore. They had a slap-up champagne dinner, though, just the two of them, in the renowned Raffles Hotel. It was September 1941.

This fine house went with the job and the red collar tabs and hatband. Its previous occupant had been a senior civilian administrative officer, now retired and gone back with his wife to face the onset of English winter after the steam-bath heat of Malaya. They took all their things with them, so, to Marion's relief, she was able to bring her own furniture from Hong Kong and feel only half-uprooted this time. With more living space than ever before, she thought yet again of bringing twelve-year-old Ben out from his boarding-school at home. It was a notion which often recurred, but much as she longed to have him with her she resigned herself again to leaving him where his education would have continuity.

So Clifford and Marion Jefferson settled into their respective spheres: he behind a General Headquarters desk, she into the inevitable round of coffee visits, cosy chats, gossipy lunches, the Thé Dansant, and the frequent hair-dos that the climate demanded if she were to stay immaculate beyond criticism. If she stopped to think about it all it was pretty boring. She was not given to intellectual pursuits, nor to idle ones, and was not tempted to enliven things with amorous adventures, the scope for which increased almost daily, as in the weeks leading to Christmas there began to be many more uniforms wherever she went in the cosmopolitan island city.

But thinking about her way of life and especially allowing it to make her feel discontented were things she had long since stopped herself doing. She was a Service wife, with

9

all that that implied, chief of which was to provide her husband with his escape from the formality and protocol and demands of responsibility. Hers was the gentle touch in an austere career. It was the life she had chosen. Many privileges as well as irritations went with it, and she had learned to accept whatever it brought her, and be thankful for it.

This fine house was the biggest material bonus so far, she thought, as she stood gazing at it. Its feeling of unfamiliarity had lasted only a matter of days. Their things had fitted in like a dream, and they themselves were soon as at home as if they had been living there for years. It was only a shame that Clifford had to be away so much. Everything had become so restless in Singapore since soon after their arrival. His inspection trips on the peninsula had become far more frequent and his absences longer. He was away now. He seemed to have been gone ages. How many days was it? She suddenly couldn't remember.

Come to think of it, she couldn't remember how she came to be here at this moment, standing outside her house, just staring at it. She was very hot. One perspired all day in the humidity, which was the worst feature of this place, but why had she been crazy enough to *walk* all the way from Robinson's department store, carrying the shopping, which was dragging her arms down and making her shoulders ache so? Why hadn't Ali brought her in the car?

And that was odd, too – where had Ali been lately? And Dolah, the indoor manservant, so unobtrusive in his presence and movements, so deft with a decanter and glass that he often seemed to magic the cool, ice-clinking drink into one's hand before one had finished asking for it.

Minah, too, her own maid: rather dour and not given to chat – which Marion had put down to longstanding loyalty to the old mistress whom she had served for so many years, and resentment at this new one who had taken her place. Perhaps, Marion had thought once or twice, Minah saw her as one of that younger generation of Europeans, who but for being a Service wife would never have known what it was to have servants; true enough, as it happened. But where *was* Minah?

Although Marion would die rather than tell Clifford, she would give up the whole lot of them just to be home in England – not merely another posting, but for good. She had seen all she wanted of the world, which seemed to her mostly made up of South-East Asia.

A quiet place, somewhere in Kent or Sussex, with Clifford pottering in tweeds, herself in twin-set and country shoes calling him in for a preprandial G & T which she'd mixed with her own hands, and Ben banging about in his room upstairs. The narrow, unambitious aspiration of a woman in her late thirties, she knew – but grant her it, and she would never once complain of the cold, or being unable to get a reliable girl to come in for just half a day a week, or that the postman called too seldom and there wasn't enough happening in the neighbourhood . . .

Perspiration trickled from her armpits and her dress clung to her, damp and hot. Her feet ached from the long, foolish trek all the way up to the suburb from downtown, and with such a weight of shopping. Why hadn't Ali driven her? Or she could have taken a taxi – even a rickshaw, though that wasn't done by a colonel's wife, and one wouldn't have come this far out from the centre anyway.

Now she noticed a curious thing – the white-painted farm-style gate was drawn shut across the mouth of the driveway. The gravel was as flat as the grass, for the gardener always restored it as soon as any tyre marks or footprints had sullied it. The car was not in sight. No servants were in sight. Marion heard herself give a little sob of alarm as she saw that the shutters were drawn fast across every window. And as her gaze traversed the lawn, she realised that, instead of flowers, the ornamental borders were planted out with the uniform dull green of vegetables.

She went to move towards the gate – but couldn't. The weight of the beastly shopping-bags seemed to be anchoring her fast. She tried to loosen her grip to drop them, but they wouldn't leave her. She began frantically trying to work her hands open-shut-open-shut, but the weight grew heavier and the pain in her shoulders intensified. Her feet would not lift. She opened her mouth to call for Dolah, Minah – but no sound would come out.

She knew she was paralysed. Some unnoticed bite, some bug activated by the stupid long walk . . . She was helpless to move, to cry out . . . even to let herself go and fall down. . . She closed her eyes.

And then came the noise in her head – a bell clanging like a summons to school, only more urgent, more insistent; and, bearing in under it, and then louder so as to match the pitch and clangour of the bell, a voice, just as insistent: '*Tenko! Tenko! TENKO!* . . .'

Marion opened her eyes wide, and knew where she really was and how she came to be there – and she burst into tears.

2 A Change of Clothes

The reason she was sweating so profusely was because the wooden hut, on the bare floor of which she was lying, stood exposed to the full glare of the sun, which had been beating on it throughout the day; and because the space in the hut, whose door was shut fast, was occupied not only by Marion, but by a small crowd of other women, who were sweating as she sweated, whose clothes were as filthy and ragged as hers, and whose bodies and hair were in equal need of washing.

The ache in her arms and shoulders and legs was real, attributable to having piggy-backed a small child over miles of rough track along which she had had barely enough strength to keep going herself. The unnecessary walk from downtown Singapore to leafy Alexandra Road had been the dream journey of an exhausted doze, following a forced march of several days' duration. Now that her eyes were really open there stood no elegant house for them to see. Home for the colonel's lady now was this oven of a hut, and her social circle was reduced to these other women internees, who, because of her surrogate rank, had elected her their leader.

It was not from self-pity, though, that Marion Jefferson began to cry when she awoke to the truth of it all. It was something less personal and far sadder that moved her to unaccustomed tears as memory of it flooded back.

'It was my fault,' she sobbed. 'I should have insisted. Should have . . .'

A hand, hot and rough-skinned, came down on her forehead and stroked it gently.

'Not your fault at all,' urged a gentle, accented voice close to her ear. 'You could not have prevented her from being bitten.'

'They blame me.' Marion's reference was to her companions. Before exhausted sleep had claimed her for an hour, and granted her the doubtful release of a phantom vision of the home she had last seen a year ago, there had been grumbles about her fitness to be leader and spokesman. That was nothing new; nor was their chief source, the once-pampered nouveau riche Dutchwoman Mrs Van Meyer, with her air of superiority to them all and resolute refusal to undertake any responsibility and none but the minimum of work. Mrs Van Meyer complained so often, and about everything, that none of it went deep. Her accusation that if Marion had insisted to their Japanese captors that their party should not be split up, their friends Nellie, Sylvia and Blanche would not have been taken off to some other destination, was nonsense. One did not insist anything to the Japanese: one humbly requested, and nineteen times out of twenty got a refusal. In any case, Mrs Van Meyer had cared no more for the departed women than she did for any of the rest of them.

It was for another loss that Marion woke to grieve immediately. On the march from their old camp to this new one, Debbie Bowen, still pretty despite her privations, her adolescence blighted by her mother's death, had suffered the bite of some unseen insect and died, with them helpless to do anything more for her than pray, led by the Dutch nun, Sister Ulrica. It was her hand that offered rough comfort to Marion's brow.

'I tried so hard to take her mother's place,' Marion said miserably, mastering the tears and hoping that none of the others had been aware of them. 'I'd made her my responsibility. . .'

'My dear, Debbie was quite old enough to know better than to wander off the track on her own. She knew the

14

insects that infest the jungle. We were all so tired, and perhaps she did not even know what she was doing.'

'I suppose you're right, Ulrica. It's this feeling of help-lessness – *nothing* one can do. . .' She started up suddenly, alarmed at the memory of the bell ringing.

'Tenko! Roll-call. Why isn't anyone moving?'

Sister Ulrica stared at her. 'Tenko? There has been no summons. Besides, we are still locked in here.'

Marion sank back. 'I must have dreamed it. I expect we'll go on hearing "Tenko!" for the rest of our lives.'

'Let us hope not,' replied Sister Ulrica, a little grimly in view of the implication the remark carried. 'Anyway,' she added as brightly as her solemn manner allowed, 'they have quite a nice little bell here. A proper one, not that dreadful metal triangle. It was ringing for something else just before you woke up. I imagine this used to be a mission station, with a school. Perhaps there will be more space. Some room for a separate sick-bay, even.'

She turned to look towards the doorway, where Rose Millar and Kate Norris squatted on their haunches native fashion, talking with Dorothy Bennett, Sally Markham, and the oldest member of the group, Joss Holbrook, who had been added to their number during their long journey. Unquestionably a lady was Joss, despite her propensity to swear, which Service life had taught Marion to associate with naval wives. Joss had volunteered nothing about herself since she had joined them after having been separ-ated from another party. Her fractured right arm was in a sling, splinted with a piece of chair-leg.

Their doctor, Beatrice Mason, was unable to move from the floor where she sat – her feet were lacerated from having walked so far. Marion had recently noticed that Beatrice, to whom they all looked for the strength that lay in her professional experience, had taken to peering closely at things as though her keen, rather hard eyes had lost some of their sharpness. Her hair was distinctly whitening and her shoulders beginning to round. But then, none of them

15

had improved under the auspices of the Imperial Japanese Army. At best, they were lucky to be alive. None of them was more than partially fit after a year of near-starvation diet and the kind of work that would have been beneath their own household servants in those languid, unthinking, often boring days preceding December 1941; and now it was the first day of January 1943.

There was a scuffle of movement near the door as the women there got to their feet, painfully and stiffly, for the long march to this camp had jarred limbs made brittle by lack of calcium; their muscles strained for want of suppleness. Marion got up too, swaying at first from momentary dizziness. Footsteps had approached along the verandah, a bar was being lifted, and the door swung open admitting a blaze of sunlight.

There were no Japanese guards with rifles and bayonets silhouetted against it, but two women, one of whom stepped over the threshold with a briskness that Marion had not seen in any woman for months. She was young, clean, neatly dressed – she even wore shoes – and enviably healthy-looking. Her shoulder-length hair was drawn back in a bun and had obviously been combed carefully.

When she spoke it was with a French accent as crisp as her appearance.

'Please do not look scared. I am not a ghost. Nobody told me you had arrived, or I should have come sooner. I am Natalie Trier. Dr Natalie Trier.'

'A doctor! Oh, thank God!' sighed Beatrice Mason, who had for so long taxed her medical skill beyond its limits, denied supplies, equipment, even the most rudimentary tools of her profession.

Marion stepped forward to greet the newcomer. 'I'm Marion Jefferson, the . . .' It was suddenly beyond her to proclaim herself. Sister Ulrica did it for her.

'The leader of the British. And I am Sister Ulrica, leader of the Dutch.'

'How do you do.' With the briefest nod and twitch of a

smile the new doctor turned at once to the stretcher cases and began examining them. It was a perfunctory check to decide who needed immediate attention. The girl beside her scribbled on a slate her brisk and confident comments. Beatrice Mason, looking on, realised how slow her mind had become compared with this girl's.

'I am Mrs Van Meyer,' announced that lady important-ly. 'Why have we been locked in here?'

The doctor continued her work without glancing up.

'Isolation. A week ago a woman brought in leprosy, so I insist on examining all new internees before they are allowed to disperse.'

'What is this place? Where are we?' Rose Millar wanted to know in a tone more reasonable than the Dutch woman's; but the response was even more dismissive.

'Not now, if you don't mind. Let's get this over first. Exhaustion, some burns and boils, first-stage malaria,' she dictated to her assistant, whose slate pencil squeaked, making one or two of the women shudder at the sound remembered from infant schooldays. The attention of them all was wrested from the two strangers by the entry of another, a European girl not far into her teens, bearing a large bowl. Dorothy Bennett, the first to peer into it, gasped, 'I don't believe it! Food!'

With a general cry the women crowded round her, pushing forward the hastily-seized halves of coconut shells which had served them so long as receptacles for any meagre rations, however revolting, that had come their way.

'Mind my bloody arm!' snapped Joss Holbrook, handi-capped by having no hand free to scrabble in the big bowl for her share. Rose filled her bowl for her with the mixture of rice and vegetables, and then insisted on filling Dr Mason's before taking her own share.

'What's your name?' she asked the girl.

'Daisy.'

'Daisy what?'

17

'Robertson, miss.'

'So?' demanded Joss, her mouth half full. 'Where are we, then?'

'It's a camp.' The child's eyes were dull and she moved her lips to match whatever was said to her, as if to help her take it in. Her few words betrayed a London East-End accent. She was in fact an orphan, trained as a servant, who had come out to the East with her employers.

'I *know* it's a camp,' Joss was pressing her impatiently. 'But what sort of a camp? How big? What's it like? You know what I mean, girl.'

'It's . . . just a camp. There was missionaries here before.'

'Well who's here now besides us? A lot? Only a few? Many guards?'

'It . . . goes up and down.'

'What – the camp or the guards?'

Joss's heavy irony and her habitually brusque manner were too much for the girl. Her bowl was empty. She turned and fled. Dr Trier noticed her leaving and called to her to fetch women to bear out the stretcher cases.

After an admonitory glance at Joss, Beatrice Mason spoke to her enviably efficient French colleague.

'Dr Trier – I'm Beatrice Mason, a doctor too.'

'That's good.' There was no gratified smile though.

'I can save you the trouble with my patients – give you all the details . . .'

For answer this time, Dr Trier turned, surveyed her, and then opened the front of Beatrice's dress to sound her chest.

'. . . They've been with me for. . .'

'Could you be quiet a moment, please? Mm. Hospital for observation.'

'But I'm perfectly all right – just a bit tired.'

'Let me be the best judge of that,' said the other doctor and moved on to Mrs Van Meyer, who greeted her gushingly: 'It is so reassuring to have a Continental doctor.' It elicited no sign of appreciation. The Australian Kate Norris changed her mind about volunteering the fact that she was

18

a nurse. She decided to keep quiet about it until asked, or Beatrice Mason mentioned it, and see how the land lay, in view of this Frenchwoman's coldly clinical manner.

The stretchers were brought in. Despite her protests Beatrice was ordered to lie down on one of them. Mrs Van Meyer, almost pleased to be told that she was suffering from the early stages of beriberi and therefore qualified for some special attention, occupied another stretcher with eager haste. The two of them, together with the others still on the makeshift litters that had borne them on the march, were carried away.

Natalie Trier turned to the room in general and raised her voice for attention.

'Before my assistants escort you all to the wash-house they will attend to any minor ailments. When you reach the wash-house you will please take off all your clothes – everything – and throw them into a pile. Daisy will bring you new ones from the store.'

'New clothes!' It sounded unbelievable to them all.

'Before putting them on, make sure you wash most thoroughly all over, with particular attention to all hair. My assistants will inspect you before you dress.'

She strode away after the stretchers. Her efficiency, together with her commanding manner, her evident good health and the unmistakable vestiges of French chic in her looks and poise, would have been enough to earn her a raspberry in other circumstances. As it was, the women were too bewildered by their new surroundings and a regime so different from their old one to do more than obey meekly.

'Not one of life's little charmers,' remarked Joss to Marion, who agreed. But the sentiments of both women, like all the rest, were almost wholly taken up with the prospect of a bath and clean clothes. In peacetime Singapore the steam heat had made both a necessity at least twice daily, and, for the more socially active, several times. Now they were about to experience it for the first time in

19

an entire wretched year. Whatever else lay in store for them in this new place all felt instinctively that, clean and decent, they would find it that much easier to face.

There was apprehension in it for Sister Ulrica, in the short term. The notion of giving up her nun's habit, worn and dishevelled though it had become, disturbed her, the more so when she learned that the clothing store of which they all had such hopes included no other similar garment. Worse still was having to undress among her companions. They rallied round understandingly. The 'new' clothes turned out to be a motley heap of cast-offs from former internees who had gone on to fates better not thought about. They were an improvement, though, on what the present women were discarding without regret and had at least been boiled clean.

Some of them were men's things, including a white night-shirt, which Dorothy picked out and showed to Sister Ulrica.

'A man's shirt!' exclaimed the horrified nun.

'Oh, I've known plenty of women wear these,' Dorothy lied. 'Isn't that right, Rose?'

'Of course,' Rose backed her. 'And with a tie round the waist it's the nearest you'll get to a habit.'

Sister Ulrica resisted no further. Her more pressing worry was overcome by the percipient Dorothy calling everyone to turn their backs while Ulrica stripped naked, washed all over, and then escaped into the enveloping garment, which reached her ankles. A large handkerchief tied round her head completed the effect. On reflection she was quite pleased with the ensemble, and that in turn led her to murmur a few inward words asking forgiveness for the sin of pride.

The only other of them who greeted the new clothing with anything but enthusiasm was young Sally Markham. Marion turned from the now diminished clothing pile, holding her own limited choice from it, to notice that Sally had made no move to help herself. She was standing watching the rest of them without seeming to register what she was seeing.

Marion turned quickly back to the pile and picked up some things which she had hesitated over for herself. She took them to Sally and held them out.

'Come on, Sally. The sooner we're washed and changed, the sooner we can go back and have another lie down.' There was no response save a vague smile, so she added, 'Oh, isn't it lovely to have running water. Come on!'

Automatically, Sally accepted the clothes from her. Marion guided her by the arm to where the water trickled, with little pressure, from pipes in the adjoining wash-house, which had no doubt been kept neat and efficient under the missionaries but was now grimy and dilapidated. She took the clothes back and placed them on one side together with her own new ones, and then helped Sally out of her filthy rags before removing her own.

Marion looked down at the girl's abdomen, fearing to see marks there that would speak of lasting damage from the premature birth in the previous camp of the baby which this so public-school-type young wife had been carrying at the time of their capture. It had been a difficult delivery by Beatrice Mason, in dangerously unhygienic conditions, which the Japanese – for all their professed respect for motherhood and tenderness towards infants – had refused to alleviate.

'Because there's nothing about it in their book of rules,' Beatrice had snapped wearily when the misshapen girl-baby had been taken away in a sack for disposal. 'They're terrified of doing anything that's not a direct order, or down in black and white. Still, nothing would have saved that poor little mite.'

Relieved now to see that Sally was not physically damaged, at least externally, Marion remained worried about her as she helped her listless moves to wash herself. Naturally this young girl had been brought low by the loss of her baby and the pain and strain her enfeebled

21

constitution had had to suffer in giving birth. Her mind too was constantly on her young husband, Peter, whom she had last seen at Singapore. By now he must certainly be either dead or a prisoner – like Clifford, come to that, Marion thought, but quickly shut off that speculation, which she had long ago forbidden herself.

'Those bastards killed it,' Dorothy Bennett had said. Her infant had also died in captivity, largely from lack of nourishment. 'I'm glad now that my Violet is out of this hellish existence – glad for her sake, I mean. But the bloody Japs should never have made Sally go tree-cutting, not in her condition.'

Helping Sally dress, Marion remembered how Dorothy had lapsed into a kind of oblivion, caring neither for her baby nor herself, and she suddenly feared that Sally might be going that way too. Dorothy had come round in her own time, but as a changed woman, a fatalist who took what each day brought, and had no scruples about selling her body to the guards she despised in return for cigarettes and small favours they might condescend to do her. But Marion, though no psychologist, guessed that this was something that had been basic to Dorothy's personality all along, and had been brought to the surface by her tragedies. Unless Sally Markham was very different underneath from the outward impression she gave of the rather naïve and vulnerable public schoolgirl, depression, if allowed to become too deep, might have much further-reaching effects on her.

At the camp it had driven Sally briefly into the arms of Nellie Keene, one of those who had been split away from them instead of coming here. It had been an innocent enough craving for mutual comfort, Marion was sure, but malicious innuendo had forced her to tackle Nellie about it, and the older woman had broken it off. Marion was equally sure that Sally had had not the faintest realisation what it might have led to, and would have been horrified if it had gone that way. Yes, she was sure Sally, though wife and might-have-been mother, was as innocent as they came, and needed watching; she might well need saving again some time.

Meanwhile Marion had her own welfare to think about. Feeling as though a whole skin of filth had been removed from her, and with her pathetic change of clothing reminding her almost of wearing a new frock for the first time, she returned to the hut with the rest of them, lay down, and like the others fell almost instantly asleep. This time there followed no bewildering, disorientated return to the house in Alexandra Road; just welcome nothingness.

3 Odd Way to run a Camp

She was not mistaken: a bell was ringing; but a real bell it was, as Sister Ulrica had told her, a melodious improvement on that clattered metal triangle at the old camp which had made every summons so startlingly abrasive and potentially menacing. This bell was insistent all the same, and its summons was reinforced by the abrupt entry into the hut of Kasaki, one of the bloodier-minded of the private soldier guards. He was flourishing his rifle with its fixed bayonet and shouting in his harsh tone – '*Tenko, tenko*! Orr prisoners up! *Hayak*! Hurry, orr women!'

'Here we go again!' muttered Rose. Kasaki gave her a glare and jerked his rifle butt threateningly. Obediently they all trooped out, blinking after the welcome sleep and the hut's gloom, into the dusty quadrangle, bounded on all sides by long, frond-thatched huts with verandahs. The sun was still hot and bright but noticeably lower towards the tree-tops. Marion felt instinctively – she had no watch – that it was four o'clock. She felt stronger and more alert for the couple of hours' dreamless sleep.

Shouts of '*Mina ichi*!' from Kasaki and the less aggressive Shinya had the women forming the accustomed single file facing the hut over which the red and white Japanese flag hung limply from its pole. It was an anxious, apprehensive moment for them all, awaiting the presumed appearance of the Camp Commandant. Would he prove a natural sadist, a bitter ex-combatant reduced to the lowly task of guarding a bunch of women, which to some Japanese minds would compare unfavourably with being a cowherd? Would he be aloof and dismissive of their welfare and needs, or a perpetual haranguer about the superiority of the Japanese race and its rightful position as leader of the Asian Co-prosperity alliance, intending to create an Asia for Asians only, without scruple about the way it extinguished the remains of European presence and influence?

Apart from the fact that some were darker-skinned than others, the women had found little difference between their Japanese captors. Almost all were short in stature – as small as the average Western woman – with a few tall exceptions. Most were bandy-legged, the result of having been carried as babies strapped to their mothers' backs, with legs astraddle. A surprisingly large proportion were evidently myopic and needed thick-lensed spectacles.

They wore funny little hats not unlike jockey caps, grey-green uniforms, and the privates had on old-fashioned puttees and strange light boots with a divide separating the big toe. They carried rifles, almost invariably topped with long bayonets which they jabbed without compunction at any woman not quick enough to move at an order. Alternatively they would swing the weapon and deliver a bruising blow with its butt. They looked, sounded and behaved like peasants thrust into uniform, which was what they were: the Imperial Japanese Army was a peasant force, totally submissive to its officers, drilled mercilessly into a relentless military machine. Against all expectation it had proved that blind obedience, unhesitating readiness to attack without fear of death or wounds, and a total disregard for personal comfort or survival, together with superiority in both firepower and will-power, were too much for the soldiers of the West, who had never seen the like.

The surprise, the suddenness, the completeness of the Japanese assault on the territories of the Pacific, from Pearl Harbor and Hong Kong to Singapore, had had a shattering effect on morale. The defeatist legend had quickly spread that these were invincible fanatics, unstoppable by any means, and all too many Allied soldiers and their commanders had accepted that without putting it to the test. There

25

had been neither the time nor the available information – less still the inclination – to rationalise the Japanese character and learn that fear, not masterful confidence, was what drove this seemingly invincible soldiery.

As these women, like others in camps scattered all over the territories and men prisoners too, were beginning to recognise, the Japanese soldier was the prisoner of his breeding and upbringing: disciplined from infancy to do without comfort, let alone luxury; to obey his superiors in all things, however unreasonable; to regard death as preferable to failure and loss of face. The news of the murders, rapes and other atrocities committed by the drunken invaders of Hong Kong had fuelled the legend of a ferociously indomitable enemy. It would have been useless for anyone to try to explain that it had been merely a violent release of pressure that had been increasing since infancy, without benefit of safety-valve.

Who, in the clubs and bars of Singapore, would have taken seriously the explanation that the Japanese male infant was petted and spoiled by his mother, encouraged to regard her as his loving servant, while at the same time was sternly disciplined not to cry or wet his bed? Or that when another came along all attention immediately shifted to him, leaving his frustrated elder brother to clamour in vain for the care which up till then had been his alone, and leave him with a resentment which he would never lose? There were more than bow-legs to show for a Japanese male infancy. Like the spoiled, frustrated Western child whose pent-up fury sometimes erupts in hysteria, Japanese soldiers could go berserk at the least provocation.

It had not escaped the women's notice from their earliest captivity that the raised voice of a Japanese officer rebuking a non-com would soon be followed by that non-com bawling out the nearest private and slapping him hard across his face – and that the private would soon be heading their way to vent his wounded feelings on them, lashing out with weapon and boot against any prisoner within

26

range. They knew now that it was his way of salvaging his temporarily lost pride. It was instinctive, unpremeditated and quite quickly over – sometimes, incredibly enough, with a little gesture of kindness in its wake – but while it lasted it was frightening and dangerous. An injury inflicted in order to restore a damaged ego was as serious as any other injury.

It was pointless, they had learned, to seek redress or plead for aid for anyone who had suffered such an assault. The Japanese officers were deaf to such complaints, because they didn't understand them. To them, the existence of a pecking order was natural and justified; and nothing was more natural than that prisoners, who if they had been Japanese would have died rather than be captured, came bottom. That the women had been non-combatants made no difference; just being women ranked them low enough.

As usual the ritual of Tenko was protracted and tedious. The guards gave the impression of being unable to count above ten, so kept getting hopelessly confused over the total of women on parade, and had to start counting again. It was a pointless exercise, practised wilfully at the guards' least whim in any weather and at any time of day or night. For the sick, forced to line up with the rest, it was an added misery.

This particular Tenko proved to be one with a difference. For a while the prisoners forgot their preoccupation with itching insect bites, blistered feet and aching legs, as they stared at the figures who emerged from the hut before them and came to the front of the verandah. One was just another typical Japanese officer, squat and slightly stout, the bespectacled variety in full uniform with leather belt and pistol holster, leather jackboots and the inevitable sheathed sword, which seemed incongruously large for him. Nothing could be read from his unsmiling round face. His companion was a complete contrast – a woman, wearing a spotless, uncrumpled white frock, white shoes and earrings. Her black hair was in a roll round her head with a kiss

27

curl at the temple. Above big, attractive dark eyes were precisely painted brows, and she wore bright scarlet lipstick which set off her exotic light brown skin.

It was she who spoke, in perfect English with the sing-song lilt of the Eurasian.

'Good afternoon, internees. This is Lieutenant Naka-mura, who is Commandant of our camp.'

She turned slightly to the officer and bowed deeply from her waist. The women copied her; the requirement to bow low to any officer, so fiercely resented at first, had long since become an automatic habit. It was not worth the inevitable beating for refusing or forgetting.

Nakamura made no gesture towards the women. He gave a brief order to the woman, turned and went back into his office. She took another pace forward, straightened her back commandingly and resumed.

'My name is Miss Hasan. I am the official interpreter and I assist Lieutenant Nakamura in the administration of this camp. This camp is the best of all in Area Three, the most efficient, and has the best production figures at the factory.' Her voice and eyes hardened momentarily. 'There is no trouble here and no disobedience. All is harmony and will continue to be. Good afternoon.'

As she turned to go there came shrieks of 'Bow! Bow!' from the guards.

'Bow-wow!' mocked Joss under her breath as they obeyed before breaking ranks. 'Knock me down with a feather – a woman helping to run a Jap camp!'

'Extraordinary,' Marion agreed. '*Running* it, from the sound of her.'

'Cheeky bitch!' but the indignant Joss was about to receive an even greater surprise.

''Scuse me.' It was the East-End twang of Daisy. 'Verna says she'd like to see you now.'

'Verna? You mean that Miss Whatsername?'

'No. Verna.'

The mystifying summons was made clear by another

28

female voice, again authoritative, calling to the women in general: 'Over here, please. All of you.'

They saw her on another verandah, a middle-aged Englishwoman in a print frock and with thick hair to her shoulders. The hair shone, and as they drew near it was again evident that here was a female who had not known near-starvation for quite some time. A cat wove around her ankles. She picked the animal up and gave it to Daisy, who carried it away through the beaded curtain doorway of what was evidently Verna's room.

'Gather round everyone and make yourselves comfortable,' the woman said with a smile. 'My name's Verna Johnson. Welcome to the camp.'

Ignoring Joss's snort of outrage at this insensitive greeting Marion stepped forward to introduce herself as leader of the British women. Sister Ulrica did likewise as leader of the Dutch. To the surprise of both Verna shook hands formally with them, but Marion noticed that she seemed uninterested in their status and when she spoke it was to the whole group, in a schoolmistressy tone that implied that if anyone was anyone's leader, it was she. Her accent was of a contrived gentility, but to Marion's ear didn't disguise a hardness beneath.

To their further astonishment Daisy reappeared through the bead screen bearing a rocking chair into which Verna placed herself, gesturing the women to come and sit around her like a class of children. Then, and greatest surprise of all, Daisy went again and came back with a large jug from which wafted the unmistakable aroma of coffee.

While they were all gasping to one another, Daisy brought out a supply of coconut shells and started to go round serving them all from the pot.

'I don't believe this!' Dorothy said to the smiling Verna, having sniffed confirmation from her portion. 'How on earth d'you get coffee?'

'From the traders.'

'You mean . . . you're allowed?'

'So long as we're good.'

'It's a bloody miracle,' declared Kate. Marion noticed that it provoked a sharp glance and a frown from Verna. Continuing to observe her, she saw a similar reaction to any other expletives. Joss, Kate and Rose in particular were free with their language. Marion had grown used to it, but now she cringed a little at their crudeness, embarrassed by Verna's obvious distaste.

Verna explained that she had run an hotel up-country before being interned. She had spent all her captivity in this camp and had come to be trusted to be in charge of distribution of the limited supplies of provisions and comforts.

'It's a thankless task, having next to nothing to manage with,' she added, 'only someone has to make sure that the factory shifts get their shares in turn.'

'What's this about a factory?' Kate wanted to know.

'It makes clothing – Japanese headgear mostly.'

'The factory's not in the camp?'

'A bit of a drive away. Absolute nightmare of a road, they say.'

'You haven't had to work there?' Joss asked a little too sharply.

Verna smiled and answered easily, 'Sometimes I wish I did. My job causes some resentment, trying to keep everyone pleased. It isn't easy, you know.'

'I'll bet,' Rose murmured to Kate. 'Coffee on the verandah, and a maid.'

Dorothy was asking as casually as she could, though not sufficiently to get past Verna, 'This food and supplies – where's it all kept, then?'

Verna returned her a direct look. 'Under lock and key. Sadly, some are not quite as honest as one could wish.'

While others were asking questions, their spirits rising under the influence of the welcome and hospitality and the comparatively orderly atmosphere of the camp, Marion heard herself greeted by her christian name from behind the group. She turned to see an old school friend whom she had re-encountered in Singapore, Lillian Cartland. Marion scrambled up and the two embraced happily. Lillian was able to give her the good news that she had with her her eight-year-old son Bobby, on whom Lillian doted more than she had on her husband, it had always seemed to Marion.

Verna saw them together and called out, 'Lillian – just the person. Duty calls me, I'm afraid, but why don't you show the newcomers round the camp?'

'Pleasure, Verna.'

'Good, then. Enjoy yourselves.' She got up and went indoors, her audience dismissed.

Marion turned back to her old friend. 'You mean we're free to wander about?'

'If Verna says so.'

'What the hell is all this?' Joss demanded suspiciously. 'Couple of women giving out orders, and I'm not sure that I'd trust either of them as far as I could throw them.' She held up her bandaged arm. 'And that's not far at present.'

'They're all right if you keep on the right side of them,' Lillian explained. 'Nakamura's as blind as a bat and doesn't understand a word of English. He's happy to let the Hasan girl look after it all.'

'And after him, I don't doubt,' Joss snorted.

'Look,' replied Lillian a trifle testily, 'Hasan may be fond of herself, and stuck up and given to tantrums. Remember she's a Eurasian, and the Japs have put her to lord it over women who, let's face it, wouldn't exactly have been inviting her round to tea in the old days. I think she worked in the prison service.'

'I thought the bitch seemed at home,' Dorothy put in. 'She's found the right bloody niche for herself.' She noticed Lillian's expression and demanded truculently, 'What's the matter? Don't care for my language, is that it?'

'Perhaps I'm old-fashioned,' Lillian mumbled apologetically.

'Please, Dorothy,' Marion said. 'We're in a new environment. It's all strange to us for the moment, but Lillian and her friends know how things stand here. I think we ought to conform.'

'It's for the best,' Lillian agreed, thankful for her support. 'Please don't rock the boat.'

'Come on,' Marion reminded her to change the subject. 'You were going to give us a guided tour.'

'That's right. Wait till you see the cookhouse.'

'A cookhouse!'

'With a wood cooker that works.'

'Hear that? A cooker!'

The women were almost dancing around her with the first enthusiasm they had shown for a year. What did it matter if a couple of favoured headmistresses were going to rule the roost? A thorough wash. Clean rags. A meal. Coffee. And now a cooker!

'This is beginning to feel like bliss,' someone said, and drew a chorus of happy agreement. Even the sardonic Joss couldn't help feeling that things had taken a turn for the better, and that their painful march towards the unknown had finished up – if not exactly in Shangri-La – at least at a place where their hopes of survival had risen a notch or two. She quickened her steps, not to get left behind the excited gaggle.

4 The Swearing-box

Further surprises awaited the women when they returned to their hut after the tour of inspection: a pile of mattresses had been issued; and at about 7.30 electric light came on in all the camp buildings, with a suddenness that startled them. With more whoops of delight, they responded to this extra lift to their morale by helping one another tidy their hair to go with their 'new' clothes, and made as much as they could of faces whose cheeks were sunken, eyes dulled and dark-shadowed, and skin scorched and lined from over-exposure to the sun.

One of them began singing 'There'll be blue birds over the white cliffs of Dover', and others joined in, reverting to humming when their enfeebled memories ran out of words. When Verna came in, first knocking politely on the door, she beamed about with evident pleasure at their happiness.

'Forgive me for intruding, but may I join you?' she asked.

Joss nudged Dorothy as if to say, 'Wait for it!' There was something about this woman's ingratiating manner that moved them all to caution; but Marion spoke up and welcomed her.

'You're all settling in well, then?' Verna went on.

Most of them chorused their satisfaction. Only Sister Ulrica had a mild plea to make.

'I really shall be grateful if I may have my habit back soon.'

'I'm sorry to say that won't be possible, Sister.'

'I do not understand.'

'Well, it was in such a state that the boiling water was just too much for it. It disintegrated.'

'What about the rest of our things?' demanded Rose sharply.

'The same, I'm afraid. They fell apart. But you're very welcome to keep what you have now.'

'That's not the point,' Rose persisted. 'I knew every stitch and patch in mine. It may have been a bloody mess, but it had come to be like my own skin.'

'Yes, sod it!' Dorothy ejaculated, making Verna show shock and disgust in turn. 'Those clothes were all we had left from the beginning of all this.'

'Dorothy, it's not Verna's fault,' Marion reminded her. 'She couldn't help it if they fell apart.'

'I do understand,' Verna was quick to nod. 'After all you've been through. However . . .'

She paused, hesitating to continue, then said, 'May I give you all a piece of advice? It may sound petty, but it's about some of your language.'

'I'm not going to believe this,' Kate murmured, as they stared and listened.

'You see, when we first came here,' Verna went on, 'we had to decide what attitude we would take towards the Japs. Of course, there were some who insisted that we should be, well, difficult . . .'

'Bloody good for them!' Rose affirmed.

Verna gave her a hard look. 'But the majority thought that that would be sinking to their level. We voted to stand on our dignity and keep up a certain code of behaviour.'

'Set the Nips an example?' Kate spoke scathingly, but Verna answered seriously, 'Yes, there is that to it.'

'You never thought that the gooder you all were, the more they'd feel they'd got you under their nasty little thumbs?'

'I'm sorry but I don't agree. We're different from them, with a different background and make-up. They expect women to be obedient, and by being so we've given them no cause for treating us anything but fairly – according to their lights. And while we were about it we agreed that

34

we'd behave towards one another as we would be doing in normal surroundings. Part of that is that we don't go around swearing.' Verna's look took in Dorothy, Rose and Kate. 'We have a system of small fines if we do. Not,' she added hastily, 'that it applies to you – at least not till you've settled in.'

'Jesus, I give up!' Rose exploded. 'We could be back in the bloody nursery.'

'Please don't feel like that.'

'Listen,' Rose began, 'it may come natural to your lot to kowtow to the Japs, but . . .'

'No, Rose!' Marion interrupted sharply. She addressed Verna. 'I'm sure we'll all do our best to fit in with your ways.' There was sarcasm in her tone which Verna could not fail to catch, but it had the effect Marion had wanted of quelling the outburst which she sensed was imminent from some of the others. Better to play along for the moment, she thought. They had made an unexpectedly soft landing after the rigours of the trek and the wretched way of life they had come to take for granted in the last camp. It was too soon to start any feuds between her group and others in this camp.

'Thank you,' Verna smiled without warmth. 'And now that that's cleared up . . . Oh dear, this isn't my popularity night, I'm afraid.' She produced a piece of paper from a pocket of her dress and handed it to Marion with a look of embarrassed apology.

Marion's eyes widened as she glanced at it, then read its brief message aloud: ' "Meal brought to room – one dollar each. Clothes from store – two dollars." I don't understand.'

'It's all very embarrassing,' Verna admitted, as Dorothy exclaimed, 'You're charging us!'

'It's the last thing we'd want to do, I assure you, but we weren't given any extra rations for you, so the food came from the shop, and . . .'

'Shop? What shop?'

'Just a little store of bits and pieces we've managed to organise.'

'I'm afraid we've no money,' Marion persisted.

'Oh dear. That does make it awkward. Still, you'll soon be able to work and pay it back, so we'll call it "on tick" for now. As to the mattresses . . .'

'Oh no!' Kate groaned. 'Don't tell me!'

'There has to be a charge, you see. It's the same for all the others.'

'Then it's too bloody bad!' Rose raged. 'All this being fair and keeping the Japs sweet and expecting us lot to join in. Well, let me tell you we're not like that. We've got guts . . .'

'Shut *up*, Rose!' Marion commanded, surprising herself as much as Rose, who obeyed. Marion said to Verna, 'We're all very tired and I dare say a bit hysterical after not knowing where they were bringing us or what would happen when we got here. Things have turned out very differently from anything we'd imagined. You'll have to excuse us while we come to terms with it and ourselves. We're grateful for a kind welcome, and I'm sure what we all need most is a night's sleep. So may we please leave it at that?'

There were one or two murmurs of support from among the women. Verna smiled and prepared to leave.

'Anyway,' she said soothingly, 'the shop's shut for the night, so do enjoy the mattresses. And thank you for being so understanding. Good night.'

She went out. For quite half a minute a bewildered silence prevailed, as each woman in the crowded hut took stock of her own feelings. Then Kate broke the ice with, 'And the first to swear . . .'

The recital of oaths which followed would have horrified a platoon of Australian infantry. Mild, sanguinary, obscene and blasphemous, each woman made her contribution according to her nature – all except Sister Ulrica, who stuck her fingers in her ears and sent up a little prayer that her makeshift outfit of a man's nightshirt would be regarded as a seemly enough substitute for her habit in the rather exceptional circumstances.

Even Marion contributed a word that she had not used since her schooldays, when she had not yet discovered its meaning. Then she giggled; and the rest of them, having let off steam, shared a good laugh before wasting no more time about getting down on the lumpy, grimy mattresses, which felt to them like beds of purest swansdown. Within minutes the hut was silent, save for snores, the whirr and flutter of many insects, and the infiltration of shrieks and whoops and croaks from the creatures of the jungle whose unknown depths enfolded this resting place of souls cut off from everyone and everything that they had held dear in life.

Only one did not sleep. Oblivious to the sounds about her, Sally Markham lay on her back, eyes open. The electric light was not switched off at night, in accordance with Japanese notions of surveillance; but Sally's eyes saw nothing. Her fingers turned and turned unceasingly her plain gold wedding-ring which she had knotted on a string worn round her neck.

She was trying to think, and finding it hard. Whenever she seemed about to lock her concentration onto anything it slipped away again, leaving her wondering what it was she had been trying to visualise or remember. Her parents, her brothers, her best school chums appeared to her, sometimes smiling, more often anxious, seeming to be calling her name as if searching for her but unable to see her lying there under their very noses. She opened her mouth to answer them but knew she mustn't; it was forbidden, and little green-uniformed monkeys would beat her with clubs if she disobeyed. And in and out of the whole miasma swam Peter's face, at times pale and emaciated, or bloody from head wounds, or, more rarely, as healthy and smiling as she remembered it at the altar when he had drawn forward to raise her veil and kiss her after the ceremony.

37

Sally's hallucinations, which recurred again and again in different patterns, were punctuated now and then by moments of awful clarity, when she knew precisely where she was and how she had got there, and that Peter was missing – and at those times she was certain she was going mad. The women around her slept, some of them tossing and squirming in the grip of their own anxious dreams of loss and pain. She was tempted to call out and beg them to help her; but before she could summon up courage to do so she had forgotten what it was she wanted of them, and was off again into her waking delirium.

She dozed occasionally. Marion had to shake her arm to wake her. A school bell was ringing, and Sally thought she was back in the dorm. It was full of movement; the other girls were up and dressing for prayers and breakfast. Only somehow the dorm had changed.

'Where am I?' she muttered thickly.

'At the new camp,' Marion told her gently, not liking the way the puzzled look didn't leave the girl's eyes. 'We arrived here yesterday, remember? Come on, Sally. Time to get dressed for Tenko.'

She was holding clothes out to her. Sally protested, 'These aren't mine.'

'Not your old ones. They gave us new ones from the store.'

'Plus a bill for them,' Rose reminded her.

'Surely you remember that Verna female,' Joss called over, struggling to dress with one hand. Despite her immobilised arm she would accept no help.

'*Vermin*, you mean,' Rose corrected.

'Here come the monkey-folk,' said Dorothy, as the door opened on the mild light of early morning. But it wasn't Kasaki or Shinya or any other guard coming in waving his rifle and bayonet and screeching in a mixture of fractured English and paddy-field Japanese; it was the slow-minded Daisy.

'Well, if it isn't the Vermin's side-kick,' Rose said.

Daisy didn't hear, or ignored her. She came up to Marion, who had succeeded in persuading Sally to start dressing.

'Good morning, Mrs Jefferson,' she recited carefully. 'Verna said to say that First Bell's for dressin' and Second Bell for Tenko and she'll see you in the cookhouse and will be obliged if you'll return all mattresses after breakfast unless you've decided to buy them.' The long message cost her an effort, and she finished it with obvious relief and shortage of breath.

'Thank you, Daisy,' said Marion quietly, and the girl left.

'This place almost gives me the creeps,' said Kate. 'Dressing Bell! They'll be ringing a bloody breakfast gong next.'

'And bringing the swearing-box round,' Marion reminded her good-humouredly. 'Let's give it a fair trial, shall we? If it seems to be leading up to anything sinister we can think again.'

The more spirited women returned comments which would have qualified for the swearing-box, but the majority finished dressing in relatively good humour, almost girlishly eager to find out what this strange and so far relatively cushy camp had to offer them next.

Other women whom they had not seen before were on parade this time. Tenko followed the usual pattern of counts and recounts, until at length agreement was reached and the sergeant in charge went in to report to the commandant. Lieutenant Nakamura and Miss Hasan, immaculate in a pressed white frock, came on to the verandah.

'Women bow!' the sergeant bellowed. They obeyed. This time Nakamura stayed, his expressionless bespectacled gaze seeming to be directed over the prisoners' heads while Miss Hasan conducted the litany.

'On behalf of Lieutenant Nakamura and myself, I wish you all good morning.'

'Regular Butlin's camp,' Dorothy hissed to Rose.

'We trust you all slept well, for hard work requires a rested body. And there is much hard work to be done. You will be given your duties later. Our camp is the most efficient of all in the area. The most efficient, the most clean, the most harmonious. The Commandant hopes this will continue to be so, as I am sure it will, provided the new internees follow the example of those already here. They will be hard-working, they will be obedient, they will be cheerful.'

'And now the Vermin will pass among you with the swearing-box,' murmured Dorothy, almost causing her neighbours to laugh out. Their grimaces were not spotted by Miss Hasan or any of the guards, and the Commandant seemed indifferent to the whole proceedings. The parade was dismissed, with glummer faces among the newcomers than before.

'There had to be a snag,' said Rose. 'Some sort of slave labour.'

'I don't think so,' said Marion. 'The other inmates look healthier than we do, wouldn't you say, Kate?'

The Australian nurse agreed, adding, 'Did you hear what she said? "Most efficient camp of all in the area." I reckon that means there's quite a few. Some of them could be men's.'

'You're right,' Rose agreed. 'We'll do some asking around.'

'Discreetly though,' Marion warned. 'I've a feeling people won't like us asking too many questions.'

They broke away and moved towards the cookhouse, from which quite a savoury smell was issuing. Marion felt like a schoolmarm at times, delivering her little warnings and rebukes. If she was aware of it, what must the other women think of her? Still, she had undertaken to be leader and she must stick with all that it entailed and be thankful that she was less volatile by nature than some of them. Having been a colonel's lady, even for a little while, had taught her enough for the role.

40

Was she even a colonel's lady any longer, though? Kate's speculation about there being men's camps in the region had quickened Marion's heartbeat. It could help them little in practical terms if there were male prisoners nearby, but knowledge of it must bring some comfort, even if her own husband were not among them. There might be some news of him, if it could be got. As always Marion put such thoughts sternly from her. Captivity, even in circumstances that gave one no moment of physical solitude, had taught her that, mentally, everyone passes through life alone. It was her life, her survival which had to concern her, and, wherever he was, it was the same for Clifford. If God or Fate decreed it they would be reunited. For the present they were apart, and there was nothing they could do about it save survive for themselves and for one another.

With that philosophical observation for the day disposed of, Marion went into the cookhouse and joined the queue towards a long trestle table, where pots were steaming and volunteers were ladling out careful portions. She found herself behind her friend Lillian, who had her son with her. He looked in reasonable shape.

'You remember Mrs Jefferson, Bobby?' his mother said, and with an effort he did. When it was their turn to be served Lillian showed a slip of paper to the kitchen helper, as a result of which an egg and some fruit were added to Bobby's plate. His mother received only the same plain ration of low-grade rice and scraps of vegetable as Marion.

'I try to supplement his diet,' she explained as they found seats together at another table, 'but it's expensive!'

Marion told her about the money her group were expected to raise to pay for yesterday's food in their hut and the mattresses.

'We haven't a bean between us. Nothing left to sell, even.'

'I've got a toothbrush and a comb in the world,' remarked Rose, who had overheard. 'They're both on their last legs but I haven't a hope in hell of paying for new ones, even if there are any.'

'Oh, there are,' Lillian told her. 'Of course, there are always a few women able to pay others to do their heavy chores for them.'

'Rich bitches, huh? Like the Dutch in our last camp.'

Joss leaned over to suggest, 'It wouldn't surprise me if that Van Meyer woman hadn't still got a few baubles stuffed down her knickers.'

Lillian frowned and darted a meaningful glance at Bobby. Joss rolled her eyes.

'Sorry. Is "knickers" swearing? I say, do you really fine each other for it?'

'Well, yes. Anyway, the proceeds go to a good cause.'

'What's that? Lining the Vermin's pocket?'

'Certainly not. They buy birthday gifts for the children.'

Joss, regarding Bobby enjoying his extra rations, seemed about to retort but merely said, 'Ah, well, they'll do pretty well with our lot around.' She went back to her own ration, chewing slowly to make it last.

Marion said quietly to her friend, 'Lillian, I don't suppose you could . . . lend us anything?'

The refusal was firm. 'I would if I could, Marion dear. It's Bobby's extra food, you see. I need every penny. Ah, here's Verna.'

'What are we supposed to do?' Rose asked. 'Genuflect?'

'And how are you all today?' Verna greeted the new faces. 'Recovered from that awful journey?'

'If not from the shock of those bills you brought us,' Rose answered bluntly.

'Well, I want to talk to you about that. I'd have come across earlier, but I have to make Miss Hasan her breakfast first. Oh, I can see what you're thinking. She found out that I used to run a hotel so she expects the full works. I don't enjoy doing it but actually it's very useful to have an "in" with her. I often pick up titbits of information, don't I, Lillian?'

Lillian agreed. She lowered her voice and asked the others, 'Did you know the Allies have started to make a comeback in Burma?'

They had known nothing of any Allied success, anywhere in the world. The only news ever given them, officially or by guards in expansive mood, had been of further crushing victories by the glorious and indefatigable Imperial Japanese Army, Navy and Air Force. Lillian's revelation caused a hopeful stir among them and served to raise Verna's stock.

'I didn't manage to get any details,' she hastened to add, 'but I'm keeping my ear to the ground. Now, to return to the sordid question of money, I've had a word with my colleagues on the Finance Committee. I'm afraid you'll have to work off your bills for the clothes and yesterday's extra food, but I'm happy to tell you that we're agreed you should keep the mattresses for nothing. There was a little comfort money left in the kitty . . .'

Joss interrupted sharply. ' "Comfort money"? D'you mean money sent by the Red Cross?'

'That's right. So we thought that in the circumstances it should go to help you all. Now I must be getting about my work. I'll see you get your duty rotas as soon as possible.'

Her departure had been preceded by a short expectant pause, as though she was waiting for their thanks for the gesture about the mattresses. None was forthcoming. As soon as she was out of earshot Joss said indignantly, 'Dammit, that money was sent for general welfare. We've every right to our full share, and no bloody committee's going to take my whack of it off me.'

Marion suggested, 'Perhaps we could ask for our share to be paid directly to us in future.'

'That's right,' Joss agreed firmly. 'She may be their leader but she's not ours. You are. You put that to them, Marion.'

'I will support you,' Sister Ulrica volunteered. 'The same applies to my people as to yours.'

Together they went after Verna, and put the case. She heard them out and then said, 'I'm afraid a matter like that isn't in the committee's hands or mine. It would have to be put to the Commandant.'

'Then we'd like to see him,' replied Marion determinedly.

Verna gave her a curious look. 'I don't think it would do any good.'

'Nevertheless, we must try. We owe it to the others.'

'I'll speak to Miss Hasan . . .'

'We'd prefer the Commandant personally. He's the one officially responsible for us.'

'He doesn't understand English. He'd only refer the matter to Miss Hasan.'

'That's his decision, but it's him we're asking to see.'

Verna sighed. 'Very well. I'll pass the request on. I only hope you know what you're doing.'

She went away, leaving Marion and Ulrica with a distinct sense of foreboding. As leaders their duty had to be faced, though, and it was not long before Kasaki came for them. With the usual prods and nudges he herded them across the quadrangle to the accompaniment of some calls of 'Good luck!' from the women who knew of their mission. But it was to Miss Hasan's room that he drove them, despite their protests.

They found that lady seated at a desk across part of which a spotlessly clean tablecloth had been spread. She was taking her 'elevenses' of coffee and biscuits. There were no extra cups in sight and no chairs drawn up for the reception of her visitors. Marion had time to take in a gilt-framed mirror on one of the walls, an arrangement of jungle blooms in a tall vase, some framed Japanese woodblock prints and a row of identically decorated red lacquer vases of graduated size.

Miss Hasan dabbed daintily at her lipsticked mouth with a napkin, consulted a piece of paper and addressed her standing visitors.

'So you are Mrs Jefferson and Sister Ulrica. Lieutenant

Nakamura has asked me to see you regarding a question of leadership which I gather you have raised. I should have thought that Verna Johnson would have made it plain to you that there is only one women's representative in this camp, and that is herself.'

Marion replied, 'I represent the new British internees, and Sister Ulrica the Dutch.'

'You do not, Mrs Jefferson. You will tell your fellow internees, both of you, that they will look to Verna Johnson only for leadership from now on.'

'I protest very much,' Sister Ulrica spoke up. 'Some of my people speak no English at all. It is necessary for me to interpret for them.'

'Then you may regard yourself as an interpreter but not a leader. And speaking of interpreters, Mrs Jefferson, I gather that the girl Christina Campbell who is one of your party speaks a number of languages, as I do myself.'

'Yes. Four or five, I think.'

'Including Japanese. I have her records. For that reason she has been transferred from here to Headquarters to serve as an interpreter.'

' "Has"? You mean she's gone already?'

'I saw the truck drive off just now. She is on her way.'

Marion was aghast. 'She said nothing to me about it. I think, Miss Hasan, that that's going a bit far, telling her not to inform her leader, even if you were going to supplant me. The poor child might at least have been allowed to say goodbye to her friends.'

Miss Hasan finished her coffee and dabbed her mouth again.

'She was not told to keep quiet about it. She did not know she was going until she was fetched just now and put aboard the truck. There is no time for sentimental farewells when there is work waiting to be done. Work and obedience, Mrs Jefferson – those are the keys to comfort and happiness under the care of the Imperial Japanese Army. You can see the agreeable results of them in the smooth running of this camp, which is due to the combined efforts of Lieutenant Nakamura and myself. Verna Johnson is your appointed leader and there is neither need nor room for any others. You will obey her or be punished. Is that clear?'

There was nothing to be done or said. Marion and Sister Ulrica murmured acceptance of the position and were dismissed.

'I hate that woman,' Marion said, as they walked away from her hut.

'One must try not to hate.'

' "Love our enemies", you mean?' retorted Marion, with uncharacteristic bitterness.

'There is some goodness in everyone.'

'Yes – in Christina Campbell too. She's who I'm thinking about just now. To be bundled out of the camp without so much as a goodbye. . . What must she be feeling? The poor child's probably not even been told where she's being taken, or what for.'

'It was a bad thing to do it so, I agree.'

Christina Campbell, like Miss Hasan, was a Eurasian, the daughter of a Scots father and a Chinese mother. In the early days of internment the superior attitude of some of the women towards those they had always regarded as racially inferior had earned Christina many a snub and gratuitous insult. Proximity and the discovery that all shared equally in suffering and humiliation under the Japanese had changed that. Christina's mixed origins and the exotic colour of her skin were no longer despised. She had become an equal sister in suffering. Her original timidity and self-consciousness had given way to a confidence worthy of her high intelligence, so at least one of that ill-used community could be said to have gained something. But in learning to accept Christina, the Women of Empire, the mighty *tuans*' wives and daughters, had discovered something which they would never have come even close to learning if their lives had continued on the predictable course on which they had once seemed set. Ironically, in their wretched situation, all had been to that extent enriched.

'Well?' asked Verna Johnson, approaching the two disappointed ex-leaders. Their faces gave her their answer.

'I did say it wouldn't get you anywhere – but please don't hold it against me. I did what you asked me to.'

'Did you know anything about Christina Campbell being taken away?' Marion demanded.

'Nothing. Honestly. "Madam" doesn't let me in on her plans in advance. The guards came and just bundled the poor girl off into a truck while you were inside there. I shouldn't be surprised if it was organised that way so that you wouldn't be around to kick up a fuss. Some of your girls did, and they've some bruises to show for it. That'll be a black mark, I'm afraid.'

'Too bad. I'd have been ashamed of them if they hadn't protested.'

'But she's only been transferred to do interpreting work. She'll be better off.'

'Yes, I expect some other Nakamura will take her under his wing. We can guess what that'll mean.'

'Maybe you've hit on it,' Verna smiled and lowered her voice. 'Perhaps our Commandant isn't as myopic as he looks and Miss Hasan would prefer not to risk having a rival about the place.'

'You really think she'll be all right? Seriously?'

'Positive. Interpreters are too valuable to be wasted, whether they're pretty or not.'

'I'm not pretty,' said Sister Ulrica, 'but at least Miss Hasan thinks I might have my uses as an interpreter.'

'You see? And as for you, Mrs Jefferson – Marion – there's a vacancy on the Discipline Committee. A member's gone down with scrub typhus. Would you care to join?'

'If I could be of any use I'd be prepared to stand.'

'You don't have to be elected. Consider it done. Good leaders are valuable, and they don't necessarily have to

47

lead from the front.'

She smiled and winked. As she smiled back Marion felt herself half warm towards this mysterious intermediary, yet the other half of her reaction to her was cautious restraint. Who was it had said she wouldn't trust either Miss Hasan or Verna as far as she could throw them? Joss. Joss, with one arm in a sling. It was a sentiment worth hanging on to.

5 Sally

It took only a few days in the new surroundings for their strangeness to wear off for Marion. She felt no loss of superiority at having to step down from leadership, merely the exclusion from personal contact with the Commandant which had been her privilege at the old camp. At least Yamauchi had listened to her representations before almost inevitably turning them down, occasionally with detectable regret. Here, the female barrier of Miss Hasan and Verna Johnson stood impenetrable between the internees and the aloof Nakamura.

But although these two women's roles might be resented by those forced to live by their rules they had at least got the camp organised. In so far as conditions in any jungle prison, adapted from what had formerly been the simplest of missionary settlements, could be tolerable, they were. Life soon settled into a routine prescribed largely by the captors' rules and partly by the prisoners' organisation of themselves.

Punctuated by the irritating and for the most part unnecessary Tenkos, the women ministered to the sick and feeble among them, prepared and cooked food, cleaned out latrines (and filled them again – they were constant prey to stomach bugs of varying kinds), practised choral singing under the enthusiastic leadership of a former missionary, mended their clothes with makeshift materials and washed them in their limited water supply, scrubbed the Japanese soldiers' floors, speculated about the proximity of any men's camps and the general progress of the war, about which no information at all was given them, and in differing ways contrived a measure of private life, even if it had to be confined to memories and imaginings.

Dorothy Bennett was the only uninhibited pragmatist. She had lost her husband and her child. She would probably follow them sooner or later, struck down by one of the diseases for which only makeshift treatment was available or by simply wasting away from malnutrition and exhaustion. As day dragged after day without anything to encourage hope or to cause her to take heed of her future, she shrugged at Fate and got what little extra relief she could in a way that almost none of the others could have contemplated. She hired her body to the Japanese guards.

Although the women were wholly under the power of the Japanese they were spared that which at first all had imagined to be inevitable: there were no attempts to violate them. The rapes of Hong Kong and elsewhere had been part of that blind savagery which had included the bayoneting of helpless hospital patients and the indiscriminate mass murder of men, women and children. The madness having passed, the captors metaphorically turned their backs on their charges as though not wishing to be reminded of their presence. As 'fourth-class women' they had been written off from the life which they were still allowed to live if they could, as though degradation and shame, along with hardship and neglect, would cause them to fade away.

The nearest that any guards had come to abusing their femininity had been through a tendency to stand and stare at them when they were taking ablutions or using the latrines. It was peasant curiosity; and on the principle that those who are held to have lost face have no more face left to lose, the women had learned to ignore it and get on with what they had to do.

Dorothy Bennett's relations with certain of the guards had been at her initiative. She had made the approaches, and the men's response had been almost shy. They were running a risk of punishment by their own superiors if caught; but they too were virtual prisoners in this lost jungle place far from home and their own womenfolk, and although some had rebuffed Dorothy a few had accepted the chance of a brief encounter under cover of darkness behind one of the huts. It had brought out yet another of those contradictions of the Japanese character. What they could have had for nothing, they had insisted on paying for out of the modest means at their disposal – cigarettes, food, little items such as needles and thread, worn cooking utensils.

Dorothy shared her spoils with the other women. They knew what she was doing, and disapproved from a variety of standpoints; but the unspoken opinion was that it was her conscience and her body, and there was no denying that some of the 'presentos' which she brought back with her helped ease the lot of the sick and suffering.

Those same sick and suffering, who had once been Beatrice Mason's charge, had been taken over from her by the brusque Dr Natalie Trier. After the initial rebuffs, Beatrice had tried hard to win her professional acceptance, but it was not forthcoming.

The hospital was in the old chapel, separate from the huts. The larger of its two rooms served as the ward; the patients, lying in facing rows, were tended by Natalie Trier's two novice nurses from among the camp's former inhabitants. Kate Norris had still not let on that she was a trained nurse and had forbidden Beatrice to mention it. A small side-room served as Dr Trier's office and examination room.

With all the newcomers settled, and the sick identified and isolated, Beatrice again offered her skills.

'Very well, Dr Mason,' she answered this time. 'You may put in a few hours here each day.'

'Thank you, Dr Trier. But I'm perfectly willing to do a full stint and share the burden equally with you.'

The cool response came like a blow.

'You are clearly in no condition for that. It is obvious that you are still suffering from fatigue. You had already experienced one near-collapse from nervous exhaustion, did you not?'

'Who told you that?' Beatrice couldn't stop herself snapping.

'You see? I did not need to be told. You have all the symptoms – touchiness, anxiety, irrational behaviour.' The younger woman carried on relentlessly. 'Your physical condition speaks for itself. The deterioration in your eyesight is not the only effect malnutrition has had on you.'

Beatrice had to lower her head and bite her lip. It was so dismissively clinical – but she knew it was true.

Her obvious distress brought a slight softening of Dr Trier's tone.

'I am sorry to be brutal. It is because I need your help that I must be so. I would rather have a colleague capable of working efficiently for a few hours a day than one who is little more than a corpse herself. I will see to it that you are put on a special diet from now.'

Beatrice pulled herself together to protest.

'The others are in just as bad condition as I am.'

'The others are not doctors,' she was interrupted. 'Besides . . .'

In a gesture that carried its own meaning the French-woman picked up a small box and handed it to Beatrice, who saw several pairs of spectacles in varying shapes and condition, some with cracked lenses.

' . . . I save them when they die,' said Dr Trier. 'Also the teeth.'

Beatrice slowly selected a pair of the spectacles and tried them on. It felt almost like an admission of defeat.

One of those who settled easily into the new camp was Sally Markham – but her acceptance of the changed surroundings and routine was really apathy. Increasingly, she was withdrawing into a state of indifference, oblivious to her friends and what was going on about her.

Daisy came across her one late afternoon at the plot of land set apart as a cemetery, contemplating the grave mounds with their pathetic crosses and inscriptions and withered tributes of jungle blossoms. As she stood, Sally rubbed continuously at the wedding-ring tied round her neck.

'Hello,' ventured Daisy. Sally returned her the vaguest of looks.

'Hello.'

Daisy pointed to the nearest grave.

'I used to work for her. Back in the old days in Kuala Lumpur before we come here. Malaria it was. The sort what goes to your head. She went screaming mad in the end. It was horrible.'

'I don't know what he died of,' Sally murmured more to herself than in answer.

'Pardon?'

'Maybe he got malaria too.'

'You . . . mean your husband? I heard he passed on. I'm ever so sorry.'

'Thanks.'

'I daresay you've got someone else to go home to. Your folks, like as not, and brothers and sisters.'

'Yes.'

'There you are then. Could be worse. Me, I ain't got no one. Me mum died when I was two, and me dad . . . I was a charity child. Not that I'm complaining, but it's nice to have somebody. . .'

'No,' Sally spoke directly to her for the first time. 'You're better off without. You only lose them.'

Daisy hesitated for a moment, then said in a lower voice, instinctively glancing round, 'Listen. Don't say nothing, only some of us has seances. With a Ouija board. Mrs Vance runs them. Her hubby often gets in touch.'

'You mean . . .'

'From the other side. You know? Whyn't you come along? We're having one tonight. Only don't tell no one else, for fear of the Japs getting to know.'

Almost automatically Sally agreed. She had forgotten about it by the time darkness had fallen, and she was back in the hut with the others, sitting on her mattress, fingering the wedding-ring. Daisy came and fetched her, pretending that Verna had asked her to go over to see her. It did not escape the sharp eyes of Joss Holbrook, though. The former university graduate and Suffragette had retained the natural rebel's alertness, and when Daisy had led Sally off into the night she slipped out after them.

The seance was being held in one of the other huts whose occupants would all have been strangers to Sally had she even noticed them. She obediently let Daisy lead her by the hand to the group squatting and sitting on the floor in one corner. They shuffled apart to make room for her, but there were no introductions or greetings – merely a nod from the tall, cadaverous-looking woman in her late fifties who had charge of the flat little piece of wood on castors, with a pointer piercing its middle.

'Now we are all assembled,' pronounced this Mrs Vance, 'place your fingers on the board very lightly . . .'

Daisy had to place Sally's finger for her. Mrs Vance's further injunction to them all to empty their minds and think of nothing was superfluous so far as Sally was concerned; her state was trance-like already.

'Is anybody there?' intoned Mrs Vance.

They sat still for some moments until almost imperceptibly the board began to move on its little runners, hovering towards the letters of the alphabet which had been marked out on the box on whose surface it lay. It began swinging hesitantly to and fro.

'Will you tell us who you are, please?' asked Mrs Vance, in a respectful tone. 'Who are you?'

After further hesitation the board made a sudden and

purposeful dart towards the letter P. Daisy gripped Sally's arm.

'Yours was a P, wasn't he? P for Peter? It may be her husband,' she explained to a frowning Mrs Vance.

'Really? Then try talking to him, dear. See if he responds. Go on.'

Without consciously doing so Sally found herself asking, 'Peter? *Are* you there, Peter? Please tell me.'

The response did not come from Peter. It came sharply from inside the hut, and it was in Joss's voice as she strode forward.

'What the devil's going on?'

'Ssssh!' hissed the spellbound circle, but Joss was not to be silenced.

'Thought as much,' she snorted. 'Come on out of that, Sal my girl.'

'But she'd just made contact,' Mrs Vance protested.

'Tommy-rot!' Joss glared at Daisy. 'I suppose you got her into this, you half-baked little ninny.'

'I was only trying to help.'

'Call this help? The poor girl's disturbed enough as it is without filling her head with this nonsense. Up you get, Sal. You're coming with me.'

She bundled her out into the dark again. They were not supposed to be abroad at this hour so Joss waited until they were safely back in their own hut before launching into Sally.

'But he *was* there,' Sally insisted with the fervour of the suddenly-convinced.

'Bosh! It's all in your head.'

'I asked if he was there and it was just moving towards "Yes" when you interrupted.'

'Somebody wanted it to indicate that for your sake. That nincompoop Daisy, I shouldn't wonder, or maybe yourself. You pushed it that way. Listen, Sal,' she urged in a changed tone, 'if you want to wish him anywhere, wish him there alive.'

'He's dead. I know he is.'

'Defeatist talk, my girl. There are dozens of camps on this island alone. He could be in any of them.'

'That's what they all say.'

'Then listen to them. It just doesn't do to throw your hand in. That's what *they* want – to undermine our morale. We've got to fight back, show 'em they can't get us down. So snap out of it, there's the girl. Won't you?'

Sally turned and smiled at her, but it was a bright, artificial smile, which did nothing to reassure Joss that this poor girl wasn't already half out of her mind.

'All right, Joss. Anything you say.'

She seemed as good as her word, though. At Joss's suggestion she joined the missionary lady's choir, and sang more tunefully than some the familiar old hymns which were its repertoire. Not many of the women from her hut were members, but Marion and Kate were.

'It's good to see Sally so much better,' remarked the former, when they got to the end of a run-through of 'Fight the good fight'.

'Yes. Almost her old self,' Kate agreed.

As a trained nurse she ought perhaps to have seen as much as Joss had in that feverishly entranced expression.

At the next morning's Tenko Miss Hasan delivered her daily address from the verandah of the official hut. Lieutenant Nakamura stood stiff and expressionless behind her.

'And now,' she concluded, switching on a startlingly sudden smile, 'our Commandant has asked me to give you some good news. Tomorrow an important officer of the Imperial Japanese Army, General Shimojo, will be visiting the camp. For this important occasion the Commandant wishes that all internees will wear their best clothes. They will also make themselves tidy and groomed in readiness for their photograph to be taken. The General has expressed the wish to show the world pictures of our new arrivals happily settled. We are greatly honoured that our camp has been chosen for the privilege. All rooms will be scrubbed, all walls washed down, and the gardens will be tended. Let us make sure all is well for this important visit.'

The smile was snapped off as suddenly as it had appeared.

'Which will you be favouring?' Rose asked Dorothy as they dismissed. 'The blue chiffon or the gold lamé?'

'She can't be serious.'

'She is, though. Look.' Dorothy's nod was directed towards the compound gates. They were open and native labourers were trundling in cartloads of plants, fruits and vegetables. A Japanese guard saw her and Rose watching and came over to them, his bayoneted rifle gripped in both hands for equally ready use as goad or club.

'Women work,' he commanded. 'Make garden. *Hayak!*'

They obeyed his order, and for most of the morning they and other women were stooped over a previously bare patch of land, scratching over the earth, making the edges symmetrically tidy and planting the imported plants in neat rows to give the appearance of having been cultivated there all along. The steamy heat bore down on their painful backs and the sweat poured down their foreheads and breasts.

And the seemingly ludicrous instruction about dressing up was implemented after all. Early next morning Verna and Daisy came into the women's hut bearing armfuls of dresses and other items, which they dumped on the mattresses nearest the door.

'There,' Verna smiled. 'There should be enough to go round. But please, I beg you, take care of them and return them the moment the General's visit is over.'

'You sure there's no hire charge?' Rose demanded, as they clustered round picking up garments that caught their fancy.

Verna laughed. 'Of course not – although we would have to charge for any damages.'

'Who do they belong to, Verna?' Marion asked seriously.

'Various people. I can't tell you more than that I had to twist a few arms to get them for you.'

'Literally, I bet,' murmured Joss. Aloud, she said, 'I'm damned if I see why we should dress up like a lot of dolls. The whole thing's a propaganda charade.'

Mrs Van Meyer, who, to her regret, had been discharged from the hospital and its marginal extra comfort, had picked out a red dress and was holding it up against her. 'Personally,' she confided, 'I like to have my photograph taken. Always I photograph well.'

'P'raps you'll be discovered,' said Dorothy drily.

'Discovered?'

'When your picture gets in the newspapers. They'll send a rescue party from Hollywood for you. Metro Goldwyn Van Meyer.'

Dorothy's joke put them all in a better mood and they set about equipping themselves with a spark of enthusiasm. Verna seized her chance to reassure them.

'I know how ridiculous it may seem, but we have to go along with such things. It isn't worth getting into trouble by refusing.'

'I don't see why,' Joss argued. 'Strikes me as a good chance for a spot of sabotage. Mess the whole affair up, and lose Nakamura and Hasan a bit of face before their precious general.'

'Please,' said Verna earnestly. 'You haven't seen Miss Hasan when she's crossed.'

'Probably have you beheaded on the spot,' Kate put in, meaning it as a quip, but Marion had read Verna's tone and anxious look.

'Better not take any risks,' she counselled. 'As Verna says, we've little to gain and too much to lose.'

'I agree,' said Beatrice, peering at her choice of dress through the unbecoming spectacles that she now wore though only one lens suited her eyesight. 'We don't want trouble, Joss.'

'Oh all right,' grumbled the natural rebel, 'Spoil-sports! It would have been spiffing to turn the old bastard's visit into a shambles.'

'Don't worry, Verna,' said Mrs Van Meyer ingratiatingly. 'We will do our best to impress the General.'

'Thank you. A little make-up wouldn't come amiss, so I managed to get you this.' She held up a single lipstick.

'Only one problem about that,' Rose told her. 'We haven't got a mirror since Christina took hers with her.'

'Yes you have,' Verna surprised them. 'The one Sally bought yesterday.'

They turned as one to where Sally was still sitting on her mattress taking no interest in the share-out of the dresses. For the first time Marion noticed that the wedding-ring had gone from the string around the girl's neck.

'Sally?' she asked, going to her. 'You've sold your ring for a mirror?'

The girl started back to awareness. 'Oh ... oh, yes. Didn't I tell you? It was to replace Christina's, only I forgot.'

She rummaged under her mattress, and brought out a small unmounted handbag mirror.

'But your ...' Marion bit off the rest of what she had been going to say. Nothing anyone said to her could persuade Sally that her Peter was alive. The ring had been her property and concern, not theirs. So the proffered mirror went the rounds in due course, as the women, instinctively making the most of themselves in the borrowed clothes, did what they could with one another's hair and felt the old sensation and taste of lipstick.

They were a grotesque assemblage as they paraded at two o'clock for the General's coming. Their emaciated bodies were devoid of female curves. Their clothes, ranging from sweeping evening-dresses to tennis frocks and kimonos, made ridiculous contrasts, while the bright red of the lipstick on the leathered, sunken faces added just the artificial touch to make them appear more like an amateur theatrical group of men impersonating women.

Only one was absent. After she had at last been persuaded to take one of the dresses for herself and had submitted to having her hair done and been given last use of the lipstick, Sally had suddenly begun to shiver uncontrollably. It looked like an attack of malaria and Beatrice had hurried the girl along to the hospital, where Dr Trier admitted her at once, though with none too sympathetic a grace. She had been ordered to stage-dress the sick quarters for the General's inspection. It had involved reducing the morning's nursing routine to a minimum, to free all able hands for tidying and straightening the room's spare contents and placing jungle blooms alongside the mattresses where no flowers had ever stood before. Sally was allocated the furthest spare bed from the door and left to shiver and shake under the rough blanket, her eyes burning unnaturally.

'She's well out of it,' growled Joss as they stood waiting in the baking sun.

'Wish I'd thought of going sick,' agreed Dorothy. 'When the photographer chap says "Watch the birdie" all start blinking. Any luck and they won't get anything worth printing.'

'Please be careful everyone,' Marion reminded them. 'Nakamura will take it out on us if he loses face before his general.'

The guards were shouting for silence, brandishing their weapons threateningly, as the gates were opened ready to receive a vehicle. A sharp order from the Commandant, who had hardly before been heard by the women to utter any word, caused his soldiers to cease their antics and line up at attention well away from the subjects of their menace. A battered and dust-caked staff car lurched into the compound and disgorged several sword-trailing officers.

Without being instructed the paraded women bowed. Miss Hasan also bowed alongside Lieutenant Nakamura, and the oldest of the visiting officers, who was obviously the General, favoured the two of them with a stiff little bow in return. A brief chat ensued, with Nakamura accompanying each of his replies with a bow and a polite sucking

60

hiss. Then the General and his staff were directed towards the ranks of women, who again needed no urging to bow as he approached to begin inspecting them.

In the hospital Sally pushed back her blanket and rose painfully to her feet, shaking visibly and clutching her arms about her, hands under armpits.

'What are you doing?' Dr Trier demanded sharply. 'Get back into bed at once.'

'Please, I . . . I must go to the lavatory.'

'You *have* to?'

'Yes. Can't wait.'

'Hurry up then. I want you back in bed and lying still by the time the General gets here.'

Sally tottered out to the nearby hospital ablutions room, which had a squatting-type lavatory, a relative luxury after the latrine pits. As soon as she was alone her trembling ceased. She unclasped her arms and stood motionless, surveying her face in the small mirror which had been concealed in one of her hands.

The photographic session proved to be an even more hypocritical pretence than the women had anticipated. When the General and the other officers had made off towards the hospital led proudly by Miss Hasan, Marion, Mrs Van Meyer, Sister Ulrica, Dr Mason, Kate, Rose, Dorothy and Joss were ushered onto the verandah where Miss Hasan's table was laid for tea for them all. The photographer, a soldier, had his camera ready on a tripod far enough back to take in the whole group. While he focused and set his shutter speed and aperture Daisy passed round with the teapot, pouring a half cup for each woman, followed by Verna with a biscuit tin from which they were each to take one.

The photographer indicated that he was ready.

'Splendid, ladies,' beamed Verna, who was directing the proceedings. 'All raise your cups, please, and a big smile from all. *All*, please. Say cheese. Cheese . . .'

'Cheese!' they responded, wearing the travesties of smiles.

The shutter clicked . . . and at that same moment Sally brought her mirror down hard against the edge of the washing sink, shattering it so that a dagger-like sliver was all that was left in her hand.

'Cheese!' again . . .

Sally slashed hard at her other wrist, so that the blood spurted in a bright scarlet fountain.

6 Dorothy

The cross at the head of the fresh mound in the cemetery plot was inscribed:

1920 – 1943
SALLY FELICITY MARKHAM
MOTHER OF ELEANOR
WIFE OF PETER

After only a few hours in the direct sunlight the blossoms which had been scattered at its foot had already faded and curled.

Too long had elapsed before Sally's body had been found for Dr Trier to save her. At the moment she had slashed her wrist almost to the bone the General and his entourage had entered the hospital door, and Dr Trier had had more to occupy her than remember that her new patient had been overlong in the lavatory and might interrupt the inspection by her return.

She was dead when they did find her, and instead of the scrubbed and tidied wash-house that Miss Hasan had smugly stood aside to bow the General into there was revealed what more resembled a slaughterhouse. Sally had taken several minutes to expire, and her blood had gushed while her heart still beat.

There followed a clamour of apologies, recriminations, excuses, orders and general fury, though not a word of pity for the wretched dead girl. As they strode furiously back towards the officers' quarters General Shimojo upbraided Lieutenant Nakamura wildly, irrationally blaming him for allowing so unseemly an occurrence to mar his inspection. All his previous complimentary remarks about the camp's organisation, its high standards of neatness and order and the docile, disciplined nature of its inmates were cancelled in a petulant diatribe. Miss Hasan and the guards trembled for the predictable aftermath. They had not anticipated wrongly. As soon as the staff car had lurched out of the camp and the gates had been closed Nakamura started screaming at his woman aide and the guard sergeant. When he had done with them, Miss Hasan almost dragged Verna Johnson into her room and abused her in language that contrasted totally with her immaculate attire and appearance and would have had the interned women marvelling at her capacity for obscenity. The sergeant, meanwhile, had the corporal of the guard standing to attention before him and was slapping his face hard from side to side. Privates Shinya, Kasaki and the rest of the ordinary soldiers came in for their share of the same treatment from the corporal, and passed it down to their own juniors.

Then it was the women's turn, though not to be beaten or slapped. The Tenko bell was rung as fast as the rope could be jerked, and when they were all lined up once more before the Commandant's hut he stood glaring at them from the verandah and for the first time addressed himself directly to them. Since he spoke no English, Miss Hasan translated from his Japanese, and her own fury ensured that no nuance of his anger was lost.

'Lieutenant Nakamura is very angry that you disrupted the visit of General Shimojo. What has happened here today has placed the entire high reputation of our camp in jeopardy. On your very first day here it was made plain to all of you, and to suicide Markham, that no disobedience or bad behaviour would be tolerated. You were told that by following our rules and learning to obey in all things at all times peace and harmony would be ensured. Yet you allowed suicide Markham to go against the instructions . . .'

'But we didn't!' Marion spoke up, heedless that her interruption could earn her a beating on the spot. Like the

64

others she was still in a state of shock at the news of Sally's death, and protested without thought for herself. Luckily, Miss Hasan was in full spate and Marion's voice was not heard.

'The Commandant says that the new intake of women clearly do not choose to take our rules seriously. Therefore they will be punished until they learn to do so. You will work in camp *and* in the factory from first Tenko until late at night. With the exception of the nun and those officially sick you will begin your double duties at once. Now bow to the Commandant. And again.'

As they bowed a second time, Nakamura turned sharply and disappeared into his office, to drown the fire of his fury in *sake* from the big bottle from which he should now have been pouring respectful bowls for his senior visitors as he accepted their compliments on the excellent conduct of his duties. Miss Hasan hesitated about following him, and so Sister Ulrica was able to catch her attention.

'Miss Hasan . . . Might I know why I am not to work at the factory with the others?'

'A nun would have stopped the suicide, is that not so?'

'Yes, Miss Hasan, as I know any of my friends would have done if they had been able.'

'We do not know that.'

'But I am certain . . .'

'Do not contradict me!'

'Miss Hasan, I am only asking to be allowed to share the suffering of my colleagues.'

'You choose to associate yourself with those who wilfully disobey? Then it is right that you should be punished with them.'

Miss Hasan closed the conversation by turning away. But discretion guided her back to her own room, where Verna Johnson came in for a further tongue-lashing while she obediently prepared the tea which Miss Hasan demanded.

Such was the immediate reaction to poor deranged

Sally's suicide. While it was taking place her shrunken body lay in the surgery, awaiting attention. The task of preparing it for burial naturally fell to Beatrice Mason. Natalie Trier, she had noticed all along, appeared more interested in studying her patients' symptoms than in actually treating them. She always took copious notes and spent her spare time writing them up with a clinical detachment that Beatrice thought matched her cool unsmiling nature.

'This is the first suicide we have ever had here,' remarked Dr Trier. She had uttered no word of pity for the victim.

'You'll be able to write it up, then,' Beatrice couldn't help observing in a bitter tone which caused the other to glance at her with surprise just as Kate Norris entered. Natalie Trier was able to turn her resentment on her.

'What are you doing in here? Only medical staff are allowed.'

'I want to help Beatrice prepare Sally's body,' the Australian replied quietly.

'Don't be absurd. This is a job for a nurse.'

'I am a nurse. A trained one.'

'Then why . . .'

Beatrice cut in. 'I'd like Kate to help me. Please – we were Sally's friends.'

Dr Trier hesitated for a moment, then went out.

'Thank you, Kate,' Beatrice said. 'We do need you, you know.'

Kate's gaze was on Sally's uncovered face.

'At least she achieved something, didn't she?' she said. 'She wiped the smile off their faces. Ruined his whole visit.'

'You surely aren't suggesting she planned that deliberately. Not her life!'

'No,' Kate said at length. 'But if she had to do it, she timed it bloody well.'

So now Sally lay at rest in her simple grave – shallow because her friends had not the strength to dig six feet down, and none but they were available to do the work. And while she rested, they worked a double routine, still doing all their camp duties but now also taking a shift at the factory, a mile or so away down the bumpy earth track that passed for a road. A moral triumph had been gained, but it was one for which they had not the physical resources to pay. By unspoken agreement they did not complain: that would have been to diminish Sally's gesture and her memory.

Mrs Van Meyer was the exception, but it was to Verna Johnson that she grumbled. That a woman of her family background should be brought so low as to empty latrines and scrape out clogged drains all day and then work with painfully worn fingers at making headgear for Japanese soldiers in the hot, unventilated, fly-infested factory, which was little more than a long hut equipped with a few old treadle-operated sewing machines, was too much to bear.

The two had met by chance in the compound early one evening, and on an impulse Verna invited the Dutchwoman into her room for a cup of coffee. Verna's cat made a fuss of the visitor. Mrs Van Meyer remarked that she found animals more reliable and sympathetic than people, and it occurred to Verna that it might be worth showing friendship to someone who might be willing to repay it with early warning of any other situations among the internees that could lead to embarrassments and the displeasure of Nakamura and Miss Hasan. She listened with attention as Mrs Van Meyer chattered on to this influential acquaintance who showed her more sympathy than she ever got from her fellow prisoners.

'You have no idea how undisciplined everyone was in our last camp,' she confided. 'The Van Meyers have always had a sense of responsibility for others, which is why I appreciate the way this camp is run. It makes one feel more . . . secure.'

'One must have order if one wishes to survive,' agreed Verna, pouring her visitor another cup of the fragrant brew.

Mrs Van Meyer was nodding vigorously. 'Order and

service. Both are in the Van Meyers' blood, of course. The family has served royalty since the eighteenth century.'

'Have they? Miss Hasan will be interested in that. She likes to be aware of any important people under her charge, so that she can mention it at Headquarters. She thinks it does her prestige good.'

'It cannot be easy even for Miss Hasan, working for the Japanese,' Mrs Van Meyer remarked. Despite her self-preoccupation it had occurred to her in turn that it would be no bad thing to cultivate friendship with someone so close to the camp hierarchy as Verna. 'We are lucky to have her, perhaps. Women are so much more reasonable.'

'When she's in the right humour,' Verna agreed in an almost conspiratorial manner. 'She's pleased just now to have acquired a real lady.'

For a moment Mrs Van Meyer believed it was herself to whom Verna referred. She said coyly, 'There are some of us who have been brought up to be so.'

Her smug assumption was shortlived as Verna continued, 'A titled lady, that is to say. You know whom I mean.'

'Titled? I'm afraid not.'

'But she's one of your group. The one you call Joss Holbrook.'

'Joss! Titled? But . . . I cannot believe. I mean to say, her behaviour, her manner . . .'

Verna laughed at the other's astonishment. 'Perhaps she prefers to remain incognito so that she can behave as she does, which I agree leaves much to be desired. Nevertheless, she is the Lady Josslyn by rights.'

'Well, well! What is the English saying? – "It takes all sorts to make a world".'

Verna laughed again and changed the subject. 'Tell me, Mrs Van Meyer . . .'

'Dominica please, Verna.'

'Dominica, then – who does your hair? It's always so neat compared with the others.'

68

'Oh, but I do it myself. Like you, Verna, I believe in keeping up standards. My own sisters always preferred my touch to their hair to that of any professional.'

'Really? Would you be willing to do my hair, Dominica?'

'But yours is so beautifully kept always.'

'Thank you. A little help wouldn't come amiss, though. And if you could agree to do the same for Miss Hasan . . .'

'Miss Hasan!'

'I feel she would welcome it if you'll let me suggest it to her. Naturally, we would pay you a little something.'

'Please tell Miss Hasan that I should be delighted. *Thank* you, Verna. It is comforting for a lady to be accepted among true ladies.'

So it was arranged that Mrs Van Meyer, with her boasted connections with the palace of Queen Wilhelmina and her continual reminders to the other women of her superior social position and wealth, became hairdresser to the former hotel-keeper and the Eurasian woman who wielded the Commandant's power by proxy; women who, in the old days, Mrs Van Meyer and her kind would have expected to defer to her and politely obey her every whim. Throughout Japanese-occupied South-East Asia such ironic turnabouts were happening, and though no one spent much imagination on it at the time it was the thin end of the wedge of change.

One factor which even such wholesale upheaval could not transmogrify was the ages-old force of Nature itself. In spite of the disruption which malnutrition and unrelieved hardship had caused to the women's body cycles, a tendency to bouts of sickness that Dorothy Bennett had been experiencing lately could no longer be attributed to anything other than pregnancy.

She had been trying to convince herself that the sickness had some other cause. But Dorothy had been a mother before, and her symptoms were disturbingly familiar.

Wondering what to do for the best made her hesitate to tell any of the others. Her loss of appetite and morning

69

sickness had not gone unnoticed, though, and there had been some speculative talk already among the non-medical internees. The matter came to a head as a result of Mrs Van Meyer's new employment and what she had learned from Verna.

A pittance wage was paid for working in the factory. Marion Jefferson was responsible for administering the pool into which the women had agreed to pay what they earned, so that it could be spent to their best mutual benefit at the camp shop. The shop's limited stock consisted chiefly of items sold to it for a fraction of their value by women seeking necessities, but there was the occasional addition of tins of biscuits and a few other comestibles contributed from the unidentified supplies guarded so carefully by Verna in the storeroom to which no access was allowed.

When Mrs Van Meyer had finished adding her earnings to the pathetic pile in front of Marion she was seen to have some left over. She made no secret that it was her tips from Miss Hasan and Verna for doing their hair. She declined to contribute the extra to the pool, which to everyone seemed merely typical of her, but later proceeded to surprise them all by producing a tin of biscuits which she had bought at the shop and inviting them all to celebrate Joss's birthday, which she had happened to discover was that day. Joss was annoyed at being made the subject of a fuss, though not so angry as she would have been if Mrs Van Meyer had told them what she had learned of her identity.

Joss submitted, however, and went so far as to admit to being sixty-eight, which surprised them all and added an excited note to the simple ceremony of toasting her with biscuits. It was at this rare moment of cheer that Rose noticed Dorothy standing uncharacteristically silent and apart. When Rose asked directly if she was feeling all right Dorothy shook her head emphatically and came out with the truth.

'You were sick on the march here,' Marion remembered.

'Conceived in the last camp,' Beatrice confirmed.

70

'I don't suppose you know who?' Marion asked.

'It's disgusting!' Mrs Van Meyer burst out. 'Pregnant by one of the guards – by a filthy Japanese. Our enemy. You dirty little collaborator!'

Marion pleaded, 'Mrs Van Meyer, please . . .'

'Whore!' raged the Dutchwoman, ignoring her. 'Carrying an enemy's child inside her.'

'Stop that!' Beatrice Mason ordered. 'This is neither the time nor the place.'

'No, it is not – for what she has done. You haven't stopped to think, any of you, I suppose, what the camp authorities will have to say when her condition becomes obvious? We'll all be punished again. It's unfair. Why should I have to suffer because of the behaviour of you British? Just when I have a nice new job and some real friends. I could kill you for this. I will . . .!'

She would have launched herself at Dorothy if Beatrice had not stepped forward smartly and smacked her hard across the face, shocking her into silence.

'Sit down and shut up,' she ordered.

'Yes,' Rose put in. 'And talking of collaborators . . .'

'That will do!' Marion intervened, drawing on the colonel's-wife authority which she no longer officially held, but which quelled immediately the babble of argument. 'Before we go any further, I think it should be agreed from every point of view that we all keep absolutely quiet about this, at least till we've thought carefully about it.'

'The *shame*!' Mrs Van Meyer blubbered, but a hard look from Marion silenced her again.

There were several questions to be faced besides that all too justified fear of Mrs Van Meyer's of what the Commandant's and Miss Hasan's reaction would be when Dorothy's condition became apparent: the question of whether an abortion would be preferable for Dorothy's and all their sakes; whether it would even be possible, given their lack of medical supplies and facilities, the unhygienic environment, and Dorothy's run-down state and the unknown duration of her pregnancy.

When calmer discussion became possible, Dorothy insisted that she wanted to get rid of the baby. Sister Ulrica was naturally horrified from the depths of her religious sensibility. Dr Beatrice Mason was matter-of-factly in agreement, but could not offer to do anything herself, for one of her hands had become infected after dirt got into cuts and cracks sustained in the factory, where her deteriorating eyesight made her prone to slips with needle and scissors. Kate Norris, the nurse, refused to countenance anything to do with it, on grounds of medical ethics. None of them dared risk approaching the still aloof Dr Trier, from uncertainty at how she would react. It was not long before Mrs Van Meyer, at any rate, knew precisely how Natalie Trier would react, for she was there when she did.

A Tenko had been called one late January afternoon to enable Miss Hasan to deliver one of her harangues. The women listened as patiently as they must, only interested in trying to detect any particular reason for it. If there seemed to be none, their discussion afterwards would be full of hope – of the possibility of an Allied success somewhere which had rattled Miss Hasan's nerve and made her seek solace through abusing the internees.

This was such an occasion. The Commandant was not present.

'. . . You are a defeated race,' Miss Hasan continued, her sallow features flushed. 'You are wives and daughters of the white oppressor who stole our countries and made us slaves. Now it is *we* who are masters and you who must obey. Under Lieutenant Nakamura's command and my administration this camp was the most efficient and harmonious in the whole of Area Three. It lost that reputation through your fault, and it is going to be through your harder work that it will regain it. Do you hear me? From now there will be extra duties for all.'

She paused for effect, and all were horrified to hear a

single voice retort, 'No!' It was Dorothy, pale and worried almost to the point of breakdown.

Private Kasaki, the humourless conscript who rejoiced in any excuse to kick or beat a woman, pointed out Dorothy to Miss Hasan.

'How dare you?' Miss Hasan almost screamed.

Dorothy mumbled confusedly, 'I'm . . . sorry. I didn't . . .'

Miss Hasan's tone had brought Lieutenant Nakamura out of his office to find out what was going on. She told him in rapid Japanese. He replied curtly and went indoors again, without having spared the women a glance.

'The Commandant has ordered internee Bennett to do extra heavy duties,' Miss Hasan announced triumphantly. 'The rest of you will work harder too, to make this camp the most perfect in the Japanese Empire. That is all.'

'Women bow!' shrieked Kasaki.

As they did so he walked swiftly to Dorothy and pushed her bent back even further down with a hard thrust. She was promptly sick.

Miss Hasan had turned away to go, so saw nothing. Dr Trier did, though. She went quickly to Dorothy's help.

'Has this happened before?' she demanded.

'No!' chorused Marion and Joss; but Dorothy herself, panting for breath as they supported her, murmured, 'So what if it has?'

Dr Trier walked away. Marion and Joss exchanged looks. 'She knows,' Joss said.

Marion nodded pensively. 'Better wait and see what she does about it. She's the doctor.'

What Natalie Trier did was to tell Verna Johnson. Not in so many words, but in a heavy enough hint when handing over the sick list that evening.

Mrs Van Meyer was the horrified onlooker. Daisy having gone down with dysentery, Verna had sweetly asked Mrs Van Meyer if she would care to replace her as her maid. The offer had been eagerly accepted. Mrs Van Meyer's outburst against Dorothy had hardened the feelings of her hut mates against the spoiled, pretentious Dutchwoman, who had come as a result to value Verna's patronage even more. She was dusting Verna's room when Dr Trier remarked pointedly to Verna, 'The fuss they all seem to be making over that Dorothy Johnson, just because she was sick at Tenko. I can't understand it. What is so upsetting about a girl being sick?'

When she had gone, Verna rounded on Mrs Van Meyer.

'Well? What's going on? You must know.'

Fearful of the ultimate consequences, Mrs Van Meyer tried to bluff that she knew nothing, but Verna was too shrewd for her and the truth emerged at last.

'Don't tell them I told you,' Mrs Van Meyer pleaded. 'They'd kill me.'

'Oh shut up!' snapped Verna, who was just as worried as she. 'How many know of this?'

'Only those in our hut.'

'Understand one thing from me. I know nothing of it. Is that clear? Nothing.'

'Yes, Verna. Of course, Verna.'

Verna lost no time in seeking Dorothy out, unnoticed by the others. She quickly took her back to her own room, where Dorothy was surprised to be offered a glass of *sake*. Then Verna came straight out with it.

'You're pregnant, aren't you? I know you were sick on parade, and about your relationships with guards.'

'What if I am?' Dorothy responded dully. She would have liked to have been left alone with the rest of the big *sake* bottle. It would probably have settled everything, one way or another.

But Verna was regarding her with what looked like sympathy, saying, 'Then it must be dealt with, don't you agree? Only fair on everyone, in view of what our lords and masters might think if they find out.'

'You'll help me?'

'Somebody's got to. It won't do to involve the medics.'

'Do you know someone?' Dorothy asked pathetically.

Verna gave her a cigarette.

'I know someone,' she said.

Her acquaintance was a middle-aged Chinese woman named May, a tough, capable woman who had performed the same service in the past, though not on the camp premises.

'It is more dangerous,' she told Verna. 'It will cost ten dollars.'

'But that's impossible. I could manage six.'

'Eight,' said May, and the deal was done, though Verna had no idea how she was going to raise the money. After much thought she took the risk and went straight to Miss Hasan with an honest report. As it happened, things proved to have timed out perfectly.

'It must be got rid of without complication,' Miss Hasan said when the heat of her angry reaction had died down. 'I cannot have any more troubles, what with a new District Commander about to take over. New commanders inspect everything. Why didn't you come to me before? Why hasn't it been done already?'

'Because I've only just learned, Miss Hasan. And I have to pay ten dollars.'

'Ten dollars! Why should you have to pay anything?'

'Because an outside woman has to be involved. She could make trouble for us, but she won't if we pay.'

' "We"?'

'It's in everybody's interest.'

'Then let everybody pay.'

'Only a few know, and they and I couldn't hope to raise it between us. Not quickly.'

Miss Hasan gave her a hard look, then went to a drawer. She took out some notes and counted ten dollars, which she dropped on the table for Verna to pick up.

'Get it done tomorrow, while Lieutenant Nakamura is away at Headquarters,' she ordered. 'And you have three months to pay it back – no more.'

Arrangements were put in hand at once. Much against Verna's wishes she was compelled to make her storeroom the venue for the operation. It was the one room in the camp to which no guard could gain access. Verna alone was entrusted with its key and its contents, and those contents included certain items that she wished no one else to see. Dr Beatrice Mason would have to be present to oversee the Chinese woman's work. Verna spent an hour shifting things around and draping old blankets over the stocked shelves before she prepared the necessities for the operation itself – a mattress, a paraffin stove and kettle, two buckets of water, a bowl, cloths and towels.

May had been summoned and was smuggled in furtively. Beatrice brought Dorothy to the hut at eight o'clock in the evening. Nakamura would be leaving for Headquarters early in the morning, so they had all the night hours as well as the following day, should the abortion prove a long process.

It did. It was eleven o'clock next morning before May said to Beatrice, 'Not long now.' Beatrice had spent many of the intervening hours walking Dorothy up and down the store hut after May's ministrations, and she was almost as exhausted as Dorothy herself.

Then came an emergency none had anticipated. Verna, who had stayed in the hut with them to make sure they did not take the opportunity to snoop among her covered-up stores, was summoned out by Miss Hasan's urgent knocking and voice. When she came in again she addressed herself hurriedly to Marion.

'There's been a hitch. The new District Commander's on his way without notice. Lock yourself in here and for God's sake keep quiet if you hear voices approach. Miss Hasan and I will keep him away for as long as we can. When it's happened, it's up to you to clear up and get away. Lock up from outside and slip the key into my room. Understand?'

'Yes. I think we're nearly there.'

'No traces, mind. If he finds anything out it will be hell for all of us.'

She slipped away to rejoin Miss Hasan, who was furious at being caught on the hop. She had ordered Mrs Van Meyer to hurry round the living huts, hospital and cookhouse, passing the message that they must be tidied immediately for inspection.

Not long afterwards they heard from inside the hut the guards on the gate being commanded to attention, and then the grinding entry of the staff car, its suspension and chassis badly strained by long use over the island's bumpy roads. Then there were voices coming nearer – and as Dorothy began to moan out, Beatrice clapped a cloth over her mouth with a gentle but firm grip.

7 Rose

Miss Hasan was finding the new District Commander a sticky customer. She had greeted him in unctuous Japanese, and been told in good English that if English was her normal tongue she should use it to him. When she had hastened to explain that the absent Lieutenant Nakamura had learned no English and relied totally on her as interpreter he frowned and made an impatient exclamation.

He was about the same age as Nakamura, heavy-featured and thickly-built with greying hair and moustache. His name was Yamauchi.

Major Yamauchi had brought to the camp with him Captain Sato, a younger, wiry, hard-faced man. He walked with a distinct strut and in his less fluent English took up such generalisations as Miss Hasan made, pinning her down to precise details, a pedantic bureaucratic type who she was glad was only visiting.

'It is such a pity that Lieutenant Nakamura was not here to greet you, Major,' she gushed to Yamauchi, who answered curtly, 'A good commander arrives when he is least expected and expects to find all in order. There has been bad report of discipline at this camp.'

'That can be explained, Major. One incident only – a suicide by one of the new intake. They are an undisciplined body whom Lieutenant Nakamura and I have been working hard to teach more obedient ways.'

Nakamura and *you*?'

'As his, er, assistant.'

'What was this suicide's name?'

'Markham, Major. Sally Markham. No self-will.'

Major Yamauchi stopped to face her and answered with patent displeasure. 'Mrs Markham lost her baby in her last camp. She had already given up husband for dead. I suppose she lost her mind?'

'You . . . you knew her, Major?'

'I know all your "undisciplined body of women", Miss Hasan. I was Commandant of the camp in which you suggest they learned bad ways.'

'I . . . I'm sure I didn't mean . . .'

'You meant, but would not have said if you had known who I was. Also Captain Sato here. He was at that camp. Now he stays here to take command.'

Major Yamauchi was watching every change of Miss Hasan's expression, grimly enjoying her growing discomfiture. He was a strict disciplinarian himself when rules needed applying and due punishment handing out, but sometimes felt that his subordinate, Sato – whom the women had nicknamed 'Satan' at their old camp – went too far. Sato was a Japanese officer, though, and while it was one thing for a Japanese officer to act rigorously, it was quite another for a civilian to have wormed her way into a position of power over fellow internees.

'But . . .' she was faltering, 'Lieutenant Nakamura . . .?'

'He will not return here. I have sent him to another place. Captain Sato remains in command here now.'

Miss Hasan turned to the Captain and bowed deeply. He watched her without change of expression.

'Come,' ordered Major Yamauchi. 'I inspect the camp.'

They went the rounds. Inevitably, after a time, Miss Hasan, Yamauchi and Sato approached the storeroom. Miss Hasan sought desperately for some excuse to dissuade Yamauchi from demanding to enter.

'It's only a storeroom,' she told him casually, drymouthed.

'I see all rooms.'

'I . . . I'm afraid I don't have the key, Major.'

'The key will be found.'

'Do you wish me to look for it now?'

Instead, he gestured to Sato, who strode to the door and tried the handle, rattling it vigorously. When the door didn't budge, Sato put his shoulder to it, but Yamauchi waved him away impatiently.

'Does not matter,' he grumbled, to Miss Hasan's great relief.

They turned away and continued their tour. Inside the hut, several deeply held breaths were expelled with a relief even greater than Miss Hasan's.

When Major Yamauchi at length departed, leaving Sato in sole charge, he lost no time in ordering Tenko and laying down his own law in his own words: 'Bad work, punish. No obey, punish. No food. Stand in sun. Many hours!' Miss Hasan was at his side on the verandah – for his English was far from good – but she looked distinctly subdued.

The Chinese woman had earned her eight dollars – and Verna her two undisclosed dollars margin for having produced her. Dorothy was very ill but under the care of Dr Trier and Kate Norris, who made no reference to the cause of the haemorrhaging that had resulted from her ordeal. She was no moral problem to them now – simply a woman needing healing. Debility made her recovery slow, but by the end of the first week of February she was fit for discharge.

She was just in time to take part in yet another farewell, which brought regret to them all. Sister Ulrica was leaving the camp.

A priest who was being allowed to do the rounds of certain camps had heard her first proper confession since being interned. There had been little enough to confess about a life of such enforced self-denial, but Sally's suicide and Dorothy's abortion had been much on her mind.

'You should have reported her intention,' he said, after she had told him of Dorothy.

'To the Japanese!'

'Anything – even that – would have been better than to allow her to take a life.'

'I spent much time examining my conscience, Father. I searched my heart and conscience, and found my answer in our Blessed Lord's taking unto himself the care of the sinner.'

'No, Sister Ulrica. It was what *you* wished. Cut off from proper guidance, you chose to divide your loyalty between your calling and those whom you regard as friends. Sister Ulrica, I am much troubled by you. And you say you even attended the suicide's funeral?'

'It seemed the only thing I could do for the poor child. It was little enough. I had no one to advise me otherwise.'

The priest folded his hands for a long silence, as he himself sought an answer.

'So I am going away,' Sister Ulrica broke the news later in the hut to which Dorothy had just returned. 'I go to a convent where the nuns care for the native sick.'

'Is that a punishment?' someone wanted to know.

'How can it be? A nun needs her sister nuns about her. I think the Father was offering me a kindness.'

'Well, you won't have us about you – us and our swearing,' Rose said, breaking the solemnity of the moment.

Sister Ulrica smiled. 'Do you remember the night when you all swore over Verna?'

'How do you know? You reckoned to have your fingers in your ears.'

'What do they say? – the air turned blue. But the Father has given me a little money. Just a little, but enough for a small party for me to say goodbye to you all.'

Hands were clapped and there was a little cheer.

'You're sure he isn't sending you away in punishment over me?' said Dorothy.

'Quite sure. But he realises, as I do, that in not going to every possible length to stop you I showed that I am empty of resources. I need to have them renewed, to rededicate my will to the wise laws of the Church.'

'I'll never understand that,' said Beatrice Mason, for whom medicine and science were the nearest thing to a religion.

'No, you won't,' Sister Ulrica smiled and pressed her hand. 'You are too stubborn. I was once, and it made me very lonely, which was one of the reasons why I became a nun. But here, with all of you, I came near to discovering too late what a great vocation it is merely to be a woman. God bless you all for showing me what resources of sisterhood and courage and fight for survival exist in women so different as all who are here.'

Someone – the speculation later was that it had been Joss, however unlikely that seemed – said 'Amen'. Then they started chattering about their party like a pack of girls.

Six weeks of the new regime had taken visible toll. The 'new' clothes had become as grubby and ragged as those they had replaced. Sato's insistence on extra and harder work, neither of which was realistically attainable, had put the labour corps of debilitated females under extra stress and brought down the threatened punishments for non-conformity. Deteriorating rations had reduced further their energy for work and resistance to sickness. It was, thought Marion in her blackest moments, as if Sato were deliberately waging a campaign of attrition which would cause them one by one simply to give up and fade away.

One who was suffering more than most from lack of nourishment was Lillian Cartland. Marion had noticed with concern how her old friend of Singapore days sacrificed most of her own meagre food to her son Bobby, whom she protected and spoiled, in so far as any child could be spoiled under such circumstances, at visible cost to her own condition.

Even Bobby protested, 'Mummy, please don't go on giving me all your food. It isn't fair to you.'

'It's what's best for you, dear,' she answered. 'Run along

and play with the other children now – but remember to keep your straw hat on against the sun.'

'Bobby's right,' said Marion, watching him move listlessly away. 'You've got to look after yourself too.'

'I'm fine – fine.' Lillian brushed off the admonition with what she herself knew to be a gross untruth. 'Anyway, I hear the repatriation list's coming through at last. Verna thinks we've got a chance, especially since Dr Trier wrote a special note about Bobby's health.'

'I honestly wouldn't raise your hopes, Lillian. The chances of any British being repatriated are very small.'

'Marion, they say you can get through to Yamauchi, because you were leader at his camp. When he comes here again for his inspection, do you think you could . . .?'

Marion had no need to hear the request out. 'I'll try, Lillian, I promise. Remember, I have to ask Verna to ask Miss Hasan if I can even see him. It will probably have to be approved by that lout Sato. Even so, you must eat, or repatriation will be beside the point for you.'

Lillian sighed. 'I've still got one spare dress and mother's brooch. Once I know we're on that list I'll sell them for some extra food to build us both up. I'm keeping them in reserve for that.'

As Marion expected, her request for an interview with the District Commander got no further than Captain Sato, who dismissed it. There was nothing left but to risk direct action next time Major Yamauchi came, for she had more than Lillian Cartland's problems to raise. There were matters she preferred not to ask Verna to take up for her.

Yamauchi was soon back, clearly intending to keep a regular watch on the camps under his control. At the end of Tenko and his inevitable reminder that the Imperial Japanese Army was continuing to sweep all before it, so the women might as well resign themselves to their lot as fourth-class prisoners and learn the humility which they had lacked when they had been the overlords of South-East Asia, Marion took the great risk of walking up to him as he moved off towards the waiting tea-table in Miss Hasan's office. Sato had found her too useful to demote. He had let her keep her quarters and her privileges, but made her aware that her tenure was insecure, dependent on the obedience of the internees. It made her more valuable than the guards in enforcing discipline for him.

She saw Marion approaching the Major and moved to cut her off, but Yamauchi had recognised his former camp leader again.

'You wish to speak with me, Mrs Jefferson?'

Marion bowed low. 'If I might, Major Yamauchi.'

Miss Hasan was about to interject a refusal, but kept quiet as the Major gave her a stern look and said, 'I will give Mrs Jefferson five minutes.'

Marion bowed again. 'Thank you, Major.' He turned and they strolled away together, leaving Sato and Miss Hasan glaring blame at each other for letting it happen.

When the brief interview was over, and Yamauchi had taken his tea and gone, Miss Hasan summoned Verna.

'I am not pleased that Mrs Jefferson was allowed to approach Major Yamauchi herself.'

'I couldn't help it, Miss Hasan. She didn't ask my permission. You know I would have referred her to you.'

'Well, go and tell her from me that she and her friends in her hut will go without supper tonight and breakfast tomorrow morning for an act of disobedience. And find out what she said to him.'

There were groans in the hut when Verna announced the punishment. Marion protested, 'It's not fair, I merely wanted to ask the Major about our friends from the old camp who were separated from us, and how they're getting on. It wasn't a thing to trouble you with, and you wouldn't have been able to talk about people you've never met.'

'That isn't the point, Marion.'

'If it'll satisfy Miss Hasan's curiosity, he knows nothing about them nowadays.'

84

'I could have found that out for you. Did you make any other requests?'

'I . . . I did put in a word for Lillian Cartland and her Bobby. She's an old friend, Verna, and I'm worried about her.'

'You had no right. There are other women and children wondering if and when they're likely to be repatriated. Major Yamauchi would show no favouritism, I'm sure.'

'So he gave me to understand,' Marion answered bitterly. 'You can tell Miss Hasan that. It'll get you back in her good books.'

'Please, Marion,' said Verna, as she left, 'don't do that to me again.'

Marion could sympathise to some extent, though there was some hostility to be endured from all sides over the loss of two meals. She was vindicated in less than a week, however, for shortly after a lorry-load of new arrivals had entered the camp one afternoon Christina Campbell walked into the hut, to be greeted with glad cries. Marion did not crow 'Now who was right?' on her own behalf, but she knew that it was her talk with Yamauchi that had brought the half-Scots Eurasian girl back to them. When she had asked him about the splitting up of their old camp she had also mentioned Christina, who had been spirited away from this new camp so suddenly and inexplicably. He had frowned with what looked like surprise, and although he had given her no answer she had had the impression that he had made a mental note that that at least was a question to be followed up.

Christina looked healthy and less emaciated than they, although the impression of relative well-being was probably partly due to the neat frock and shoes she wore. Dorothy remarked on them, with snide inference.

'I was working for high Jap officials,' Christina explained without resentment. 'They expected me to be smart.'

'What else did they expect?'

'Nothing you wouldn't have given them,' Rose put in,

and Marion thought she detected Christina's relief at being spared having to give an answer.

'You never came across Yamauchi?' Marion herself asked.

'Not until yesterday. You've no idea how I felt when he said I'd be coming back here to live. It was awful being taken away from you all so suddenly.'

'You know Satan's in charge now?' Rose said.

'Anything's better than actually having to live among the Japs.'

'Speaking of men,' Rose said with a wicked intonation, 'did you hear anything about *our* men? Where any of them are?'

'Not specifically,' Christina answered. But she returned a secret look which made Rose's heart jump. She sensed that Christina had something to tell her when they could be alone.

She had thought correctly. When they were able to get out of earshot of the rest Christina said, 'Rose, I didn't want to say anything before the others, but . . .'

'*Yes?*'

' . . . when I was at HQ yesterday one of the natives approached me. He knew I was an internee because of my armband and that I was being sent back here. He said he's part of their underground and that he's in contact with some prisoners from the men's camp nearest here. I asked him about your Bernard and Kate's Tom . . .'

'*Christina!*'

'It's all right, Rose. They're alive and they're both there.'

Heedless that anyone, friend or guard, might be looking, Rose gave Christina a tight hug and a kiss on the cheek.

Although Christina had come back among them to live her duties at Headquarters continued. She was ferried there in the supply truck each day, a jolting, shaking journey which she nevertheless thought worthwhile to be able to be back among her friends.

After a few days of it she sought out Rose again. In a

86

place of concealment behind a hut she drew out from inside her official armband a tiny screw of paper. She handed it to Rose, who unrolled it greedily.

'Be sure to destroy it,' Christina warned. 'Promise.'

'Give me a chance to read it!'

'Yes, but then you must destroy it. And don't tell a soul you've received it. Not even Kate.'

'You haven't one for her?'

'No. And she's inclined to be a loudmouth.'

The note from Bernard was short enough, but sufficient to lift Rose to ecstasy.

'He wants us to meet! Night of the Jap Emperor's birthday, next Thursday. He says the guards in both camps will be too busy celebrating.'

'Japs always get blind drunk when they celebrate,' Christina confirmed.

'I know. It won't be any trouble. There's that place where the wire sags.'

'Where have you to go?'

'Somewhere between the two camps. A hut. He'll send instructions via your native friend the day before.'

'Rose, I can't go on doing this – acting as a go-between.'

'You must. You're our only link.'

'That native's risking his life every time. If they find out, it wouldn't just be you and I who'd pay . . .'

'Just this time, Christina – please. Let me see Bernard just once. Then perhaps something else can be worked out.'

'All right. But destroy that message now.'

Rose said, 'It's the first I've heard from him in all this time.'

'I know, but sentiment's full of risks. *Now*, Rose.'

'All right.' Reluctantly, she scanned the brief message for the last time and then tore it into tiny shreds which she slipped into the slimy ooze of an open drain. Then the two women went opposite ways.

29 April was the day marking the birthday of that reputedly divine being Hirohito, 'Son of Heaven', 124th in direct

lineage from the Emperor Jimmu, the first to ascend the Japanese throne in 660 BC. Hirohito had succeeded in 1926 to begin a reign designated *Showa*, which in English meant Enlightened Peace. Only the Japanese called it that any longer, as they celebrated it with ritual and liquor, which invariably went straight to their heads. Rose Millar's and Bernard Webster's chance of reunion could not have been more timely.

They had lived together unmarried in Singapore for a number of years before the invasion. Bernard was in his forties, a journalist and broadcaster whose patch had always been the tropics. He was tough and outspoken in private as well as professional life; and since Rose, his junior by a decade, had possessed all the arrogance and self-sufficiency of the attractive, well-off lady of leisure, their association had been one of stormy passion, intense love-making alternating with furious quarrels, punctuated with intervals of calm in which to regain breath and work up towards the next outburst. There were few dull moments. They deserved one another in every sense, and although there had been constant threats on either side to walk out for good they knew that they were bound together by something far more compelling than marriage vows. They had missed one another acutely during imprisonment. It was almost a natural outcome that they should be the first couple to find a chance of brief reunion, and they both seized it without hesitating over the considerable risk.

On the day before the festivities Christina brought Rose another little paper roll, this time a sketch map of the way to reach an abandoned ruin of a hut about a quarter of a mile from the women's camp. Seeing what it was Christina handed it over with misgiving.

'Honestly, Rose, I was hoping it would be a note calling it off.'

'Thanks a million!'

'I know it sounds heartless, but I'm thinking of the risk to so many people if you get caught. Not just you and

Bernard. The native, me, all of us in this camp and the men's. There could be the most awful reprisals.'

'The Japs will all be too drunk to notice.'

'They were drunk when they raped and murdered at Hong Kong and other places. Can't it be enough to know that each of you is alive and well?'

'For Christ's sake, this is what we've been longing for all this time. If it had been any of the other women they'd have grabbed the chance.'

There was no dissuading Rose. She felt drawn towards Bernard as inexorably as she had been after each of their many fights and brief severances. He would be feeling the same about her. He would never have called their rendezvous off, and she wasn't going to. She told Christina as much with all the vehemence that had once been hers when she was in a position to demand her own way. The Eurasian girl parted from her, wishing she had never become involved and wondering whether it would be better for everyone if she were to confide in Marion Jefferson, who, if persuasion failed, might find some way of preventing Rose.

She did nothing, though. Her mistake had been to bring the first message. Rose was aroused now, and Christina could see that it would take more than Marion or the whole lot of them to stop her going to her meeting.

By one of those unexplained whims of the Japanese, Blanche Simmons was suddenly reunited with her friends as blasphemous and ebullient as ever. Apart from some minor sores and boils and a scalp infection – a matter of course for the women – she was the same old Blanche. Her cockney spirit was still indomitable, as the shrewd Joss did not fail to notice as she watched Blanche's eyes on one of the Japanese guards and heard her mutter to herself, 'One of these days . . .'

Joss edged close and murmured, 'Never mind *one* of these days. Why not Thursday?'

'Thursday?'

'Emperor's birthday. Give 'em something to remember it by.'

'Such as what?' Blanche asked eagerly.

'Mess up a few machines at the factory, maybe.'

'You're on!'

'A little fire, too, perhaps. Somewhere near Satan's quarters.'

'His *hind*-quarters, for choice. I'm with you all the way.'

They decided to go it alone, two matchingly defiant spirits. But Blanche's closest friend had always been Rose, and she told her the plan, confident of recruiting an ally. To her surprise, Rose objected almost vehemently, asking her to call it off.

'Not ruddy likely,' Blanche retorted. 'You gone soft, like some of the rest of 'em?'

'No. But there's bound to be an almighty stink . . .'

'That's the idea. Sod them and their bleeding Emperor.'

'There'll be punishments all round. Early curfew. Cut rations.'

Blanche snorted. 'S'pose you'd sooner we all stood round singing' "Happy birthday, dear Emperor"?'

'You don't understand, Blanche.'

'Oh yes I do. Soon as I came here. You've all caved in, save that old Joss. Well, me and she reckon it's time we started fightin' back.'

Rose had wanted to keep her secret, even from this old friend whose reappearance she had welcomed more than she had said, but which threatened to prove so untimely. She could hold it back no longer.

'Blanche, listen – do it if you want, but not tomorrow. Any day but tomorrow.'

'What's so special?'

'I . . . I'm meeting Bernard.'

Once it was explained, Blanche's attitude changed completely. She went quickly to Joss and put it to her that since it was the Emperor's birthday, there would be unlikely to be any factory shift to make it possible for them to do any sabotage. There wouldn't be long to wait for another opportunity. Joss grunted sourly, but had to agree.

From then on Blanche was Rose's eager helper in her adventure. She assisted her to make what she could of her appearance. When the time drew near, they waited with shared impatience for the evening to advance, bringing growing darkness and an intensified volume of shouts and singing from the guard hut where the Japanese celebrations had started early. At last, making sure none of the other women saw them go, they crept off together to that weak part of the stockade where Blanche could hold up the barbed wire strands for Rose to wriggle through.

'Now hold it for me,' Blanche surprised her friend.

'What d'you mean?'

'I'm coming with you.'

'No fear. Two's company, three's a crowd at times like this.'

'Won't be no fun alone out there, gettin' to the place. I'll just come to see you there safe, then I'll beat it back. Promise.'

Rose didn't hesitate further. She was glad of the comfort of a companion to find the way through the undergrowth in the direction Bernard's memorised sketch had indicated. She held up the wire and Blanche followed her through.

It was a frightening enough journey, even so. Used to being herded among others every hour of every day and night for more than two years, they felt eerily alone in the semi-jungle, threading their way along what had once been a track but was now overgrown. Creepers snagged their feet and made them trip more than once. Fronds and low branches caught at their legs and thighs. Sometimes they had to force them back to get by.

There were sounds all around: the stirring and calling of creatures and birds and monkeys. It did not do to imagine what unseen things crawled and slithered at their feet. At one point a greater sound petrified them into halting and crouching motionless and silent. Men's voices, talking the native tongue, approached, and two figures strode past, almost touching the girls, who waited with held breath until they were well past.

At long last they were able to make out the sloping roof of the hut which was the rendezvous. The singing from the camp was still audible. At least it would help guide them separately back there, if the singers hadn't all passed out into drunken slumber by the time Rose was ready to return.

There was light enough to see that the hut was rotted and broken and that there was no one waiting in it.

'Looks like you've beat him to it,' Blanche said. 'Want me to stay with you till he comes?'

Rose did. They moved to the hut and sat down to wait.

'What if he can't come after all?' she began to worry.

'Relax. He'll come.'

'I'm glad you did, Blanche.'

'Poor substitute, but at least I'm company.'

The wait must have seemed longer than it was. Rose began to fret again.

'If he'd kept me waiting this long in Singapore I'd have stood him up. God, I feel sick.'

'That'll be a nice way to greet him.'

'I'm frightened.'

'What of?'

'Of what I might feel at seeing him again.'

'You know what you feel. It's what's kept you going.'

' "Love" was a word we never used – except in the middle of sex, and that's different.'

'Yeah.'

'It belongs with words like "marriage" and "children". We didn't talk about them, either.'

'No strings, you always told me.'

'It suited us fine.'

'And now?'

'I don't know if it's him I love – or just the idea of him.'

'Well, you better find out, 'cos here he comes.'

Blanche had been the first to hear the approaching male voice, softly calling 'Rose?'

'I'm off,' she said, scrambling up. 'Don't do anything I would.'

She was gone; and from another direction there loomed towards Rose a form which she believed she could never have mistaken in any circumstances. The familiar voice made her cry out mentally, but she would not have been Rose if she had not greeted him with, 'For goodness sake, what kept you?'

'Same old Rose,' Bernard answered – and then they were hugging one another closer than they had ever hugged before.

They stood back at last to survey one another; each saw a very changed version of the image so often dragged back from memory for fear that neglect of it might make it evaporate. Bernard's comfortable bar-counter bulk had all gone. He was angular, bony, hollow-cheeked and sunken-eyed. There were sores on his skin and his ill-cut hair was spiky and silver in the moonlight. It didn't need his expression to tell her what changes he was marking in her.

There was an awkward silence between them, neither knowing what to say. Bernard was able to break it by fumbling in the pocket of the bush jacket which hung about him. 'I've got something for you. Best I could do, I'm afraid.' He produced a small jar. 'Yeast extract. Good old Vitamin B.'

'Where on earth did you get that?'

'Local tuck shop.'

'Share it?'

'It's for you.'

'I can't take it back with me, and I'm not going to eat it in front of you.'

'All right, then. No spoon, though.'

He put his arm round her and guided her into the ruined hut. They sat on the floor and shared the sticky yeast, dipping their fingers to get it.

'Before I forget,' Bernard said, 'that girl Kate Norris in your camp – tell her Tom Redburn sends his love.'

'He might have sent her a note.'

'He can't, poor sod. He's in a cell.'

'Cell?'

'Solitary. Nips caught him stealing some paper.'

'Is it . . . awful?'

'Not much fun. I'll spare you the details. You won't want to be passing them on to her.'

'Have you. . .?'

'We've all had our turn, Rose . . .'

Strangely, she wanted to put off any emotional exchange. It was as though she needed to re-establish mundane contact first.

'That was the nicest meal I ever had,' she said, savouring the last of the yeast from her fingertip.

'You wait till we get back, old girl. We'll have a right old blow-out, by God we will.'

'Do you think we will . . . get out of here?'

'There are rumours through the natives. Looks as if the Allies are starting to turn things around.'

'They'd better hurry.'

His arm went round her again. 'We'll survive, you and I. We've toughened ourselves up on each other.'

'Yes.'

'And soon as we get back, we're going to do something we should've done long since. Get married. I love you, Rose.'

'I love you, Bernard.'

They sank to the floor in each other's arms.

8 Christina

The commotion over at the Japanese quarters had changed tone so abruptly that the women awoke and sat up on their mattresses to listen. The raucous singing and laughter had stopped. Now there were shouts of command and abuse, passed down from one man to another, and soon the scuffle of running feet was heard.

'Christina,' Marion called along the hut. 'Can you tell what they're saying?'

'A woman's escaped. They're going looking for her.'

'Oh God!'

It was only now that, glancing round the hut, Marion noticed Rose's absence. There was nothing unusual about that. Their variety of intestinal bugs had most of them on the trot, day and night, but suddenly Blanche burst into uncharacteristic tears.

'It's Rose,' she sobbed. 'They'll kill her!'

The whole story came out for the first time. At Rose's insistence only Blanche and Christina had been in the know. She had been certain that Marion would forbid her expedition if she learned of it. Marion would have indeed, and her alarm now was mixed with anger at the girl's stupidity, not only on her account but for all of them, the men prisoners at the other camp included.

'You should have told me,' she stormed at Blanche and Christina.

'You're not our leader any more,' Blanche snapped back defensively. 'Would you have had me tell Verna?'

'Even that would have been better than keeping quiet. Anything that would have stopped her.'

'Nothing was going to. She'd have found a way.'

These fruitless speculations were brought to an end by the hut door crashing open. A half-dressed, bleary-eyed guard swayed there, waving his rifle dangerously at them all. Miss Hasan and Verna, both looking the worse for wear and obviously having shared in the revels, followed him in. Miss Hasan shoved him aside, something even she would not have dared do if he had been sober.

'You fools!' she almost shrieked. 'There'll be hell to pay for you all this time.'

'We don't know what's going on,' Marion tried bluffing.

'Do not lie to me! Rose Millar sneaks away from camp, and you don't know about it? Well, you will all pay, you will see.'

She turned and left unsteadily, followed by Verna, looking apprehensive that she would come in for a share of the blame. The guard swung his rifle around, covering them all in turn, and it seemed that at the least movement from any of them he would open fire. As it happened it would have done no harm, for in hastening drunkenly from the guard room he had quite overlooked the fact that his weapon was unloaded. But they were not to know that, and it was a moment of relief when he spat towards them all and went staggering away.

'To be free . . . just one of us,' said Blanche.

At that moment two shots were heard some distance away. The women stared at one another in horror, with the exception of Beatrice Mason. She had risen from her mattress and was making the few changes that differentiated her night clothing from what she wore in the day.

'Get dressed, Norris,' she told Kate curtly. 'Dr Trier's going to need our help – if any help's possible.'

At the hospital a new shock awaited them. Natalie Trier was not there, and when Beatrice questioned the Dutch assistant on duty she was told that the doctor had gone.

'Gone?'

'For repatriation. They took her and two others and their children tonight in a truck.'

'Dear God, why didn't you send me word?'

The woman shrugged. She was an old inmate of this camp who had worked with the French doctor since long before the new women's coming. Beatrice had not failed to notice how Natalie Trier's grudging acceptance of her had been reflected by the assistants.

'She left no messages?'

'Nothing special. She was just taken off.'

'Typical Nip,' commented Kate. 'They keep you waiting without news, then whisk you off without a word to anyone else. Like they did to Christina.'

'The notes on the present patients are still here, though there doesn't seem to be much else,' Beatrice confirmed, searching the desk. 'Right,' she told the Dutchwoman. 'I'm taking charge of the hospital now. Help Norris get the operating-table ready, and pray hard that we might be in time to use it.'

The operating-table was literally a table, a plain wooden one, with a smaller one beside it for instruments and equipment, all of it makeshift. Beatrice gave orders for the paraffin heater to be lit and a bucket of water brought to the boil in readiness. As a steadfast atheist, she did not pray that any of it would be of any use; she merely hoped and made ready, helped by the shaken and shocked Kate, the Dutchwoman and a Chinese girl.

At length a dread procession was seen coming in by the gates. The guards Shinya and Kasaki were bearing a form between them, without benefit of stretcher, one holding the feet and the other the armpits. At an order from the sergeant, his voice hoarse and slurred with drink, they carried Rose into the hospital and dropped, rather than placed, her on to the operating-table indicated by Kate. Then the Japanese left them to it.

Beatrice swiftly moved forward to lift the lid of one of Rose's shut eyes and then to feel for her jugular vein.

'She's alive,' she said. 'Just about. The wound must be in her back. You two turn her gently to expose it.'

Kate and the Dutchwoman turned Rose very slowly. Her dress was torn and dirty, and the many earth stains and lacerations pointed to her having been dragged part of the way, rather than carried. The wound itself was just below her waist, just to the side of her spine. It was small and dark and bleeding only slightly. Beatrice peered closely through her defective spectacles.

'The bullet's still in there,' she said grimly. 'That's all we need.'

'At least she can't feel anything,' offered Kate.

'Because she's concussed into the bargain. That's something else we could do without. Right, Norris. Get the following: another bucket of water boiled up; every dressing there is in the place; alcohol; tweezers, knives, narrow-bladed and sharp; needles and fine undyed thread.'

Kate was staring back.

'We haven't got half those things.'

'*Get* them. Go back to the hut – to the other huts, if you have to. Beg and borrow those things, but don't come back without them, because there wouldn't be any point in it.'

Kate hurried away. With her hutmates' help she gradually amassed all the items Beatrice had listed, although some of them came in far from conventional forms. The tweezers were a pair of Victorian silver sugar spoons which Verna donated. The knives were the two blades of a pair of scissors, taken apart and quickly sharpened using stones. A nail-file was contributed, some needles and a reel of plain cotton wound round a stick, pieces of mosquito net, a handkerchief with a flower embroidered in a corner, a small scrap of silk, a sliver of soap. A child offered a safety-pin, almost reducing Kate to tears when she saw that it meant that he would have to keep constant hold of his shorts to stop them slipping down. She accepted all the same.

Cockney Daisy and the Dutch and Chinese assistants were meanwhile obeying Beatrice's order to scrub every inch of the room in which Rose lay, walls, floor and furniture included. Even Verna brought an unopened bottle of Lysol disinfectant. Such a commodity would have been invaluable to the hospital all along, but it was no time for Beatrice to stop and ask why it had only just been produced.

In this makeshift way the preparations for the essential operation were made. Beatrice had to insist on the removal of two guards whom Captain Sato had stationed in the sick bay in case Rose should come round and talk. It took some convincing him that their presence constituted a grave risk of infection, but at length he yielded, so long as they remained immediately outside the door.

Beatrice and her assistants donned makeshift overalls, back to front, sleeves rolled up with scarves covering their hair. Strips of mosquito net were tied across their mouths and noses. The bucket of water steamed in the background and the bizarre assortment of instruments was spread out neatly on a cloth on the side-table.

Using a rag soaked in *sake*, also contributed by Verna, Kate cleaned the wound and the surrounding skin. Beatrice finished soaking her arms in the bucket of cooling water, and turned with her hands held high, thankful that her recent infection had cleared.

'All ready?' she asked. 'Right. Let's get on with it.'

It would have been a major challenge to a full-time army surgeon, fit and confident and as adept at removing bullets as tonsils. The bullet's position so close to Rose's spinal column gave Beatrice no leeway to manoeuvre with her clumsy instruments. One assistant held the room's single electric bulb, but Beatrice still had to work with her head craned to one side to focus through the one good lens of her spectacles. Perspiration from heat and tension streamed down from under her hairline and was mopped constantly by the Dutchwoman, leaning across from the opposite side of the patient. Kate constantly held Rose's pulse, fearing that the worst thing of all would happen and she would wake up and start to scream with the pain. There was no means of putting her under again if she did.

After what seemed ages of careful, precise probing with the two scissors blades in separate hands, Beatrice slapped one of them into Kate's free hand and ordered, in a shuddering breath of apprehension, 'Tongs'. Kate automatically repeated 'Tongs', and placed Joss's Victorian silver pair firmly in Beatrice's palm. Beatrice grasped them and stooped again towards the open wound.

In the dormitory hut, further sleep was out of the question. A Tenko had dragged them all out into the night and kept them standing while the still fuddled guards made even more futile than usual attempts to agree on how many were present. Sato raved in Japanese and Miss Hasan in English, telling them that there would be a further cut in rations until those who had helped Rose get out of the camp owned up. Then Christina was kept back after the rest had been dismissed, and taken by a guard into Sato's room.

'God knows what they'll do to her to make her talk,' Dorothy said, back in the hut. 'If they found Rose with her feller they'll be bound to suspect that it was Christina fixed the meeting. She's the only one who could have.'

'Then,' said Marion, 'she'd have been the last one likely to give Rose away.'

'What's that supposed to mean?' Joss demanded.

'I've been thinking,' Marion answered. 'When the Hasan creature came staggering in here to bawl us out, did she or didn't she distinctly say that it was Rose who'd gone?'

'She did.'

'But how did she know it was Rose without having to have a Tenko first and find who was missing?'

'You're right!' Joss exclaimed. 'She knew already. Someone had told her.'

'That's what I'm saying – but scarcely Christina, who'd organised it.'

'I am not very sure,' put in Mrs Van Meyer, whose only

contribution to the night's proceedings had been a flow of complaints about her lost sleep and now the further ration cut. 'I have never trusted that girl since she went off to work for them at Headquarters.'

'Was taken off, you mean,' Marion corrected.

'How do we know? That was perhaps just a story for us to believe. Then she could later be put back amongst us to spy on us. See how she has become like a sleek cat since she went to work for them. She has put on weight. Her clothes are like new.'

Even Marion had to concede that much, but she could not bring herself to believe the accusation.

'Are you saying that she set up Rose's meeting because the Japs told her to, in order to get Rose shot and give them the excuse to cut our rations?'

'Balderdash!' Joss agreed. 'They could knock any of us off whenever they felt like it without going to those lengths. And they're always cutting the rations. At this rate there won't be any left to cut.'

'I do not mean such a thing,' snapped Mrs Van Meyer angrily. She had not yet forgiven Joss for possessing a title. She had kept the knowledge of it to herself, rather than let any of the others regard Joss as anything but a cantankerous and eccentric old ex-Suffragette.

'What then?'

'I mean that Christina did arrange the meeting. The night when she knew the guards would be celebrating would be ideal. But then, too late, she realised that she must be the suspect for having arranged it, because she only has been outside the camp and able to get a message to the men. So she does not wait for the Japanese to become sober again and work that out. She tells them that Rose has gone.'

'To meet her feller?' Dorothy mocked. 'That'd be a dead give-away that Christina had fixed it.'

'I do not imagine she mentioned the man at all. She would merely say that Rose had escaped.'

'Where to?'

'Does it matter? To escape is enough.'

'Why didn't we all go, then?'

'Because . . . because maybe we were afraid, or thought it would be fruitless. Rose is a headstrong girl.'

'The Japs don't know what each of us is like,' Joss snorted. 'We're all alike to them – fourth-rate white trash.'

'Verna knows us, and Miss Hasan has some ideas of the way we are.'

'From your gossiping while you're prettying them up – and buttering 'em up.'

'Do stop it, Joss,' said Marion testily. 'We have to work this out. I don't like the implication, but what Dominica's saying does have logic.'

'Thank you, Marion. I would have you all know that I do not do their hair to be in their favour. A Van Meyer hairdressing for a half-chat! I do it because I think it is useful to be in some of their confidence and perhaps hear things.'

'Like hell!' muttered Joss, but only to herself.

'Then why have they got Christina in for questioning now?' Dorothy wanted to know.

'We can't be sure that they have,' Marion had to admit. 'It's probably just for show, to keep us from being suspicious.'

'Wait till the bitch comes back here. I'll throttle her with my own hands.'

'You won't touch her, Dorothy! Not by word or sign will any of us show any suspicion. If the Hasan hadn't been drinking too much for caution, and let Rose's name drop by accident, we wouldn't have any reason to believe she'd been betrayed at all.'

'Then how'd they find out? There weren't any guards on duty. No . . . Oh, streuth!'

'What it is Dorothy?'

'. . . nothing.'

'Come on. What have you remembered?'

'Well, Shinya told me he'd volunterred to stay on duty. He doesn't drink. I wanted him to meet me, but he wouldn't. Whatever you lot think, he's a decent type. Takes his job seriously. If he says he'll keep guard while the rest go on the piss, he'll do it properly.'

'He didn't much, did he?'

'He couldn't be everywhere, one man. Rose must've watched till he was well away from her before she went.'

A silence fell. They had talked round the topic and seemed to have come full circle. The Eurasian girl, a low-paid tourist guide in civilian life whom circumstances had forced these *tuans'* wives to live with and treat as an equal, had thrown in her lot with the present lords of South-East Asia as readily as Miss Hasan had more blatantly done.

'They know which side their bread's buttered,' Joss remarked, and everyone knew just what she meant.

'I tell you something,' Mrs Van Meyer said to Dorothy, with a gleam of malice in her eye. 'Your Jap friend Shinya – it was no doubt he who shot Rose.'

'How the hell can you say that?'

'He was one of two who carried her in, but you say he was the only one sober of them all. The rest could not have hit an elephant in the daylight.'

Dorothy swore at her; but, with a sinking feeling in her stomach, she realised that the Dutchwoman was probably right.

'Remember,' Marion was reiterating, 'whatever we suspect about this business, whatever we might think we can work out, we keep it strictly to ourselves. Only Rose knows the whole truth, and we simply do not say anything until we have her version.'

'Supposing she lives to tell us it,' said Joss.

'She'll live,' said a weary voice from the doorway. An exhausted Beatrice Mason, supported by Kate Norris, came tottering into the hut and almost fell onto her own mattress. Kate opened her clenched hand and released something which fell with a small thud on to the upturned box which was all the table they had. They peered and saw a blood-smeared bullet.

Naturally, Beatrice had to be told their suspicion. As their sole doctor now she had risen in status among them, and as one of their original party from the old camp, where Christina had also been, it was felt that she had the right to know. Blanche was drawn into the discussion too, as the one who had helped Rose get out. She confirmed Christina's role and flatly refused to add her support to her condemnation.

This was two days after the incident. Rose was reported to be fully conscious at last, but Beatrice Mason sternly refused her visitors and parried all enquiries by saying that it was too early to give an opinion of her general condition.

Beatrice sat alone on the verandah edge with Marion, digesting what she had been told. She sighed. 'What I wouldn't give for a drink!'

'You and me both,' Marion agreed.

'I'm past it Marion. I'm getting old – and to think that in Singapore I was almost classed as young.'

'Weren't we all, compared with the old memsahibs? Perhaps it'll give you a new lease of life, stepping into the perfect Trier shoes.'

'Her shoes wouldn't fit me, Marion. Too narrow. Too hard. She'd have been writing Rose up in one of her case histories. Apparently she's been collecting material all this time for a book on practising medicine under adverse conditions. We've all been objects of study for her.'

'Well, she missed out on the way you managed to operate on Rose. I bet she couldn't have done better with a pair of scissors and some sugar tongs.'

Beatrice turned to her old friend and said seriously, 'I haven't been telling people, but you at least ought to know – it's unlikely Rose will ever walk again.'

'Oh, Beatrice, no!'

'She's paralysed from the site of the wound. She can

improve generally, so long as there are no complications and given decent nourishment – and I don't frankly see much prospect of that – but she won't walk, ever.'

'What can we do?'

Beatrice shrugged. 'Nothing, except visit her when she's well enough. Try anything to take her mind off it – if that's ever possible.'

Their moment of grave contemplation together was broken by a woman's voice. It was Lillian Cartland, gaunt from her self-imposed near-starvation. She was holding Bobby by the hand, which at his age he hated.

'Dr Mason, I went to the surgery, but there was only that Australian nurse in charge. I really can't have my Bobby's boils neglected like this.'

'Lillian . . .' Marion began, but Beatrice cut across her wearily.

'Let's have a look at your neck, Bobby. Mm. Splendid! Clearing up more quickly than I'd dared hope.'

'They look worse to me,' Lillian frowned.

'They might look it to you, Mrs Cartland, but I'm here to tell you they're not.'

'Are you sure you can *see*?'

Marion saw Beatrice's lips tighten at the slighting allusion to her eyes.

'*And* he's got sores all over his bottom. Show the doctor, Bobby.' Before the boy could protest, which he did, his mother had pushed him round and pulled his shorts open at his thin waist. Beatrice looked in, then said, 'What can you expect, when you keep him sitting by you in the shade all day instead of running about with the other children. He needs exercise.'

'Exercise! On this diet!'

'Far better than a diet of apron strings.'

'You just don't understand, Dr Mason. He's always been delicate and weak, hasn't he, Marion?'

'Lillian, I think . . .'

But the discussion was not to be continued. Beatrice

Mason's eyesight was not so defective that she couldn't see Captain Sato and Miss Hasan making their way purposefully towards her hospital. She jumped up and hurried after them, leaving Lillian Cartland to exclaim an outraged '*Well!*'

Beatrice almost ran into the side ward where Rose lay. The Dutch assistant was cowering in a corner. Sato and Miss Hasan stood on either side of the patient, bending menacingly towards her. Sato was shouting in Japanese.

'Who helped you escape?' Miss Hasan translated. 'Who helped you contact the male prisoner? You must answer Captain Sato.'

'Leave her alone!' Beatrice raged. 'This patient is very sick indeed.'

'She has only herself to blame for that,' Miss Hasan retorted. 'Herself and whoever helped her. Who was it?' she demanded of Rose again.

'No one,' Rose answered faintly. Her cheeks were deathly pale. 'I did it myself.'

Miss Hasan translated rapidly for Sato, then asked, 'How?'

'A native was passing. I waved him to come over to me. I gave him a message to take to the men's camp. I paid him with a little brooch.'

'Captain Sato says he does not believe you.'

'It's the truth.'

'There must have been someone else. Who brought a message back, arranging where to meet?'

'The same native. I'm telling the truth. Please go away.'

'Please, Miss Hasan,' Beatrice put in. 'She's seriously ill.'

Miss Hasan ignored her, translating Rose's last reply to Sato. He glared at the pale, helpless girl for some moments, then shrugged and spoke again for Miss Hasan to translate.

'Captain Sato says he does not believe you, but he will let the matter rest for the present. I am to tell you, though,

106

that your stupid action had worse results than perhaps you know. You may have survived, but your lover was killed.'

Rose began to scream. Her cries were so rending and her accompanying struggles so painfully ineffectual that even Sato and Miss Hasan could not stand the sound and sight. They left hurriedly. Beatrice hurried forward to give Rose what comfort she could, holding her like a hurt child.

9 Beatrice

'I still don't believe,' said a perplexed Marion that evening, 'that Christina would take the risk of acting as go-between and then decide to give them away.'

'Perhaps she was riding to the Nips' orders all along,' said Dorothy. 'She's close enough to them. Look at the way they're looking after her.'

'But why Rose? Why not Kate as well, and her Tom? Why not a whole bunch of us, if they want an excuse to thin our numbers down?'

Joss gave one of her snorts. 'Who says Rose was set up and betrayed at all? Perhaps Shinya saw her getting through the wire and raised the alarm instead of shooting at her.'

Beatrice shook her head. 'Rose and Bernard were together quite some time before the Japs came for them. She told me. It's her one consolation to cling to.'

'Then,' said Marion carefully, 'someone knew she was going, and waited till she did, rather than risk giving a false alarm and spoiling the Nips' party.'

'Christina knew,' Dorothy persisted. 'She knew it all. It's got to be her.'

'Circumstantial evidence,' Joss snapped.

'Well, Verna seems convinced enough,' said Marion. 'It's Christina she wants before the Discipline Committee. Whatever we do, remember to say nothing at all about her carrying those messages. If she isn't in with the Japs, that could get her shot.'

'Good riddance!' thought Dorothy, but only conveyed it with a scowl.

The committee met an hour later under Verna's chairmanship. It was a wary affair, with the internee members deeply suspicious of Verna's exact standing with Miss Hasan and the Japanese. But before Christina was sent for Verna made no secret of her suspicion of her.

'She works at Headquarters. She's better nourished and clothed than any other internee, so she's getting favours for which she'd be expected to do favours in return. Miss Hasan had her in her room for some time after the incident, but she hasn't punished her at all.'

'You've no idea what that interview was about?' Marion asked.

'Marion, I want to stress that I'm one of *you*. I have some responsibilities which set me apart a little, but I'm still just an internee. Miss Hasan only tells me what she sees fit.'

Marion felt the nudge of Joss's knee at this.

'I think we'd better have her in,' decided Verna. 'Dominica, please . . .'

Mrs Van Meyer, grumbling that she should be picked out as messenger, went to fetch Christina from the hut. While she was gone Verna reiterated, 'I must say how shocked I am at this whole business. The lack of thought for others, for all of us. The whole camp and the men's might have been put into jeopardy.'

'Whereas it's only Rose's life that's in jeopardy,' murmured Beatrice.

Christina was brought in by a stern-faced Mrs Van Meyer, who had changed her mind and decided to enjoy the role of wardress. The pretty Eurasian's glance darted from one to another of them and she moistened her lips nervously.

'Sit down, please, Christina,' invited Verna sweetly. 'There's nothing to be afraid of.'

'I'm not afraid,' replied Christina, who pointedly remained standing.

'Good. Now you know why the Discipline Committee

109

wish to hear from you. In view of certain circumstantial evidence, it's only fair to give you the chance to put your side of the story.'

Christina lifted her chin defiantly. 'All I have to say is this. I'm British, and I've always been proud to be. If it's accepted that everything that's meant by the term British honour applies to women as well as to men, and *if* you consider me British, then you'll know I would never betray a friend.'

There was an uneasy silence for some moments before Verna asked, 'Is that all?'

'Yes, thank you.'

'Any questions, anyone?'

There were none.

'You will be told the decision,' intoned Mrs Van Meyer sepulchrally, and led Christina out.

There was nothing more to discuss. Everything had been argued and speculated over already. They took a vote which resulted in four in Christina's favour and three against, excluding Verna's as chairman. The result meant that there could only be a finding of not proven for lack of evidence. Marion was deputed to carry the decision to Christina, which she did with pleasure. It was coldly received, and Marion's attempt to reassure the girl was brushed aside. Christina made no attempt to hide the fact that the accusation had offended her deeply, and that the committee's divided vote had not cleared her completely.

Rumour had done its nasty work, moreover. Word had quickly spread about the camp that Christina had sold out one of her friends to the Japanese, with the result that she was cold-shouldered for it as well as for working at Headquarters and looking so healthy. At Headquarters, the District Commander had heard the talk about her down his grapevine and watched her curiously as she stared into space over a translation she was supposed to be doing for him.

'You are feeling ill?' Major Yamauchi asked.

She came to with a start and shook her head.

'Then you must work,' he reminded her, not unkindly. '*We* must work. There is much still to do, serving the Emperor to liberate the East from the white oppressor.'

'I am British, Major Yamauchi.'

'On one side only. Your mother's family have known what it is to live under white servitude.'

'My mother loved a British man enough to marry him,' she retorted spiritedly.

'Yet rumour reaches me from the camp . . .'

'Rumour is a liar, Major. If Rose Millar was betrayed it was not by me. Ask Captain Sato, Miss Hasan – anyone. They must know who it was.'

'Pass me water.'

Christina passed over the carafe. Yamauchi took a little lacquered pill-box from his drawer and swallowed one of the pills with the water. He indicated the food which had just been brought in for his luncheon.

'Eat it,' he said. 'I do not want.'

'I . . . I feel guilty eating your food, Major, when the others are on reduced rations and blame me for it.'

Yamauchi answered without emotion, 'Here is food. I am ill and cannot eat. You are hungry.'

She had been eating much of his food for as long as she had been working for him, hence her well-nourished appearance. He looked sick and drawn. But today, with last night's accusation still vivid in her mind, she could not eat. Yamauchi shrugged and bent to his paperwork again.

Yamauchi's pain was as nothing compared with Rose's. His was spasmodic, like a rising, cresting, breaking wave; and if it did not spend itself naturally, there were the contents of the little box to ease him through it. Beatrice Mason had no drugs to ease Rose's constant suffering, which did not diminish of its own accord. She slept little, and so had to endure it. Apart from the limited nursing she could receive, all that could be offered was kindness by those who attended her and in brief visits from her friends.

111

The visits were few. Neither Rose nor those who came could manage more than a little effort and pretended optimism. Blanche came one morning, to learn from Beatrice that Rose had managed her first consecutive couple of hours' sleep, and had benefited much from it.

"Ullo, 'ullo, 'ullo!' Blanche breezed in, with Beatrice's permission. 'Hear we're quite perky today, then.'

Rose returned one of her now rare smiles. Blanche, who had been the most regular of her visitors, was more aware than the others might have been of a change in her friend. Something more than the boon of sleep was responsible for the tranquillity about her; but there was something unnatural to it which troubled Blanche.

She held out a little bunch of jungle flowers.

'Brought you these. Bit droopy, but not much choice, eh?' She put them in Rose's hand.

'They're very nice, Blanche. Very pretty. Thanks.'

'How are you, then?'

'Could be worse.'

'That's the spirit. Anything you'd like?'

Both recognised the fatuity of the question. The hopelessness behind it and other such bedside observances was largely responsible for the brevity and awkwardness of sick-visiting in such a place.

'Like?' Rose answered. 'Only to know Bernard's OK.'

'Oh, surely. I mean, them guards are no marksmen. It were just a sheer bit of luck, them getting you . . . I mean . . . What I meant was . . . Oh, Gawd!' Her voice trailed away from the attempt to redeem her gaffe.

'You don't have to, you know,' Rose said.

'Have to what? Be so bloody stupid?'

'Be so careful. It's of no moment, after all.'

It stung Blanche. Some drooping flowers and her sympathy were all she had to offer. Rose had accepted the former and seemed to be spurning the latter.

'Do you have to be so bloody kind?' Blanche couldn't stop herself saying.

Rose smiled into her eyes. 'But of course. At least I can still do that.' She snapped off the smile and turned her head away in an unmistakable gesture of dismissal. Blanche hurried out, getting a curious look from Beatrice, who had been about to enter.

'What's all that?' Beatrice demanded.

'Enjoying my remaining pleasure – the ability to hurt.'

Beatrice snorted. 'Nothing wrong with hurting, if it gets your spirit up.'

'For what?' Rose answered bitterly, and there was nothing Beatrice could reply.

Behind a hut, Lillian Cartland and her Bobby were arguing. The cause of it was a small jar of yeast.

'No, Mummy,' the boy was protesting. 'You eat it. You gave me your egg yesterday. It's not fair you should give me all yours and have nothing.'

'Please, Bobby, eat it up. You're young and need it.'

'You need it, too. Mummy, you're getting so thin.'

'I'm all right. Once they repatriate us I'll start eating properly again and I'll soon put it back on. Ladies are always trying to lose weight,' Lillian tried joking.

Reluctantly, Bobby dipped his finger into the jar and carried a blob of the sticky brown extract to his mouth. Just at that moment Joss came round the back of the hut.

For some time she had been becoming more obsessed with the idea that they should all be waging a constant campaign of sabotage against the Japanese. Little support was forthcoming from the others; there seemed too little they could hope to do, and the risk of reprisals for any success was too great to make it worthwhile. Still Joss persisted, and filled in much of her spare time snooping about, looking for discarded odds and ends to hoard against the day when she should hit on a plan in which they would prove useful.

At sight of one another Joss and Lillian froze. It was a moment before the older woman registered what was going on there, but when she did she sprang forward, recognising the jar of yeast for what it was.

'Where the hell did you get that?' she demanded. 'Pinched it from the patients did you? Answer me?'

She had seized Lillian by the shoulder and was shaking her violently. Bobby cried out, 'Leave my mummy alone. Let go of her!'

His high-pitched cry reached Marion, who was passing the front of the hut just then. She came running.

'Joss! Lillian! For heaven's sake pipe down. The guards will hear.'

'Something worth their hearing,' Joss answered grimly. 'Look at this. Yeast. A whole jar of it, pinched from the sick for this spoiled little brat to get his fingers into.'

'It wasn't stolen,' Lillian insisted, scrambling to her feet. 'Marion, please.'

'How did you get it, Lillian?'

'I . . . I earned it. Working for Verna.'

As it happened, Marion had only just left an irate Mrs Van Meyer. That lady, whose self-importance had survived two years of imprisonment and had been renewed by the dubious privilege of acting as hairdresser to Verna Johnson and the almighty Miss Hasan, had just suffered a setback. She had been informed by Verna that her additional services as domestic servant had been given to someone else – Lillian Cartland.

'She needs the little money I can give her to buy extra food for her child,' Verna had explained. Mrs Van Meyer had been unable to protest in the face of the seemingly good cause, though she shared the general view of the women about Lillian's over-protective attitude towards Bobby, which had only brought him and his mother general dislike. Mrs Van Meyer had just been venting her feelings on Marion, who could not bring herself to feel overly sympathetic.

'I work for her for only a little pay,' Mrs Van Meyer

had complained. 'I only do it because I hope to hear things to the advantage of us all.'

Marion took that with a large pinch of salt; but she could believe that Verna paid only a pittance for the work, certainly not as much as would buy a jar of yeast extract, even if that commodity were ever for sale at the 'shop'. Beatrice had complained that there was little available even for her patients – yet now Marion was looking at an almost full jar of it, clutched in Lillian's hand.

'Verna gave you that?' she said.

'Y . . . yes. For Bobby.'

'But you've only just started working for her.'

'It was . . . a sort of advance on my wages.'

'Yeast extract?' exclaimed Joss. 'It's as scarce as gold dust.'

A blinding suspicion hit Marion. She said to the boy, 'Bobby, dear – just run along for a few minutes, will you? There's something I want to talk to Mummy about privately.'

The boy looked at his mother. She nodded miserably and said, 'Do as Aunt Marion says, darling.'

He still hesitated. 'I didn't even want it,' he told Marion. 'Like Mummy's egg yesterday. I wanted her to eat it, but she made me.'

'I understand, Bobby. Run along, please.'

He went. Marion turned to Lillian, who could not return her gaze.

'Tell me the truth, Lillian. You sold Rose, for a job and food for Bobby?'

Lillian kept her eyes still cast down. 'For Bobby,' she admitted dully. She raised her eyes appealingly to Marion and to Joss, who was looking on aghast. 'He's so delicate. He'll never survive. But I never dreamed they'd shoot her – never, never!'

'*My* God!' Joss ejaculated.

Lillian faltered, 'She's . . . going to get better – isn't she?'

115

Marion didn't answer. She asked instead, 'How did you know about Rose getting out of the camp?'

'I overheard her and Blanche planning it. I waited till I saw them go to the wire, and Blanche helped her to get through.'

'Was it Verna you told?'

'Yes.'

'You didn't mention Blanche as well?'

'No.'

'Rose was enough,' Joss snorted. 'What's female for Judas?'

Lillian pleaded, 'Marion, I feel so dreadfully about it. I know it was an awful thing to do. I just saw the chance of getting in her favour, for Bobby's sake not mine. Finding we weren't on the repatriation list was the last straw, and watching him get thinner and sicker . . .'

'He's about the healthiest looking brat in the camp,' said Joss. 'So he should be, at the price of two women and a man.'

Lillian stared at her. Marion opened her mouth to silence Joss, but she was too late.

'Rose with her life touch and go. Her man dead. And Christina despised all round for something she didn't do.'

Lillian was weeping now. Marion said, 'That won't help, Joss.'

'Don't come the old girls act, Marion,' was the retort. 'She may have been your friend from way back, but we're living strictly for the present now. And don't say there must be some way of explaining it away, because there isn't. Everyone's got to know.'

'Oh please!' Lillian sobbed. She had known the risk she was running, but the awfulness of it only came home to her now.

Realisation became reality later that day. Joss had flatly refused Marion's request to her to say nothing to the others until she could think things out. She went straight to the hut and told those who were there. Not long afterwards when Lillian entered the wash-room she was seized by Dorothy and Blanche, who had been waiting for her. While Dorothy held her securely, forcing her arms so tightly behind her back that she found it too painful to wriggle, Blanche began hacking at her hair with Mrs Van Meyer's scissors, those same ones that had been taken apart for Rose's operation. Tufts of hair fell onto the terrified Lillian's shoulders and drifted down to the floor. Only the arrival on the scene of Bobby, and his anguished cries – which brought Marion running – saved Lillian from a complete cropping and perhaps real injury. Even so, it took heated persuasion for Marion to get them to release their victim.

'I'll go and tackle Verna about it myself,' she promised them. 'If we create any more incidents for Hasan and Sato to hear about we'll all be in even worse trouble. We're none of us in a fit state to work harder or get less rations, so we'll have to forgo the luxury of vengeance.'

'Your old school pal!' Dorothy sneered. 'Never mind what she's done to Rose.'

'I *do* mind. I'm thinking of what the Japs might do to us – and what *we've* done to Christina.'

The latter reference sobered them. Lillian, shocked and weeping, was released roughly, to stumble away led by the hand by Bobby, who was crying too. Marion said, as much to herself as to Dorothy, 'That isn't the Lillian Cartland I knew. I don't suppose any of us knows what we might do for our own children if we had them in this place.'

They dispersed quietly, each thinking her own thoughts. Mrs Van Meyer made a point of seeking out Christina, who was sitting alone on a verandah edge. She told her the news. Christina showed neither relief nor surprise.

'All this has put years on me,' the Dutchwoman moaned. 'And you, Christina – you must hate Lillian worse than any of us. How could she let them accuse you, while she kept quiet and took advantage by stealing my job for her reward?'

Christina stared ahead of her. 'Perhaps I should thank her,' she mused.

'*Thank* her?'

'For showing up what people still think of me, and just who my friends are.'

'Ah yes. Of course, *I* knew it wasn't you. I told the committee so and gave you my vote. But the Van Meyers have always been good judges of character.'

Marion had gone to Verna's room. As soon as she announced her business Verna put on a defensive look.

'Believe me, Marion, when Lillian reported the escape to me I had to tell Captain Sato. If I'd kept quiet he would soon have found out, and then . . .'

'I understand, Verna.' Marion still distrusted and despised this woman, but she needed her help. 'As you know, Lillian is an old friend of mine, and I can see how far she's deteriorated. Quite frankly, I don't think she's responsible for her actions, and if she gets any more treatment like she's just experienced she'll snap completely. There could be some further incident that will bring down wrath on us all.'

'Oh no! I sometimes wonder how much more even I can stand, Marion.'

'I'm thinking of Bobby, too. Everyone calls him spoiled, but what does that mean in a place like this? It occurred to me . . .'

'Yes?'

'If I could be allowed to see Major Yamauchi and put it to him. I mean to say, the Japs do owe Lillian a favour on their own account.'

Verna was looking distinctly relieved. 'I'd been thinking along those lines myself, and wondering how to approach it. You and Yamauchi – that's the way. I'll see Miss Hasan and try to arrange it. For the sake of peace, I think there's a chance she'll agree.'

Miss Hasan did consent to Marion's seeing the District Commander. He came to the camp next day and received her alone in Sato's office. He sat at the desk while Marion stood before him.

'It's her little boy I'm so worried about,' she went on to explain. 'Knowing how much you yourself care for children . . .'

'All Japanese love children, Mrs Jefferson.'

'Of course. That's why I thought you might consider taking some action.'

'You want I punish all prisoners who treat mother and boy bad?'

'Oh no, no. That would make them even less popular. What they need is a fresh start. To be somewhere else where they are not known.'

'Ah so! You think I should move them to other camp?'

Marion framed her answer carefully. 'I had thought that, in your wisdom, you might decide that was the best solution, Major.'

He nodded vigorously. 'Such is my decision.'

'Thank you very much, Major. I'm sure it is for the best.'

'You say nothing to anyone. They will go very soon.'

'Very well.'

'How is prisoner Millar, Mrs Jefferson?'

'As well as can be expected, sir. Dr Mason says she will never be able to walk again.'

Yamauchi got to his feet, signifying that the interview was ended.

'Tell prisoner Millar she is fortunate not to be dead,' he said. 'It is only by mercy of Japanese conquerors that she is not.'

Marion gave him her deep bow, thinking yet again what extraordinarily contrary beings the Japanese were.

There was unconscious irony in what he had said, though. Rose Millar was thinking how unfortunate she was to be still alive.

She had lost Bernard, she knew, and with him the only future she had had to contemplate from this dreary waste

119

of years, as the last of her youth decayed. Now she knew that she would never walk again.

It had not needed Dr Mason to tell her; in fact, Beatrice had not done so. Rose knew it with the intuition of one who had come within an inch of sudden death, only to be spared for a lingering one. And there were the physical signs. She had no bodily sensation from the waist downward. She could not move in bed and was already experiencing the misery of bed sores. Everything she needed to do had to be done with help, and she could read the distress in the expressions of those who tended her. There were no drugs, no medicines; only makeshift dressings and pads to ease the contact between her elbows and back and the hard, lumpy mattress. She was incontinent, and conscious of her own smell. Even the release of sleep came only briefly. When Beatrice once asked her if there was anything else she would like her to do for her, Rose answered, 'Yes. You can finish me off.' She meant it.

The natural resilience of the human constitution kept her alive, though. Days passed, and weeks. Lillian and Bobby had left the camp. Mrs Van Meyer was restored in her place as Verna's domestic help. The women moved wearily between factory and camp, with exhausting toil at each place to deplete what was left of their energy and hope. Meanwhile, Rose lay helpless, knowing that her body was literally rotting away.

One day Kate came in from the side ward and told Beatrice quietly that the first signs of kidney infection had shown themselves.

'Uraemia next,' said Beatrice. 'At least that would be a peaceful end.'

'We can't let her die,' protested Kate. 'There must be something we can do.'

'Under these conditions, without drugs or medication, she is going to die anyway. It's merely a question of the cause.'

'Miracles do happen.'

'There speaks the Christian, not the would-be doctor.'

'You've seen it happen, Beatrice – people we'd given up for lost.'

'They had the *will* to live. Rose hasn't the will or the incentive. I just hope it happens quickly, for her sake. The alternatives to uraemia don't bear thinking of.'

'Septicaemia?'

'Or gangrene.'

Kate shuddered.

Rose's friends had been doing their best to cheer her up with visits, but even these were proving a repugnant experience.

'Christ!' gasped Blanche, who had only just managed to get out of the hospital before having to retch. 'Can't you do anything for her, Beatrice?'

'Don't you think we're doing everything we humanly can?'

'I don't mean that. I mean put an end to it.'

'With any luck she'll go soon, God willing.'

'Luck! You could help her out – a pillow over her face or something. Don't look like that. I thought you didn't believe in God. I'd do it if I had the guts.'

Beatrice said, 'If I once started that sort of thing, where would it end? Do you suggest I suffocate all patients who become terminally ill?'

'You did it for Dorothy's Nip baby. You helped put an end to that.'

'That was different.'

'You could do it for Rose. No one need know.'

'Yes they would. *I'd* know.'

Over her breakfast of egg, fruit and coffee, served by Verna, Miss Hasan asked, 'How is the Millar woman? Still deteriorating?'

Verna had paid Rose one visit and wasn't intending another.

'In a dreadful state. A mass of sores and infections.'

Miss Hasan licked her fingers. 'Don't expect me to feel sorry for her after all the trouble she caused.'

'She should be out of your way soon,' said Verna, with one of her rare sarcastic retorts. 'They say she's refusing to eat.'

Miss Hasan put down her cup. 'Who said she could refuse?'

'Dr Mason can hardly make her.'

'If she can't I'm sure Captain Sato can. We have had one suicide in this camp. We will not have another. She will die in God's time and not before. Captain Sato will agree, you'll see.'

Sato did agree. He donned the cotton mask over mouth and nostrils which all the Japanese habitually used as a guard against infection and stormed into the hospital, followed by a guard carrying a bowl of soup. If he was shocked by Rose's condition he did not show it. He ordered Beatrice, 'Prisoner eat. I say.'

Rose, though near to comatose, understood and shook her head weakly. Sato gestured the guard forward.

'You eat. No women have food till prisoner eat.'

Rose's eyes caught Beatrice's. A feeble message passed. Beatrice took the bowl and spoon from the guard and advanced a spoonful of soup towards Rose's mouth. With a great effort she accepted it and managed to swallow. Sato stood watching as several more spoonfuls went down. Then he marched out, and Beatrice and Rose were left alone.

'Want any more, dear?' Beatrice asked.

Rose shook her head. In her weak voice she said, 'My nanny used to spoon-feed me when I didn't want my supper. She said I wouldn't grow up to be a big strong girl.' She almost managed a laugh. 'The poor thing should see me now.'

Beatrice was glad of the excuse of putting down the soup bowl to avert her head for a moment, while she mastered unaccustomed tears.

'D'you know, Beatrice, it's my birthday tomorrow,' Rose was saying.

'I didn't know that, Rose. You should have said before.'

'It doesn't matter. Yes, thirty. The age for settling down, my mother used to say. You know what? That night . . . Bernard asked me to marry him. After all our years together. Perhaps we would have settled down.'

She paused to muster her strength to go on talking.

'When I was little I used to make nanny put me to bed early on the night before my birthday. I thought it'd make the morning come quicker. Now . . . I hope it'll never come.'

Again a message passed between her eyes and Beatrice's; a long, earnest look, more eloquent than words.

The Tenko bell was ringing. The women dragged themselves from their mattresses after another night of familiar torment from flying insects, lice, stomach upsets and other pains, and the wild dreams caused by their disordered digestions.

'Sod off!' growled Blanche.

'I don't want to hear another school bell as long as I live,' said Dorothy.

'Morning, Beatrice,' greeted Joss, as their doctor came slowly in. 'What sort of night?'

Beatrice stood at the end of the hut and addressed them all.

'I wanted you to be the first to know – Rose died peacefully a little while ago.'

'Thank God,' said Marion quietly, after it had sunk in. The others echoed her and Mrs Van Meyer crossed herself.

'We'll say just a short prayer for her before the second bell,' Marion added, and they bowed their heads. 'Oh Lord, we thank you for releasing our dear friend Rose from any further suffering. Grant that she may now know the peace and joy of everlasting life.'

They joined in the Lord's Prayer. Beatrice Mason stood silent, her expression one of unfathomable memory.

10 Verna

Rose's death seemed to have cast a blight on the lives of them all. Its symbolism was too obvious. She had been the only one to have flown the coop, however briefly, wanting nothing more than the reassurance of her man's company for a half-hour. It had cost her her young life, in a squalid end. He had died as well. A betrayal had been provoked, with the inevitable reprisals and a worsening of relationships between captors and internees and among some of the women themselves. Nothing good had come out of it, and what remained seemed diminished still further.

The hope of contact with the men's camp where Bernard had been had seemed to die with him. It was revived briefly when a passing native one day furtively beckoned Kate to the wire and gave her a message of greeting and encouragement from her Tom. The native indicated a stone at the foot of one of the stockade posts and said he would place there any further messages which might be given him; but there had been only two in a month, and they were merely brief and personal, with none of the hoped-for news of the war's progress.

The one encouraging sign was that the morale of the Japanese was sinking too. They were looking shabbier, with no replacement for worn uniforms and equipment, and a general air of apathetic despondency.

'Like 1917,' said Joss, the only one of them old enough to have clear adult memories from the First World War. 'Our boys and the Jerry bogged down in the mud, unable to move. The U-boats making us short of everything at home, while the Navy kept Germany on starvation rations. There seemed no end to it – but there was.'

'Roll on, then,' said Kate. 'God, but I hope the Satos of this world get spared for their come-uppance.'

'And the Hasans. Talk about collaborating! And she's taking more of it out on Verna these days, I notice.'

'Don't shed any tears for that two-faced bitch,' said Dorothy. 'I'd still like to know where she got the yeast extract she gave the Cartland brat.'

That knowledge was not to be long in coming. Fittingly, it was acquired by the one who had narrowly escaped the collaborator's punishment from which Lillian Cartland had been lucky to be rescued by being transferred away from the camp.

Christina Campbell looked across from her desk at Headquarters and felt genuine concern for Major Yamauchi. He had treated her strictly but fairly, showing respect for her skill as a translator which had singled her out to work for him, yet giving her no favours, other than the benefit of the food he himself could not eat. His appetite had been steadily decreasing. He had more frequent recourse to his lacquered pill-box. His face was often grey and he clutched his stomach behind documents which he held before him to prevent her noticing.

One oppressively hot morning he could not prevent himself groaning and leaning forward onto his desk. Without being told, Christina hurried across with a glass of water. He fumbled out one of his pills and swallowed it.

'You're ill, Major Yamauchi,' she said, stating the obvious and knowing that he would not thank her for sympathy.

'No time be ill,' he snapped, hissing with the pain inside him.

'You have been working so hard,' she insisted. 'You've had no rest, what with so many staff transferred to the front . . .'

125

He returned no rebuke this time. He had collapsed onto his desk, breathing noisily, his eyes closed.

Christina ran out and summoned the startled sentries. The outcome of a series of orders and a brief argument was that one ran off and came back soon with two orderlies carrying a stretcher. Major Yamauchi, ashen and groaning, was lifted onto it. Christina tucked his pill-box into one of his pockets and watched them carry him away.

Her next move was back towards her own desk; but as she moved her eye caught a metallic glint and she saw the Major's bunch of keys hanging from one of his open desk drawers. Her instinct was to shut the door and search the desk for any papers that might give news of the war situation, but she left the door as it was, so as to hear anyone approaching.

She searched hastily, her knowledge of Japanese script enabling her to take in quickly the heading of each document. She had come across nothing of the kind she sought when something else took her eye. It was a letterhead bearing a red cross in one corner and an inscription in French: Comité International de la Croix Rouge. The letter was in Japanese, and as she read it Christina's dark eyes widened.

She did not have long alone with it. Footsteps approached. First thoughts of taking the letter back to her own desk were abandoned, for fear it would be missed before she could replace it. She tossed it back into the drawer and moved round the Major's desk, to appear to be placing papers of her own in one of his trays.

The lieutenant who came in gave her a suspicious glance but evidently saw nothing untoward in the Major's secretary handling his papers. He saw the dangling keys and locked the drawer and all the others.

'I hope Major Yamauchi is all right,' Christina said in Japanese.

'It is a stomach ulcer,' the young man told her. 'The

doctor warned him, but he would not stop working. A fine example of dedicated Japanese officer.'

'Yes indeed,' Christina said, and bowed. The lieutenant ushered her out of the office and locked it.

'You go back to your camp when the truck is ready,' he ordered. 'Wait for orders when to come back here.'

'Thank you, sir.' Christina bowed again.

'Marion!' she said breathlessly when the bumpy ride was over and she was back in the hut. 'Come outside, please. I have something to tell you.'

'If it's the war news,' Marion answered triumphantly, 'I can tell you. Our native brought us a message today. The Allies have landed in New Guinea.'

For a moment Christina forgot her own news. Her eyes shone.

'Two thousand miles away, mind,' Marion said, 'but at least they're heading in this direction. What is it, Christina?'

They had left the hut, out of earshot of everyone else.

'Yamauchi collapsed. A stomach ulcer. I managed to look at some of the papers he keeps locked away. There was one from the Red Cross. A load of parcels were sent for us. They reached Headquarters on the fifth and were stamped out on the twelfth . . .'

'That's marvellous . . .'

' . . . of *April*!'

'April! Are you sure? Sure they weren't for some other camp?'

Christina shook her head. 'For us specifically. Yamauchi signed for them and marked them out. Twelve parcels including two medical. Think what that might have meant for Beatrice. For Rose. For all of us!'

'Listen, Christina, keep this to yourself for now, will you? Not a word to the others, or they'd go berserk.'

'What are you going to do?'

'Tackle Verna,' Marion answered grimly.

Verna was in her hut. She, too, had visibly come down

127

in the world. Her frock was grubby, her hair no longer neat from Mrs Van Meyer's attention. Miss Hasan had been venting her recent spite by putting pressure on Verna to repay moneys owed for various things. Verna had had to give up both Mrs Van Meyer and the girl Daisy and do her own domestic chores. She was not best pleased to be found by Marion on her hands and knees, cleaning her worn rug.

'What is it?' she snapped. 'Haven't you seen anyone doing housework before?'

'Red Cross parcels,' Marion answered without hedging. 'There was a consignment back in April for our camp, but we don't appear to have had them.'

'What makes you think that?'

'A Red Cross note listing them and signed out to us by the District Commander.'

Verna had got to her feet, rubbing her hands on her dress. Before she could speak again they both registered the sound of an aeroplane engine. It was something they had rarely heard. They turned their heads to the rush ceiling, but did not go out to the verandah to look. The plane droned over, at some height, and away.

Verna turned back to Marion. 'Yes, there were parcels However, if you remember it was in April that Rose Millar fouled everything up for us all by sneaking out to meet that man. So Miss Hasan, not to mention Sato, felt that under the circumstances you didn't deserve the parcels. They were sent to the convent.'

'As a punishment? I thought you considered yourself one of us, Verna. Why didn't you say?'

'Because those parcels were for everyone, not just the lot in your room. For everyone in the camp. If they'd heard what had happened there are some who'd probably have lynched Rose Millar.'

'A paralysed girl! You mean that, don't you?'

'When it's life against death, I'd have understood.'

Marion left her in disgust. But as she made her way back

to the hut a thought suddenly struck her. It made up her mind that secrecy was no longer what was needed. She called them all to silence and proceeded to tell them what Christina had found out and what she herself had realised.

The outcome was that some time after the evening's last regular Tenko, and the fall of darkness, she and several more of them made their way back to Verna's quarters. Having listened to ensure that she was alone they entered without knocking. She was lying in bed, filing her nails.

'What's all this?' she demanded, alarmed by their grim expressions. 'What the hell's going on?'

'You're coming with us to our hut,' said Marion, as Dorothy grabbed her and Joss clapped a hand over her mouth to stop her cries, 'where your Jap friends are less likely to hear. You've got some explaining to do, Verna.'

Though she struggled and tried to call out they got her across the open ground to their hut and pushed her in. The door was shut and Verna found herself hemmed in by menacing stares. None of them had seen Marion Jefferson so deeply angry before, but she controlled herself with great effort as she addressed Verna.

'You're to listen to me as if your life depended on it – which it probably does. I want you to explain those Red Cross parcels. Food and medicine.'

'I . . . told you what happened.'

'You told me they were given away to the convent because of what Rose did on the Emperor's birthday. That was April the 29th. But those parcels had been signed over to this camp on the twelfth – over two weeks before. Why hadn't they been issued?'

'Miss Hasan told me to hold them back.'

A low, animal-like growling was welling up in the women's throats.

'Miss Hasan told you nothing of the sort. Those parcels went into that storeroom which you're so careful to keep under lock and key. You kept them as stock for your so-called shop, to dole out just a little from time to time and keep up the scarcity value of everything. It's why you were able to produce a bottle of Lysol for Rose's operation. That Lysol could have been in the hospital all along, like so many other things. Patients needn't have had half their suffering. Rose might have been alive still.'

Even Beatrice Mason couldn't keep back an outburst. 'Twenty-six dead. Twenty-six!'

'I'm right, aren't I?' Marion went on relentlessly.

'No!' Verna insisted, shaking with fright.

'It's true,' shrilled out the cockney voice of the girl Daisy. 'She wouldn't let me near the storeroom when I worked for her – never.'

'You killed my patients,' Beatrice accused.

'No – no,' Verna insisted. 'It was Hasan. She made me do everything she wanted. She's responsible.'

'Liar!' shouted Dorothy, swaying forward towards their captive.

'Don't give us that,' said Blanche.

'Marion, please help me. Please make them listen.'

'Well?'

'Everything I've ever done or not done has been because of her. I got the mattresses and other things for you, and she made me responsible for paying her for them. I've never been able to raise enough. She's bled me for all sorts of other things. Always me, so I'd have to push it on to you. She threatened me with the punishment camp if I told you. Nobody comes back from there. They all die . . .'

'Like my patients,' said Beatrice, and turned away.

For some minutes it was touch and go whether Verna would be thrown to the ground and half done to death. The pathetic, appealing figure she made held them back from her. The anger which had been about to boil over into violence receded just in time.

'Do what you like to me,' Verna half sobbed, 'but she's the one you should get.'

Marion addressed her companions, drawn into a menacing group round Verna.

'Look, recriminations aren't going to bring Rose or the others back to life. It's what we can do to help the present sick and ourselves that matters now. Verna, you can start by handing over that storeroom key.'

'I can't, Marion. Miss Hasan took it away from me. Honestly.'

'Break the door down,' someone suggested vehemently.

'There's always a sentry. You know that,' Verna warned.

Marion turned to Christina. 'When do you go back to Headquarters?'

'When I'm ordered. Perhaps not until Yamauchi's back at his desk.'

'That could be ages.'

'Doubt it,' Beatrice put in. 'I don't imagine the Jap army takes much account of ulcers, so long as a man can prop himself up in an office chair. Yamauchi's not the type to lie down for long.'

'Then we've got to be patient till then. As soon as you get back there, Christina, it's imperative you mention that there's a rumour here about some Red Cross supplies not having been released. Tell him a few of the specific items you've heard were in it. Don't admit having read the list, or he'll simply punish you and will feel he's justified in doing nothing further. Just play it as a rumour, and trust that he'll want an explanation from Hasan for taking things into her own hands.'

'Unless he's known all along,' said Dorothy cynically.

'I doubt that. Jap he may be, but Yamauchi's a regular officer who does everything by the book, good as well as bad. If it's true that things are turning the Allies' way, he's going to have to start patching his reputation together against the day when he has to stand up and be investigated. Will you do it, Christina?'

'Of course,' Christina agreed unhesitatingly, to appreciative murmurs. 'I'm sure you're right, Marion.'

Joss spoke up, causing Verna to turn to her.

'And *you* won't be tipping off Hasan meanwhile, will you?'

'I swear I won't. I loathe her as much as you all do.'

'Oh no you don't,' Joss snapped. 'Nobody else could.'

Beatrice's prognosis proved accurate. They had to wait only two days before Christina was ordered to Headquarters to resume her work for the District Commander. Major Yamauchi looked more drawn than ever and quite unfit for work, by normal standards; but prisoners of the Japanese had learned early that their captors drove their own subordinates unsparingly, which was a prime reason why prisoners could expect no leniency. Yamauchi had superiors of his own, and, together with his pride, his need to be seen to be carrying on regardless of personal discomfort remained paramount.

Christina had rehearsed her tactfully casual mention to him of the camp rumour, and thought she managed it convincingly. Yamauchi listened inscrutably, displaying no incredulity or anger. He gave no promise of an investigation; but Christina was sure the point had got across, and had genuinely surprised him.

That afternoon they were lined up to fetch water from the stream just beyond the gates of the camp. As they stood in the water, hauling up buckets to others waiting on the banks, Dorothy said:

'Can't wait to see Beatrice's face when she claps eyes on this so-called water. She'll blow a gasket – it's filthy.'

'A disgusting stink. It gives me vapours,' said Mrs Van Meyer.

They did not notice the approaching aircraft engine's noise. The first they heard was a series of explosions some distance away. Then the guard threw himself to the ground and they did the same, some of them diving down into the stream.

'Holy smoke, it's one of ours!' exclaimed Joss.

'Bombing Headquarters,' Marion gasped.

More bombs were falling, and the explosions were getting closer.

'Don't tell me they've overshot,' muttered Joss, and then screamed 'Look out!' as a bomb fell just over the hill.

Instinctively the women and guards began running for the camp. They slowed down in horror as they approached.

Two bombs had exploded, one in the middle of the compound and the other beside the hospital.

Marion could see that the wooden look-out tower had been damaged and one of its occupants hung motionless over the side. The hospital building had caved in at the corner that had taken the force of the explosion. Faint cries could be heard from within. Several women in the compound were screaming or moaning, and one or two were writhing with horrible injuries.

Some women had scrambled up already and were making for the hospital. Marion saw Beatrice's white hair in the lead and Kate following her with a limp. Some guards were up and tending to wounded colleagues. Sato was struggling to rise but could not because of a useless leg. He kept shouting, 'Prisoners go room. I order, prisoners go room.' No one paid any attention.

Nearby Marion saw Dorothy bending over a Japanese. He was Shinya, and he was dead. There was a movement on the ground which attracted her eye and she saw Daisy Robertson. Marion moved towards her. Daisy raised her head and stared, unrecognising, back. Only then did Marion see, with horror, that one of her arms was shattered almost to ribbons. She hurried to her and knelt, to cradle her and half-sob soothing words, which got no answer.

Those guards who had recovered themselves by now were mindlessly trying to herd the women back into a corner, clubbing frenziedly with their rifle butts as though the unintentional bombing had been herald to a mass escape. They were too late, though, to thwart the seizure of the contents of Verna's storeroom. Its door had been torn off by the blast, and the camp children were running

133

in and out with packages of foodstuffs and medicines, some of which, it was found later, had been there far longer than the suppressed April consignment. The children knew that the Japanese would never strike them, however much they might shout orders at them, as they were doing now, and carried on conveying the packages to the hospital and quarters, watched helplessly by the uniformed men.

Marion found Miss Hasan. The Eurasian collaborator was no longer her immaculate self. She was lying twisted in the dust near the verandah edge, quite still. She would never again issue her high-handed orders or impose her vengeful mass punishments.

The arrival of Major Yamauchi's car was unnoticed by Marion. She heard his voice as he shouted in Japanese to the guards: 'Stop those looters. Drive them into that corner. Use your bayonets!'

To her horror, he drew his revolver and raised it.

'Stop! Please!' she could not prevent herself shouting at him. He either did not notice or simply ignored her, and fired twice. She was relieved to see that his aim was over the women's heads.

She stared at this usually reasonable man whose sunken cheeks were flushed unnaturally from the heat of his near-hysteria. His voice rose almost to a screech as he demanded, in English, to be heard.

'Prisoners! You will be punished for this. You will be staked out in sun. You will be shot. You who are enemy are defeated women.'

He waved his revolver recklessly.

'Go back your rooms or I shoot.'

His glance fell at last on Marion, with whom he had so often had rational discussions of mutual benefit and to whom he had almost always behaved with a courtesy shown her by no other Japanese, high or low. He pointed the revolver at her, and the gesture seemed to symbolise the seriousness of his intent.

She stood and stared back at him for a moment, then

134

turned and walked towards her quarters, hearing him rave after her: 'Prisoners! Defeated . . . !'

'But not for long,' Marion said quietly as she walked. 'No – not for long!' And no shot came.

11 Survival

Far, far longer was to pass than Marion or any of them could have foreseen. Had they been told then, late in 1943, that they would still be imprisoned but alive in August 1945, they would have returned derision. Rather than give them courage, it would have made some at least despair.

Day by day they could struggle on, sustained by the hope that something else dramatic might happen which would spell an end to it all. To have known that there were another two years to endure of starvation, sickness, degradation and lack of comfort in any form would have been too much for some, and they would have surrendered that will to live which was the chief element in their managing to do so.

Their captors gave them nothing to cling to. The Russians' destruction of the German armies at Stalingrad; the overcoming of Italy, and her change of sides; the 'round-the-clock' bombing of Germany; the D-Day landings, leading to the end of the war in Europe: all these momentous happenings in the world at large passed unknown in their community where time was measured by the rising and setting of the sun and the sounding of Tenko summonses between.

Each month, each week of deprived misery made further inroads into their constitutions and sanity. Cut off from the world, seemingly lost to memory, they felt themselves turning into zombies, soulless corpses bearing only a semblance of being alive.

The Japanese shared their ignorance of the war situation. It was not the way of their High Command to circulate bulletins detailing the setbacks their fighting forces were suffering throughout the Pacific and the East: that General Douglas MacArthur had kept his promise to return to the Philippines, and had wrested them back from their occupiers; that since February 1945 the US Air Force had possessed the island of Iwo Jima, won at the cost of twenty-six days' bitter fighting and many casualties, but soon transformed into a base from which to bomb the Japanese mainland, only 700 miles away; that British and Indian uniforms were once more in Mandalay and Rangoon.

Such news as this was not disseminated, particularly to those cast-off Japanese soldiery who were unfit for any duty beyond guarding women and children in forgotten jungle camps.

As punishment for looting during the bomb raid, the women had been transferred to the prison – substantial buildings of grim aspect, built of stone and with most of the windows barred.

Instead of huts, they now occupied cells, each with a primitive toilet, European style but seatless, which had to be used to wash in as well as for its intended purpose. The water supply to it was a single tap, emitting a feeble flow, from which they also had to drink. A bare electric bulb provided the lighting, but it was enough to enable them to see how sadly one another had deteriorated in this place.

Beatrice Mason's hair was almost completely white now. Her eyesight had worsened to the point where she could scarcely see, let alone work on as a doctor. Kate, her nurse, had changed from a girl to a prematurely aged woman, her Australian toughness eroded. She limped from the lasting effect of her wound in the bombing.

Joss Holbrook, in her early seventies, was scraggier than ever, an effect added to by having lost tufts of her hair, leaving bald patches exposed. Her injured left arm had never healed; but nor had the glint of determination ever left her eye.

Dorothy Bennett, by contrast, had let go. Ironically, it

had been the friendship of simple Private Shinya who had kept up her morale at the old camp. She had never given herself to him, as she had to the other guards, for whom she felt only repugnance – they had merely taken advantage of her willingness to trade her body for cigarettes and other small luxuries. Status and language had kept a barrier between him and her, but in some way he had become a substitute for both the husband and child she had lost. Following his death in the bombing a heavy depression and lethargy had fallen upon her. She could not hope to replace his friendship with that of other guards, and no longer felt the urge to make lovers of them. The present had become as empty as the future for Dorothy Bennett.

Robust, pugnacious Blanche Simmons had died. She had been caught smuggling in food to occupants of the punishment cell, so had been thrown in to join them. She had had beriberi and her fellow inmates were forced to listen, in helpless horror, to the 'beriberi song', an eerie wailing sound emitted as death approached.

Marion Jefferson was still the one to whom they all naturally turned for leadership. She was as haggard as any, her hair was greying, and she found herself more frequently ill, after long deprivation of essential vitamins. Like Joss in particular she kept the spark of hope alight inside her. Every time an aeroplane's engines were heard – and that was becoming ever more frequent now – she told herself that it was another good omen.

She was right. On 6 August, the four powerful engines of a US Army Air Force B-29 bomber roared into life on the island of Tinian in the Mariana Archipelago. The pilot's name was Colonel Paul W. Tibbetts Jr, and the aircraft was named *Enola Gay* after his mother, who had probably never heard of Hiroshima in her life. Neither had Marion Jefferson; and anyway, *Enola Gay* and her dreadful mission were to remain unknown to her for some time yet.

'*Tenko! Tenko!*'

It was just another unnecessary counting of heads: fewer

of them now. Then there followed the address from Captain Sato, an older, shabbier Sato depending much on the walking-stick with which he had returned from hospital some weeks after the bombing. Christina translated. She was still the healthiest of them all, but no longer resented by any of them for it, following her clever uncovering of the Red Cross parcels.

Sato gave them his usual sort of thing: 'In Okinawa your forces have suffered great defeat. Many American and British ships sunk and many lives lost.' (Okinawa had already been in American hands several weeks by the time Sato announced this.) 'The Australians have suffered great losses in Borneo, where they tried to attack the oilfields. The brave Japanese forces have driven them back into the sea.' (The oil wells of Tarakan had been destroyed in May by the Japanese themselves, retreating from the Australian invasion. Labuan, Balikpapan and other outlying areas of Borneo were securely in Australian hands.)

As she listened, with her usual half-attention, Marion noticed the lack of conviction in Sato's tone, for which Christina made no attempt to compensate in her translation. She felt a nudge from Joss and followed her quick glance towards the wire stockade. A native, whom they recognised as their message bearer from the men's camp, was trudging along the dusty track with a load of wood on his shoulder.

'Postman,' Joss hissed from the side of her mouth. 'Perhaps we'll get a bit nearer the truth.'

He had brought a message, they found afterwards. It was a rolled-up scrap of paper, left at the foot of a fencing post. The message was in Malay. So far as Marion could make out it said that the Allies had taken Brunei.

'So much for Satan's bulletins,' Joss crowed. 'Hey, what's this?'

Her keen old eyes had spotted another piece of paper, larger and not rolled. It was concealed only accidentally, having blown or fallen into a clump of vegetation. Marion reached in and pulled it out. It was in Japanese and meant nothing to either of them. They were startled from their concentration on it by the grating voice of Sergeant Kasaki.

'Give that me.'

Palming the smaller scrap with the message in Malay, Marion handed over the larger one.

'Where you find?'

Marion pointed in the bush. Kasaki glanced at the document. In a reflex response his eyes turned skyward. Then he slapped each of the women once across the cheek and stumped away.

'Little bastard!' murmured Joss; but Marion was looking thoughtfully after the retreating Japanese, who was reading the paper as he went.

'Did you see how he glanced up at the sky?' she said. 'Bet you that was a leaflet – like the sort our planes used to drop on the Jerries during the phoney war, when we were all itching for them to get on bombing.'

'I don't think he liked what he read,' Joss agreed. 'Probably far nearer the truth than anything he's been told.'

When they got back to the hut they found an agitated Christina awaiting them. They told her their news first. She nodded impatiently.

'There have been showers of them near Headquarters. A stray one must have got blown over here. It all ties in.'

'Ties in with what?'

'Yamauchi told me not to come to work any more. I'm to stay in the camp all the time.'

'Why's that?'

'He wouldn't say. I asked if he was displeased with my work, but he said it wasn't anything like that – just orders from higher up. I could tell he was worried by some papers which had come in this morning. I thought, as there might not be another chance, I'd better try to get a look at them.'

'Good girl, Christina!'

'It's . . . not good news. There was an order from Saigon that any question of defeat or peace was rejected.'

'Whoopee!' someone cried. 'They're really getting close to it!'

'What's "not good" about that?' Joss asked the serious-faced Christina.

'It went on to say that when the Allies make their all-out attack on South-East Asia all prisoners, civilian as well as military, are to be massacred.'

A dreadful silence hung over them all, until Dorothy said, in the flat voice which was her only tone nowadays, 'I always said that was how it would be.'

She had, and they had argued that such a thing would never be contemplated -- not even by the Japanese.

'You're sure you read it right, Christina?' someone asked.

'It isn't the sort of thing you make mistakes about. I managed to read it twice before I heard Yamauchi coming and had to skip back to my own desk.'

'I can quite believe it,' said Beatrice Mason. 'They've had no qualms about killing us off slowly through starvation and disease. Why not this way, then?'

'But in cold blood. . . !'

'They'll manage to stir their blood up enough for that purpose. No surrender for them, remember. Why should they let us live if they're determined to die?'

Joss spoke up, and her tone was crisp with the authority of her age.

'Look, don't let's waste time bellyaching about it. If they're going to do it, they're going to do it.'

One of the fainter-hearted began to cry, and Mrs Van Meyer asked fearfully, 'When do you think . . . ?'

Joss interrupted her. 'You mean, will they put up a notice – "Grand Slaugher at Tenko Tomorrow"?'

'It's no joking matter, Joss,' Beatrice snapped.

'Damn right it isn't. The question is what are we going to do about it?'

'Do?'

'For God's sake, we're not just going to line up obediently and let them shoot us. How many are there of them?

Yamauchi, Satan and Scarface, plus how many guards? – five or six at any time. They're not likely to bring in extras for the ceremony. They won't expect much opposition from a bunch of half-starved females who aren't even supposed to know what's in store for them.'

Another woman, Joan, said incredulously, 'You're not suggesting we try and fight them?'

Beatrice agreed. 'Most of us are hardly able to walk, let alone fight.'

'And we've nothing to fight with.'

Joss turned on them. 'Speak for yourselves, but they won't get rid of me as easily as all that. As to weapons – shall we show them now, Marion?'

'High time, I'd say, Joss.'

'Right.' Joss strode to her mattress, seized its corner with her one sound hand and arm, and jerked it back. Between the planks, which raised it a few inches from the floor, they saw a collection of stones and sticks of various sizes.

'Mine's the same,' Marion told them. 'I won't show it now, in case anyone comes in. Better cover yours again, Joss. We've been collecting them for quite some time, just in case. We didn't say anything to the rest of you, for fear of causing any panics. There's plenty here to share out amongst us all, and plenty more waiting to be gathered. The idea is for each cell leader to pick her fittest members . . .'

Joan was still incredulous. 'Sticks and stones against rifles and bayonets . . .'

Joss leered grimly. 'Surprising what you can achieve with a well-thrown stone – especially against a man, if you aim low.'

The tension was relieved by some laughs. Joan was still trying to work out the long-term implications.

'Even if we did overpower them . . .'

Marion explained. 'We'd have Yamauchi and Sato as hostages. We'd have access to the radio. We could probably

142

make contact with the natives. We know we've some friends among them.'

'And the men's camp.'

'They'd probably have shot them first.'

'Then if it's going to be as bad as that we've nothing to lose anyway,' Joss retorted.

'Joss is right,' said Marion. 'We've also no time to lose. You'd better hear how Joss and I have figured it out.'

'Quick – while Dorothy's out of the way,' Joan surprised her by saying. Dorothy, who was suffering one of the periodic bouts of dysentery, had dashed out of the cell before the 'weapons' were revealed. They had arranged that certain cells' lavatories were to be used solely for washing purposes and others for their proper function. The one in here was for washing in only.

'What about Dorothy?' Marion asked.

'She's in with the Nips. Maggie, too.'

Maggie had already been in the prison camp when they had arrived here after the bombing. She was a very thin girl from North of England working-class background who had, in her mid-twenties, made her way with a friend to Singapore. She had worked as a barmaid, and perhaps something else on the side, making the most of her natural sexiness. That asset had wasted a good deal during three years' internment, but she had not forgotten the tricks of exciting men, and, like Dorothy's less artful practice, had used them on the guards to gain favours, though insisting to the other women that she hated the collective Japanese guts.

'Maggie's all right,' Joss said firmly. 'She's still one of us at heart. As to Dorothy, I don't think she'd betray us, but she's not as stable as she was.'

'I agree,' Beatrice said. 'We daren't take any risks. Quickly, Marion. Let's hear what you and Joss have thought up.'

It was a rudimentary scheme. Each of the ones chosen was to be issued with two or three stones, which they should have about them whenever a Tenko was called. It was assumed that if they were going to be shot the guards would line up at the front of the parade, facing them, instead of scattered around as usual. It would be Marion's responsibility to give the command to start their attack as soon as she judged the Japanese were about to fire on them.

She and Joss had spent much time discussing it, unbeknown to the others.

'They could march us out in small groups, or singly, and do it in the jungle,' Marion had pointed out.

'Being Japs,' Joss said, 'they'll have us all on parade first – *and* try to count us for the last time. You'll know clearly enough what they have in mind.'

Marion prayed that she would. A mistaken order from her could provide the excuse for the very massacre they only suspected might be coming.

The chosen ones were armed and everyone was sworn to say nothing to any of the other camp inmates. There were only enough missiles to go round the small band of mainly British and Dutch women and one or two Eurasians sharing quarters with them.

Enola Gay had flown over Hiroshima at 33,000 feet on 6 August and left in her wake 'a black boiling, like a barrel of tar, where before there had been a city'. Three days after, the port and city of Nagasaki had been even more comprehensively obliterated. Just under a week later, against the wishes of the most die-hard of his military commanders, who wanted to defend the homeland to the last breath of the last man, woman or child, Emperor Hirohito gave the order for unconditional surrender.

On 25 August, in the far-off prison camp where none of these things were known, the summons to Tenko seemed to carry a more ominous sound.

12 Last Tenko

It had an eerie quality this time. In their first camp, where Tenko had been a new and degrading experience, it had been announced by the beating of a suspended iron triangle with a bar of the same metal, an unrhythmical, discordant clatter, full of urgency and arrogance. At the second camp, formerly a mission station, it had been a less imperative summons on the bell in the little wooden belfry. The ritual by then had long been taken for granted, and the bell's small clangour came as nothing more than a nuisance in the dreary stretch of monotony.

This purpose-built prison had a siren, hand-cranked, rising from a deep-pitched grinding to a nerve-penetrating wailing before taking what seemed endless minutes to subside again. Its starting up invariably produced that clutch of chill to the stomach that people back at home had felt every time the air-raid warnings began to sound.

This morning's Tenko was unique: no artificial summons of siren or bell – merely voices. Voices shouting in Japanese and grotesquely imaginative English were part of any Tenko, but this time they were all that was to be heard; almost as if, it seemed to Marion, there was some need for hush and stealth. It was not a pleasant feeling. Those entrusted with the makeshift weapons concealed them in places they had contrived in their flimsy, worn clothing. To the surprise of the women not in the secret, those who had walking-sticks hobbled out on to the parade ground using them. Joss's arm was back in its sling, which bulged unnaturally, while any keen-eyed observer would have noticed the apparent widespread increase in arm and leg injuries.

145

There were no challenges, though. The Japanese seemed preoccupied. There was no pushing or thumping, and, biggest surprise of all, no counting. It was noticeable, though, that the guards lined up in front of the rostrum, where they were commanded by Sergeant Kasaki to stand at ease, with their rifles and bayonets aslant, their faces giving nothing away.

Kasaki's ringing command made the tensed-up women jump, and Kate swore as she nearly spilled the stones she carried in an arm sling.

'Major Yamauchi come. Women bow!'

They obeyed; some, of necessity, extra carefully.

Yamauchi and Sato appeared from a doorway and made their slow way to the rostrum from which, in this camp, parades were conducted. Kasaki saluted and asked a question in Japanese.

'What's that?' Marion hissed to Christina.

'He asked if they should count us.'

Yamauchi shook his head, saying something.

Christina licked her lips. 'He said not to bother. Just to .. get on with it.'

Marion's fist tightened round a stone big enough to fill her palm. She had marked the guard nearest to her for her target. He seemed to catch her eye, and shifted his rifle slightly, but he faced forward again as Yamauchi began to speak in careful English, not troubling to summon Christina to translate as he did for his lengthy harangues.

'You are wondering why I come to camp today. It is necessary I carry out order from His Majesty Japanese Emperor . . .'

'Get ready for it,' Joss ground out to Joan beside her.

'. . . This is to be for British women last Tenko . . .'

Marion could feel herself beginning to tremble – not from fear, but from the strain of holding her frayed nerves at this pitch.

'. . . I have to tell you war is ended. Now there is peace . . .'

146

It was so unexpected that it was almost an anti-climax. For some moments most of them stood in stunned silence. Yamauchi said some more words, but no one was listening to them. Then reaction came.

Marion felt the tears burst out and cascade down her cheeks. Joss's hand fell open and the stone she had been gripping fell with a thud to the baked ground. A Dutch woman began a prayer of thanks in her own language.

Kate Norris broke the spell of disbelief.

'Yippee!' she yelled. 'It's over. We've won!'

She seized Christina and hugged her to her. All around, women and children followed suit, mingling laughter and whoops with tears and prayers. The Japanese were ignored, though Yamauchi carried dutifully on.

'The Japanese have surrendered. In the past British and Nipponese have been enemies. Now must be friends. I will read you pamphlet dropped from plane by British.'

'Quiet!' shouted Marion, who had caught his words. 'Listen, everyone.' In semi-silence they obeyed as Yamauchi read:

' "At last the Allies have defeated completely the Japanese. The Japanese Emperor, on behalf of the Japanese nation, has accepted unconditional surrender. The necessary arrangements for the implementation of the surrender are now being made between the High Command of the Allied and British forces. Be of good cheer. I know that you will realise that on account of your location it will be difficult to get aid to you immediately, but you can rest assured that we will do everything within our power to release and care for you as soon as possible." '

He lowered the paper and addressed them directly. 'This is good news for women, but they must not be excited or without control. They must obey orders and keep tranquil.'

A babble of derision and protest drowned him out. Marion, aware of what might happen next, stepped forward and addressed him loudly. 'Major Yamauchi, I should like

147

to discuss things with you at once, on behalf of everyone here.'

He stared back for a moment, as perplexed by the turn of events as anyone; but then he nodded and ordered Captain Sato in Japanese, 'Mrs Jefferson and I will use your office. No one is to touch the women. Understand?'

Sato saluted. He had had his instructions beforehand. A sharp order sent the guards doubling away to their quarters, out of harm's way. Those women who saw them go egged them on with a jeer. Most ignored them; they were too preoccupied with rejoicing.

Major Yamauchi politely stood aside for Marion to enter Sato's sparsely furnished office. It held only a desk and chair, with a box beside the wall providing the only other seat. Without hesitation, Marion walked round the desk and took the chair. She indicated the box.

'Please sit down, Major.'

Yamauchi bowed stiffly and obeyed. Looking at his worn uniform, his sick features framed by his grey hair and moustache, and the defeated slump of his shoulders which he had neither the strength nor the will to suppress, Marion could almost feel sorry for him.

'So, Mrs Jefferson, you have won,' he said. 'It is good news for you.'

'It certainly is.'

'But not for us.'

'Major, perhaps you would tell me the exact situation. The events leading up to the surrender. I thought . . .'

'You are surprised that honourable Nipponese forces do not fight till finish? It was original intention, but then our Emperor give new order.'

'Why?'

'British and Americans have done terrible act to my people. They have made a bomb more big than any other bomb. Two city have been completely destroyed – Hiroshima and Nagasaki. Many thousands women and children have been killed by terrible injuries. Even babies . . .'

His voice almost broke. Marion remembered his once having shown her a photograph of his wife and daughter holding his grandchild. He made the effort to go on. 'Japanese Emperor, in order to save all from total destroying, accepted terms of surrender.'

Marion said, meaning it on both counts, 'I'm glad the war is over – but I'm very sorry it had to end in such a way.'

Momentarily his shoulders stiffened and he sat erect on the box.

'If Japanese fight only human forces, without doubt they win.'

She let it pass. Outside, women's and children's voices were chorusing 'Land of hope and glory'.

There were some not singing, though. Dorothy was one. Maggie Thorpe was another. Ironically, these two who had been excluded from the others' plan to resist to the death were the very ones who were now discussing taking the law into their own hands and having revenge on their former gaolers. A few other women made a conspiratorial group with them. Seeing the others throw down the missiles and sticks they would no longer need had brought it home to them how they had been suspected of disloyalty, and they were planning to show the rest of them how they really felt. As Marion and Major Yamauchi talked, these women were already gathering up some of the discarded makeshift ammunition.

'Nothing definite has been arranged about our release?' Marion was saying.

'No. Nothing is known. There is still much negotiation to be done. Women must wait. They must stay under control of Japanese soldiers.'

'I'm sorry, Major Yamauchi, but . . .' Marion began to protest. He interrupted her.

'It is the order of your Admiral Lord Mountbatten. He say so for your safety. Some Japanese do not obey order of our Emperor. They continue to fight. Also, many native do not wish for return of Dutch colonialists to island. They too make trouble for you. As officer and loyal servant of Emperor, I obey order of Admiral Mountbatten. I will endeavour to protect women till arrival of British forces.'

It made sense, and there was no alternative. Marion said, 'Thank you.'

'But,' he added with a meaningful look, 'there must be no demonstration, no bad feeling between women and Japanese. No acts of revenge. Otherwise, women will be in much danger.'

Marion got up and he followed suit.

'I'd better go and explain all this to the others,' she said.

'Please,' he said, and bowed her out.

Already, though, the vengeful group, led by Maggie and Dorothy, was making its way towards the guards' quarters. The sounds of revelry receded behind them as they crouched low to pass the guardroom on their way to Captain Sato's small room beyond. When they were under his window Maggie straightened up and peeped in.

Sato was slumped dejectedly on a chair, his walking-stick hooked on its arm. He had taken off his belt, with its scabbard and holster, and the weapons lay on his plain table. Maggie stopped again and nodded to the others. They moved stealthily towards the door.

Crossing the compound towards the rostrum, from where she proposed to try to make herself heard, Marion saw it already occupied by Kate, Joss and a few others. They were fumbling with the knot of the lanyard which secured the Japanese flag, the red ball on a white ground, at the top of its pole.

'No, Kate!' Marion called. 'Leave it.'

'Why the hell should we?'

They turned resentfully towards her. She hastened to explain what Yamauchi had just been telling her, concluding, 'He guarantees to protect us, provided his men are not provoked.'

They left the flag alone, but Kate shrugged and told

Marion, 'You'd better tell Maggie and some others that, then – if it's not too late.'

Marion stared uncomprehendingly. Kate pointed in the direction of the guards' quarters. Marion understood and hurried that way.

The avengers burst into Sato's room brandishing their sticks and stones. His hand went automatically to where his pistol should have been, before he remembered it wasn't there.

'Hello, Satan,' Maggie sneered. 'We thought we'd pay you a little social call.'

She got between him and the table, the other women surrounding him. Dorothy seized the back of his chair and tugged hard. He was thrown out of it, only just managing to stay on his feet. Maggie saw his glance towards the door.

'Weren't thinking of leaving us, was you? 'Cos we got a few scores to settle first, Haven't we, girls?'

Dorothy spat towards him. He tried desperately to pick up his chair to defend himself, but one of them had grabbed his walking-stick and reversed it, to get the crook round his injured leg and heave, bringing him down into a corner. They crowded around.

'Wondering why we don't use your gun on you?' Maggie continued. ''Cos shooting's too good for the likes of you. We want to enjoy this. Now, who's first? What about you, Dot? He's lorded it over you longer'n the rest of us.'

Dorothy had a substantial stone in her hand, which she instinctively half-raised. As he lay helpless in the corner his eyes engaged hers. He did not cringe or show pleading or fear. He said nothing. Dorothy suddenly found the stone strangely heavy. She could lift it no higher.

'Go on!' Maggie encouraged. 'Remember your baby? Smash his ugly face in!'

Still Dorothy remained immobile, and during that moment of hesitation Marion reached the room and rushed in.

'No!' she cried. 'Stop it.'

Maggie turned on her viciously. '*Oh*, no, you're not stopping us. We know all that bastard's done and what he deserves.'

With a swift stride Marion placed herself between them and the defenceless Japanese.

'If you lay hands on him, or any of them, you'll be putting us all in danger. There are facts you don't know.'

'And facts we *do* – like how he tortured and drove sick women till they snuffed it . . .'

'And does behaving the same way achieve anything? Less than an hour ago some of us were prepared for the worst and ready to fight for the lives of all of you. Thank God there wasn't any need. We're safe, so long as we do what's been ordered – by our own forces. Don't throw that away now, after all these years.'

Maggie looked hard at Sato, who returned her his emotionless stare. Then she turned and vented her frustration by hurtling her own stone into another corner of the room.

'Aw, come on,' she told her companions. 'The yellow sod ain't worth it.'

They trooped out, leaving Marion with Sato. She made no move to help him to his feet, and he gave no expression of thanks. She turned and went away.

She took the earliest opportunity to explain the situation to them all, assembled in their long dining-hall. She could almost feel hostility levelled at herself for seeming to be aligning herself with the official orders. It hurt a bit, but she could understand it.

'So long as we're not expected to go on kowtowing to the little buggers,' Joss snorted.

Kate said, 'Do you mean to say Sato and co. will still be free to roam about with their guns?'

'As I told you, it's for our protection now.'

'What's to say they won't take it into their own heads to shoot the lot of us – especially if it's true about those bombs you say we dropped?'

Marion could only repeat patiently, 'I have Major

Yamauchi's assurance that his men won't harm us if we don't provoke them. Whatever we may think of him as a Japanese, he's always played it by the book – more or less. His Emperor's ordered Lord Mountbatten's instructions to be followed, and they will.'

'I take it there won't be any more Tenkos,' Beatrice said sharply.

'Better not be,' Maggie said. 'I'm not bowing to another Nip as long as I live.'

'Don't worry,' Marion assured them all. 'No more bowing – and we've had our last Tenko.'

A small cheer went up. Marion went on.

'I've discussed other matters with Major Yamauchi. It's essential we stick to our normal routine – sanitary arrangements, care of the sick, etcetera.'

'I'm not scrubbing no more floors,' from Maggie. 'Nor lugging garbage.'

'You won't have to. I've told Major Yamauchi and he's arranging for some coolies to be sent in.'

'Poor buggers. British Empire, here we go again.'

'All right, Joss. I'll take the responsibility of keeping details, so that our people pay them for it when they come for us.'

'What about food?' Dorothy wanted to know.

'As I've said, there'll be an extra ration of rice. We'll be able to buy extras from the locals, who can come in to trade now.'

'Oh, aye? And how do we pay for it?' demanded the obstinate Maggie.

'I was coming to that, too,' Marion answered, as patiently as she was able.

There was, of course, one source of extras that was in the minds of them all – the prison storeroom. When it was opened by Major Yamauchi, after an appeal by Marion to the expectant throng to ensure that the contents were pooled for their common benefit, he was jostled aside and nearly knocked down in the rush.

153

Squealing with excitement they pulled down things from the shelves, revealing blankets and towels, mosquito nets and rolls of material suitable for making up into clothing. Incredibly, there were piles of brand new Japanese uniforms and boots, although the soldiers had been going about like scarecrows. Everyone had been deprived through some unfathomable quirk of Japanese mentality.

Hopes of food were largely disappointed. There were hundreds of tins, but all contained either condensed milk or butter, welcome enough but not offering the range of nutrition they so desperately needed. The most precious find came last.

'Beatrice, Beatrice!' Kate called to the doctor, who was standing back from the mob, not much more than a surging blur to her fading eyesight. She groped forward. Kate took her arm and pulled her to a side shelf. There were packets, bottles and boxes, dozens of them, in many sizes.

'Medical supplies?' asked Beatrice, peering in horrified.

Kate was near to tears. 'Yes. Quinine, vitamins, bandages, disinfectant. All the things we've been crying out for.'

Beatrice murmured, appalled: 'All the time. They had them all the time.'

Yamauchi watched as some of the women tried on items of Japanese uniform. 'Women happy now?' he remarked to Marion beside him.

'Yes.'

'You wonder why I have not open store long before. We did not know how long war last. You would have receive more things if Allies had not blown up Japanese Red Cross ship bringing many parcels. It is because of this we must save other supply. You blame American submarine, Mrs Jefferson. Not Japanese.'

A look was all the response she was capable of giving him.

13 Last Bows

The native traders soon began to emerge from their jungle villages, bringing eggs, scrawny chickens, fish, fruit and vegetables. There was not a lot, and the quality was poor, but to the women and children who had had to subsist on rations less than they would normally give a pet cat, which would have turned up its nose at them, the extra food represented luxury. So did the items of Japanese uniform that many had taken to wearing.

Human nature being what it is, though, it did not take many days of this captive freedom to start some of them grumbling about the delay in the rescue operation. It was not enough to know that technically they were no longer internees; they wanted to *be* free.

Kate Norris, with the knowledge that Tom was only a few miles away from her in a camp that was also no longer a true prison, fretted about being reunited with him. She approached Marion, who spoke to Major Yamauchi, who in turn pointed out that there was much unrest among a native population wary of any moves to return them to European colonialism. Their volatile mood made them a danger to anyone travelling about the roads. The only safety for Europeans and Japanese alike was to stay on in their artificial communities until the Allies got through to them.

'Sometimes I think I'll risk it and just nab a truck,' Kate said. 'It can't be a long drive. The natives won't exactly be manning roadblocks.'

'Why don't you?' urged her confidante, Maggie Thorpe. 'I'll come with you.'

'For one thing, the Japs aren't likely to leave keys in the ignition of unguarded trucks.'

'So we get one of 'em to. Pick the right one, promise him a note to the Allies sayin' what a grand little chap 'e's bin to us. He might even make sure there's petrol in the tank.'

Kate was hesitating now, but Maggie was determined.

'There and back in an afternoon. No one'd ever know. If they did find out what could they do? We're nobody's prisoners now, remember.'

It was easily arranged. One of the guards to whom Maggie had been in the habit of making herself available proved only too willing to ingratiate himself, and the following afternoon the two girls were lurching and jerking along the jungle road in a small ration truck, with Kate driving and both uninhibitedly singing 'We'll be coming round the mountain . . .'

The only natives they saw were working at the roadside, cutting back foliage with machetes. The girls waved, but none of the men or women waved back, while the infants with them just stared.

At one point they saw a small car approaching. It was obviously Japanese.

'What do I do?' Kate wondered.

'Put your foot down hard, and make the bugger move over if necessary.'

'Easier said than done with this clapped-out heap. My foot *is* down hard.'

The two vehicles passed. Maggie, craning her neck, yelled to Kate, 'Stop!'

Kate applied the badly adjusted brakes with a thump, which brought them to a juddering halt and almost pitched them through the windscreen.

'What is it?' She noticed that the car had stopped, too, and was reversing gingerly back towards them.

'That weren't no Nip,' Maggie grinned. 'Unless he turned white from shock at seeing us.'

The car was level and its occupant climbed awkwardly

out. He was a white man all right, probably years younger than his straggly, unkempt hair and long beard made him look. He wore a torn shirt and shorts, revealing thin, hairy chest and legs.

'Stone me!' he gasped, and his accent was cockney. 'It wasn't a mirage, then.'

The two girls also got down. Kate asked eagerly, 'Are you from the men's camp? Camp 3?'

Maggie chaffed good-naturedly, 'He's certainly not one of our conquering heroes, from the look of him.'

He grinned. 'Always susceptible to flattery, that's me.' He became serious for a moment. 'What the hell are you doing? I volunteered to pinch a car and come to your camp to find out how you were.'

'Our very idea, too,' Kate answered. 'Do you know a Tom Redburn?'

The man said guardedly, 'Yeah, quite well. Used to be in our hut.'

'Used to be?'

'Like, he's . . . in the sick bay just now.'

'What's wrong with him?'

He replied with a forced laugh, 'Nothing the sight of you wouldn't cure. Listen, though. You gotta turn back. Some natives in the village near us have gone berserk. A Dutch couple tried to get their house back. They shot 'em both. Tell your lot it's best to stay put till the troops get through.'

'I've come out to see Tom.'

'Not a chance, love. You'd never make the camp, let alone get back safe. Won't be long now. Cor!' he sought to jolly them along. 'You're the first bits of skirt I've seen since we came here.'

Maggie spoke up. 'You're the first bloke we've seen . . . without bandy legs.'

He turned his attention to her. 'You got a bloke at our camp?'

'No. Free and easy.'

'That's me, too.'

Looking him full in the eyes, Maggie said, 'What we waiting for, then?'

As Kate looked on in disbelief they moved as one to the back of the truck and climbed in. She could only wander over to the car, to sit in it and wait.

On 2 September, five days after this encounter ('Why the hell *should* I have bothered asking his name?' Maggie had demanded of the scandalised Kate as they drove back to camp. 'Wasn't his name I wanted from him.'), the Japanese Foreign Minister, Mamoru Shigemitsu, signed the surrender documents aboard the battleship USS *Missouri* in Tokyo Bay. The women heard nothing of it, and a fortnight later they were still incarcerated without sign of forthcoming release. For mental torment, it was probably the worst time of all their long imprisonment.

But by the morning 17 September had been crossed off the calendar with still no news and yet another day of bored idleness in prospect, a single shout, relayed and chorused, ended in concerted cheering as a camouflaged jeep drove through the gates and two British officers leaped out.

'By George, the cavalry!' Joss cried.

From all parts of the prison except the hospital the women and children came running to cluster and clamour around these two incredibly healthy-looking young men, a captain and a lieutenant dressed in jungle greens and wearing broad, though slightly embarrassed, smiles.

'Where the dickens have you been?' Joss demanded.

The Captain, who was about twenty-five, saluted her. 'Sorry. We didn't know you were here till a week ago, and had a bit of trouble reaching you.'

'Where are the rest of you?'

'Liberating other camps. We started off in teams of four, but there were many more camps than we realised.'

He raised his eyes to look beyond them at Sato approaching. There was still arrogance in his limping progress and scowling face, as though he were coming to demand the meaning of this intrusion. A call from behind in Japanese halted him, though, and Major Yamauchi appeared. He carried his sheathed sword in arms outstretched in front of him.

The women made way. He came up to the British officers and bowed.

'I am Major Yamauchi. Headquarters have telephoned to inform of your arrival. This is Captain Sato.'

'Captain Brooks, Lieutenant Curtis.' They did not salute or offer any courtesies. Yamauchi proffered the sword. Brooks took it from him.

'Thank you, Major,' he said quietly. 'From now you are under my command, but we shall be working together.'

He handed the sword back. Yamauchi bowed very formally.

Joss said, 'This is our leader, Marion Jefferson.'

Marion stepped forward to shake hands with both young officers, saying, 'I can't tell you how glad we are to see you. There just aren't words.'

The young men looked down at her gaunt face, unsightly with sores, and her incongruous mixture of Japanese military clothing and a skirt made out of a piece of the material from the stores.

'You've obviously had the hell of a time,' Brooks said, feeling what a fatuous understatement it was, but knowing no other way to put it. He and Curtis had seen several other camps already, but all had been men's. It had moved both of them more deeply than they would show to see women and children so degraded; and yet, in this brief acquaintance, they could sense a higher degree of enduring morale and purpose than the male prisoners of war had shown.

'We'll do our best to get you out of here as soon as possible,' he continued. 'With any luck it'll only be a matter of days. In the meantime . . .'

He nodded to Lieutenant Curtis who turned back to the jeep and heaved out a cloth bundle. Although it was rolled

159

up it was obvious what it was. The throng began to cheer. They continued to do so sporadically, and with renewed vigour soon afterward, when they stood about the rostrum to watch the officers haul down the Japanese flag and rip it off the lanyard to replace it with the Union Jack.

Captain Brooks slowly raised the Jack up the pole, with Curtis stiff at the salute beside him. There was no cheering. A profound silence had fallen, broken here and there by the murmur of prayers of thanksgiving and some unquenchable sobs of relief. It was only after the Captain had secured the lanyard again and stepped back to make his own salute that the cheers broke out once more and the two grinning young men jumped into their jeep and drove swiftly off across the compound to avoid being mobbed.

At evening mealtime the officers sat down to share the women's meal, with Marion seated between them. Every woman in the camp had dressed herself up as best she could. They had been busy doing each other's hair and what lipstick they had been able to buy had been liberally used. Their table manners and mode of conversation automatically became more decorous in the men's presence.

It was not of their own experiences that they wished to tell; nor did they pour out their grievances about the way they had been treated. All they wanted was answers to questions, some of which astonished the young officers as they began to realise how utterly cut off these women and children had been from all that they themselves had taken for granted as it happened and as it was superseded by other news:

'What happened to Hitler?'

'How bad was the bombing at home?'

'Are the Royal Family all right?'

'Is Sheffield still OK?'

'Who's the top film star these days?'

'Did that chap Sinatra get anywhere?'

The answer that caused the greatest surprise, among the

other nationalities as well as the British, came to Joss's question. 'Is Winnie Churchill still lording it?'

Captain Brooks shook his head. 'Far from it. We had an election and Labour swept the board.'

'I don't believe it!' Beatrice exclaimed.

'Spiffing,' said Joss.

'What, to sling him out after all he's done!'

'It's social reformers we want now, not warmongers.'

'Dammit, he led us to victory, didn't he?'

'No politics, *please*,' Marion begged.

'It is not a nice subject for ladies,' pronounced Mrs Van Meyer. 'I am sure Captain Brooks and Lieutenant Curtis wish to relax.'

She gave them a coquettish smile. Maggie nudged Kate and murmured, 'I could relax them better than what she could.' Kate, who had never quite recovered from her shock at Maggie's brazen behaviour with the prisoner of war, returned her a look of mock reproval.

News of the evacuation came through more quickly than they had dared expect. A few days later Brooks addressed them.

'You'll be leaving tomorrow in two separate batches. The sick and mothers with children will go first. The rest of you, plus the walking wounded, will follow on later. You'll be driven to the airstrip and then flown by Dakota to Singapore, where you'll be temporarily billeted, either privately or in hotels.'

'Bags I Raffles,' Joss shouted.

'You never know your luck,' he smiled, and carried on. 'Since the airstrip is some distance from here you'll need to take food for the journey. Mrs Jefferson will be supervising arrangements for that. I'm afraid you'll have to wait for the Red Cross issues you've been allocated till you reach Singapore. Now, I'm sure there are questions, and I'll leave Lieutenant Curtis to answer them while I carry on checking the records.'

One sort of question which Curtis was not faced with

had already been widely asked: what information did he or the Captain have of husbands and fiancés? It had been painful to them not to be able to help. Neither of them had been serving out East when the Japanese invasions had occurred and knew none of the men personally. They had dealt with thousands in recent weeks, but could remember few individuals' names. Marion diffidently asked about Clifford, whose senior rank might at least have brought him to their notice, but they had nothing to tell her. What she did learn, to her surprise, was that Major Yamauchi had quite some time before made an enquiry on her behalf through Japanese channels, but without luck. She was grateful for the gesture, and that he had spared her the extra suspense by not telling her.

It transpired, too, that Yamauchi had handed over a list of women and children known to have menfolk in the nearby camp. With some hesitation, after his experience of other male camps, Brooks decided to arrange a visit during the last day here. The excited party were driven over in two trucks, with an armed Japanese escort under Curtis's and Sato's command.

The majority who were left behind posed for Captain Brooks, who took photographs of them in the camp surroundings and doing various activities they had become accustomed to. The excursion parties returned while this was going on, and all were noticeably subdued.

Kate, who had been one of them, reported back to Beatrice Mason in the cell occupied by the chronically sick. Beatrice sensed her emotion rather than saw it with her weak eyes.

'I thought we'd had it bad till I saw them,' Kate told her. 'They've lost twice as many.'

'Your fiancé? How is he?'

'They had to point him out to me. I didn't even recognise him.'

Kate bit her lip and moved away to pretend cheerfulness to one of the women lying there. A glance was enough to tell her that this one would not be making any journey back to Singapore.

Beatrice said, 'Kate . . . I'm sorry if . . . I realise things have tended to fall more and more on your shoulders lately. And I may have been a bit short with you at times. My dashed eyes. Once we're back and I get some decent glasses . . .'

'I understand, Bea,' Kate spared her.

'Thanks. If you should decide to train further – become a doctor – I'll be only too glad to give you a reference or anything of that sort.'

'Thanks.'

'Do you think you will?'

Kate was only half considering. Her mind was full of the pathetic memory of Tom Redburn, lying there emaciated yet swollen and stinking with body fluids, his faded eyes showing his shame at her seeing him in such condition.

'I don't know,' she answered Beatrice. 'I shan't be able to think about anything till we're away from here.'

The rest of them had packed up most of what little they had with the impatience of children about to go on holiday and trying to make the waiting pass more quickly. Most of the talk, as they sat about unoccupied, was of the future.

Marion's priority was to reclaim the house in Alexandra Road and hope either to find Clifford already there, or at least to be joined by him soon. She wondered what state it would be in – what state he would be in, come to that. For all her deterioration from a handsome, comfortably-off colonel's wife to an emaciated scarecrow-figure, she knew she had been one of the luckier ones. She had had her share of the common diseases – dysentery, pellagra, beriberi and the like – but she had always recovered. Unless a full medical check-up revealed anything more fundamental, she could reckon she had come through intact.

So had Christina Campbell, which was less surprising from the physical aspect, in that she had had the benefit of extra rations for working for the Japanese. Translating

163

was neutral work, and her value as an insider at Headquarters had earned her the women's gratitude, overcoming any jealousy. Marion asked her what she planned to do after repatriation.

'I'm not sure,' the still-pretty Eurasian girl answered. 'I may go to Scotland.'

'You've relations there, haven't you?'

'My father's family. Now my mother's dead there's nothing to keep me in Singapore.' She hesitated, then said, 'Marion, do you remember someone called Simon Treves?'

'No. Should I?'

'He was one of your husband's young officers. It was he who got me on the ship when they were turning people away.'

'Oh yes,' Marion remembered. 'He'd only just been posted out East, hadn't he, poor boy?'

'That's right. We . . . saw quite a bit of each other in that little time. He came across me while I was tourist guiding. We . . . made a sort of pact. He said, "See you in England after the war".' Almost to herself Christina added, 'I wonder if he meant it.'

Mrs Van Meyer sat down beside Dorothy, who was smoking a cigarette, staring into space.

'All on your own, Dorothy?' The Dutchwoman said.

Dorothy didn't trouble to look at her. 'Might as well get used to it.'

'My dear,' gushed the older woman, 'I know how you feel. I also have no one to go back to, but we must make the best of things. You are younger than I am, and I dare say once your skin has cleared up and your hair has been attended to you will catch another young man. If you take my advice, though, it might be as well not to mention your, er, friendship with some of the guards.'

Dorothy turned at last to stare at her. She jumped up and flung the cigarette from her.

'Get stuffed!' she swore, and hurried away, leaving the Dutchwoman staring after her.

Joss – the Lady Josslyn – was discussing the common subject with Yorkshire Maggie, the former Singapore barmaid.

'It's strange, suddenly having nothing left to fight against.'

'It's grand, I reckon.'

'What'll you do now, Maggie?'

'I've not thought.'

'You've family, haven't you?'

'Oh aye, a brother and two sisters. They've gone their own way now, though. Mum died when I was ten. And Dad . . .' She broke off, then shrugged and said, 'Reckon I'll stay on in Singapore. Go back to the bar where I worked – if it's still there. What about you?'

Joss had begun to say she was not sure what she should do when their attention was distracted by a strange sight. Two Japanese had emerged from a doorway and were making for a distant corner of the compound. What was strange was that though one of them, Sergeant Kasaki, was in uniform, complete with sword, the other was bareheaded and dressed in a simple white robe with a sash round the waist. Into the sash was tucked a shorter scabbarded sword. This man walked with the aid of a stick, and was obviously Captain Sato.

'What are they up to?' Maggie wondered. 'Will I fetch Captain Brooks?'

'No – hang on,' Joss breathed, almost as though she feared her voice would interrupt what the men were doing. As the Japanese turned a corner out of sight Joss got up and beckoned Maggie to follow, putting her finger to her lips.

They rounded the corner cautiously, to see Sato and Kasaki come to a halt some distance away, out of all sight of people in the camp. Sato stood for a moment in silent contemplation of the ground, then knelt suddenly and placed his short sword before him. Kasaki drew his sword and stood behind him, waiting.

165

From their distance they could just hear Sato's low voice reciting in Japanese as he knelt, straight-backed and head up. After some moments he stopped speaking and, without looking down, reached for the little sword. With a swift movement he drew it from its scabbard and clenched its pommel in both hands, turning the blade inward towards the side of his abdomen. Simultaneously, Kasaki grasped his long sword and slowly raised it to shoulder height . . .

Joss pushed Maggie back round the corner and pulled her quickly away across the compound.

'Christ almighty!' Maggie said.

Joss said, 'At least it's an honourable death. I could almost respect the blighter.'

When they reported it that night to the other women someone said, 'Good riddance. I hope Yamauchi's next.'

Christina gave an alarmed look at Marion, who said, 'I don't think so. I've a feeling he'll see it through.'

'What do you think will happen to him?' Christina asked.

'He'll be rounded up and taken in for questioning.'

'I hope they hang him,' Mrs Van Meyer said emphatically. 'And now I wish to get some rest before the journey.'

'I shan't sleep a wink,' Maggie doubted.

Marion said, with a little embarrassment, 'I think we should say a prayer together.'

'Yes, Marion,' Mrs Van Meyer agreed sincerely. 'I think that would be most fitting.'

All in the room fell quiet, sitting or lying on their mattresses, some with closed eyes, others with them open, staring into memories of the past and uncertainties for the future, as Marion groped for unaccustomed words:

Dear Lord, we thank you for bringing us safely through our years of captivity and for giving us the strength to survive all the hardships they entailed. We . . . we ask you to forgive our enemies, and to help us to do the same.

'On this night, when we are about to be released, we remember especially those of our friends who did not survive. We pray for their

souls, in the certain knowledge, that they will live in our hearts for ever.'

14 Raffles

'Bags I Raffles,' Joss had said when told that some of them would be accommodated in Singapore hotels. It had gained her an ironic cheer of disbelief; yet it proved the astonishing reality for the whole group of friends.

'Cor!' Maggie exclaimed. 'All the time I spent in Singapore, and never so much as seen inside the toffy-nosed place.' Now she was a non-paying guest in this fabulous and luxurious hotel, one of the most romanticised in the world.

They had flown in a workhorse Dakota, temporarily fitted with bucket seats along each side of the fuselage, which had carried everything from troops, bombs, weaponry and supplies, to stretcher-case wounded, parachutists and even mules. It smelt of them all, overlaid with aviation spirit, and was stiflingly hot. They dozed and looked down with difficulty through the portholes at the deep-blue Pacific and its plentiful scattering of islands; each musing separately on this limbo between captivity and freedom in a world much changed from that in which they had lived more than three years ago.

Landfall at Singapore was a bewildering experience for enfeebled minds and bodies accustomed to a strict routine, however disagreeable, and now pitched into the midst of the chaos of milling crowds of strangers. Many of them were former prisoners like themselves. Others imminent hospital cases, uniformed men and women of several nationalities and races, civilian photographers, newsreel camera crew, volunteer services women with trollies of tea, cool drinks and biscuits. The roar of aircraft engines

168

revving for take-off added to the noise of a thousand tongues, so that the perspiring co-ordinators, with their armbands and clipboards, had to shout to make themselves heard and muster their respective flocks.

A middle-aged Indian Army major, whose name sounded like Jackson, managed to convey some words in the name of Lord Louis Mountbatten, Supreme Allied Commander South-East Asia, welcoming them to Singapore and to the renewed protection of the British flag. The photographers darted about, pushing them into groups, calling for smiles, thumbs-up and Churchillian V-signs, until at last they were firmly shooed away by a rather rumpled, jolly woman, middle-aged and with a cultured voice, who introduced herself as Phyllis Bristow, the Red Cross Welfare Officer responsible for the new arrivals.

'Best to get the bumph-work over as quickly as possible, don't you agree?' she breezed at Marion, who helped her guide the party towards a table where officials of that extensive and, as they soon showed, fast-working and highly efficient organisation Repatriation of Allied Prisoners of War and Internees, known inevitably as RAPWI, took details of names, next of kin and other pertinent particulars. There followed tea and biscuits ('A cup and saucer!' Mrs Van Meyer exclaimed), and issue to each of cigarettes and soap. It all took quite a time before they were at last moving out of the reception-hall into the dusk, to find transport waiting.

And then, incredibly, it was Raffles, as majestic and serene-looking as if nothing untoward had happened around it at all, as if it had been a case of 'Business as Usual' through all this time.

It was illusory, if not at first glance. The presence of an armed British soldier on guard at the main entrance, which had itself been moved from its old place, was the first abnormal sign. In that traditional place of Eastern rendezvous, the foyer, the plaster was grubby, the woodwork scratched and scuffed, the metal rails dented and lacking their usual brilliance, while instead of the usual scattering of immaculately frocked ladies and tropical-suited gentlemen seated with their drinks at little tables there was a crush of figures, military and civilian, a babel of conversation in several languages, a haze of smoke from innumerable cigarettes and pipes. And yet, as a reminder of old times, Marion noted the 'boys', the hotel servants of widely varying ages, clad in their heavily starched high-necked white tunics, white socks and felt slippers, and behind the reception desk a Tamil in a perfectly pressed white shirt and a tie, working alongside a female RAPWI officer.

Phyllis Bristow went over to confer with the officer. There was comparing of lists, puzzled inability to agree, then what looked almost like an argument before Phyllis came back to say, 'Look, I'm frightfully sorry but your rooms are still being cleaned after our last intake. I can only suggest you grab some dinner, by which time . . .'

'I could eat a horse,' Maggie assured her.

'Given NAAFI rations, you might have to. Major Jackson, will you be an angel and take my girls in to dinner?'

The officer beamed. 'Nothing would give me greater pleasure.' Mrs Van Meyer was standing beside him. He turned and offered her his arm, with a little bow. 'Allow me, madam.'

'*Enchantée*,' she beamed, and the rest trooped in after them. Only Marion held back.

'Excuse me,' she said to Phyllis Bristow. 'I know you're very busy, but my husband and I were parted here in Singapore, and I wonder if there's any chance at all of tracing him?'

'It's Mrs Jefferson, isn't it?' She glanced at her list. 'Colonel Clifford Jefferson? I'll do my best to set enquiries going. You'll appreciate that things are rather chaotic.'

'Oh, I do, and I'm sorry to bother you. Only . . .'

'Quite understood. Run after the others and have a tuck-in, Mrs Jefferson. I'll do all I can.' Thankful at least to have set something in motion, Marion obeyed, only now beginning to remember what hunger, which she had learnt to suppress into forgetfulness, felt like.

The big dining-room was as crowded as the foyer. The women, grubby and still dressed in their mixture of Japanese and self-made garments, entered shyly, noticing the gleam of napery and silver, the well-pressed uniforms, the smart Chinese waiters. But there were no outraged stares at their unkemptness, no wrinkled noses at the smell they exuded as they passed the other early diners. There were only smiles of sympathy and greeting, and soon they noticed that many of the tables were occupied by people whose condition reflected their own.

'Have to take what grub comes up in the rations for now,' Major Jackson apologised as he got them seated at a big round table just vacated. 'Still, if there's anything at all I can do for you . . .'

'A stiff drink wouldn't come amiss,' Joss replied promptly, although it earned her a reproving look from Mrs Van Meyer.

The Major winked, tapped the side of his nose meaningfully, and stopped to speak to a waiter before going about his business.

They stared at the table-cloth, with its centrepiece design of Malay orchids, as the nimble waiters re-set their places.

'Knives, forks, spoons!' Kate marvelled.

Beatrice picked up her main-course knife.

'What I would have given for this at the operating-table,' she mused.

If Mrs Van Meyer thought that was in bad taste, she was even more horrified when the food appeared. It was tinned sausages and mash. The others cheered it.

'Good old bangers!'

'Bread. White bread!'

Even more miraculous seemed the glass which the waiter

placed beside Joss. It was a gin sling. She took one sip, closed her eyes, and let out a deep sigh.

'Home at last,' Joss sighed again, and tucked into the bangers and mash.

Work went on unceasingly for the RAPWI and other personnel coping with the flood of the dying, the disabled, the chronically sick and the merely starved and bewildered converging on Singapore by the plane-load. As they had done all over Europe and anywhere else that prisoners of war and internees had been discovered the men and women of the relief services worked selflessly to ensure that their charges got the treatment, accommodation, food, clothing and anything else that they most needed, with a minimum of delay and red tape. Processing their particulars went on day and night, and as soon as possible they were back on aeroplanes, being flown to their homelands or wherever else they chose to go.

There were secondary activities, though, regarded by some of the officers engaged in them as a priority. One of these was Major Smithers, an Englishman of twenty-five with a generally grim expression on his pudding face and a doggedly determined manner to match. He shared a crowded office in Raffles Hotel with Phyllis.

A copy of the list of names in every incoming draft handled by Phyllis Bristow and her colleagues automatically landed in Major Smithers' 'in' tray, and he left none unscrutinised.

'Another camp leader, I see – a Mrs Marion Jefferson.' he observed to Phyllis, who was telephoning, trying to rustle up further supplies of the avidly read *News from Britain* bulletin.

'Don't you dare!' she warned him, tugging at her dishevelled hair while she waited for an answer to her call. 'She's as exhausted as the rest of them, not to mention worried about her husband.'

'Tomorrow, then,' he promised her. 'The sooner we get

172

full details of Jap commandants, the sooner we can prosecute and hang 'em.'

'If that's your pleasure,' Phyllis said, aware that it was. 'Oh, hello – it's about *News from Britain* . . .'

The wonder of using baths, washbasins, and lavatories behind closed doors, of putting on the pyjamas they had been issued, of brushing their hair, of cleaning their teeth, and, at last, of sliding between sheets and sinking their heads into pillows was a sequence of delights for the women; they felt it impossible they should ever take it all for granted again as long as they lived. Some were in proper bedrooms, others in converted sitting-rooms. Each had been issued with a 'brick' (British Red Cross) parcel containing clothing, toilet and sanitary things, and basic aids to restoring their appearance and morale such as hairbrushes, combs and small mirrors. Flowers had been placed wherever a vase could be stood.

Gradually, though, the chatter, the splashing, the singing all subsided, and while the lights burned on in the RAPWI offices, the telephone rang, the transit huts seethed and the aeroplane engines rumbled, the sweetest slumber these women had ever known drowned out all memories and concerns.

Marion's instinct had been to start a letter to Ben. In pencil, she had begun it 'My darling Ben . . .' before realising that she was automatically using the tiny script she had adopted for keeping a diary on scarce scraps of paper at various stages of her imprisonment. She crumpled the page up and began again in the luxury of her former bold hand; but she had got no further than ' . . . my almost grown-up son . . .' before she found she could keep her eyes open no longer. Even then, sleep would not come. She knew she was too comfortable. Not until she had got down on to the carpeted floor, with just a blanket under her and a sheet over, and with no pillow, did she share the deep sleep of her companions. She slept untroubled by dreams and awoke feeling wonderfully refreshed and relaxed.

173

Chattering happily the women went down to breakfast, in the confidence of their clean skins and clothes, brushed hair and make-up. Phyllis Bristow, tidier and less rushed than when they had last seen her – though she had slept only five hours – came to ask after them and request them to stay on the premises all day for such necessary formalities as medical inspection and the taking of details that would speed their dispersal.

Marion had her own inquiries to pursue, and was determined to waste no time going about them. She knocked at the RAPWI office door and went in, and came face to face with the very officer who had been about to seek her out.

'Just the person I was wanting to see, Mrs Jefferson,' Major Smithers greeted her, standing up to shake her hand and indicate a chair. 'I've some information that's just arrived . . .'

Marion's heart leaped. 'You've heard something?'

'Heard?'

'About Clifford. My husband.'

He looked apologetically at his file of papers as he had to reply, 'Not about your husband, I'm afraid. I had an inquiry from above about a certain Major Yamauchi. I thought you could help fill me in with some details.'

Her mind was not on Yamauchi, however. 'It's days since Captain Brooks, at the camp, promised a cable would be going off. Surely it doesn't take all this time to get some sort of answer.'

He put down his papers and answered patiently, 'Mrs Jefferson, my department's War Crimes, but I do know a bit about the other things going on. There are hundreds of cables flying about like the one that'll have been sent about your husband – thousands, more like. They have to be processed by London first and then God knows where other inquiries might need to be made to locate him.'

'But I don't care about *where* he is at this moment. I just need to know if he's *alive*.'

'Of course. But the one detail depends on the other,

174

doesn't it, so please try and bear with us. Meanwhile, about this Major Yamauchi . . .'

Marion had got up. Throwing reasonableness to the wind, she snapped, 'I really can't be bothered,' and walked out.

Christina was experiencing similar lack of success in trying to find out anything about Simon Treves, the young officer she had known so briefly but whose memory she had cherished throughout captivity. Her difficulty was not of quite the same nature as Marion's, though, as she explained to Beatrice Mason.

'Because I don't count as an official fiancée, or anything, the powers-that-be say they can't make official inquiries.'

'Nit-pickers,' Beatrice agreed.

But the Eurasian girl's resentment went deeper still.

'They were fobbing me off. Remember that five pounds pocket money they gave us each? The officer had a directive on his desk. I could read it upside down. It said he could use his discretion how much less to give to anyone who wasn't white.'

'I don't believe it!'

'He saw me looking at it, and covered it with another piece of paper. I could tell by the way he looked at me that he was wondering how much he could reasonably deduct, but decided he'd better let me have it in full. So you see, so far as all the rules are concerned, I'm "unofficial".'

Beatrice touched her brown arm. 'Christina, whatever the colour of your skin, you're still British.'

'But that still means different things to different people, doesn't it? I wonder how much else hasn't changed at all.'

Their conversation was interrupted by a lot of noise from the street below the windows of the large lounge in which they were sitting with many others. There was a general movement to look out.

A group of women – a mixture of Chinese, Malays, Indians and Eurasians – was passing along the street, guarded for their own protection by an armed British

175

soldier and an Indian one. Passers-by had stopped to form a menacing little crowd, waving their arms and fists and shouting in various languages: 'Shoot them!' 'Death to collaborators!' 'Japs' whores!' 'Traitors!'

' "Japs' whore",' Dorothy Bennett reflected, turning away from the sight. 'I suppose that's how they'd see me.'

'Who cares?' said Maggie, her constant companion now. 'Apparently that lot do.'

'Well, I'm in the same boat then. To hell with 'em. We weren't collaborating, no more than that stuck-up Dutch bitch was who you say used to do those women's hair for 'em.'

'People get funny notions,' Dorothy said. 'The way they wouldn't trust us towards the end. The time we came near to scragging Christina. I suppose there are some would call her a collaborator for acting as interpreter – or the goody-goody Marion Jefferson, for having her heart-to-heart talks with Yamauchi, when they'll say she should have spat in his eye instead.'

'Oh, everyone'll excuse her. Colonel's lady, doncher-know? Jesus, to think of going back to being a barmaid! Wish I could get out from under somehow.'

'I know what you mean,' Dorothy agreed. 'Listen, Maggie, I've been thinking. You know the bungalow I told you I've got here – if it's still standing we could move into it.'

Maggie stared. 'Thought you said you never wanted to go there again.'

It was true. Dorothy had declared more than once that she had no wish even to revisit the bungalow where she and Dennis and their baby had been happy together until the coming of the holocaust of which she was the only survivor. She had said she would put it on the market – assuming that it still stood.

Now she shrugged. 'Can change my mind, can't I? I wouldn't mind getting away from this lot. Put them and all the rest of it behind and try to start afresh. The so-called "anonymous suburbs" would be just the place for that. Why don't we go out and give the place the once-over?'

Her usually dull eyes had begun to glow at the prospect of something constructive to do about her future. Maggie had no hesitation.

'Nowt to lose by it. I'm game.'

'Tomorrow, then, when we're allowed out. We'll go tomorrow.'

'By gum. Come on, Dot.'

'Where?'

'The bar. While I've the chance to be on the right side of one – and Raffles bar, at that – I'll buy you a bloody drink.'

It was almost at the same time, in a conversation between two other women, that a similar decision was taken, but for a different reason.

In a bathroom, Marion and Christina were engaged in a mutual-assistance session – trying to get their thin bodies and coarsened, blemished skins back into as good condition as they were able, with the aid of a loofah, a razor and a pot of conditioning oil. Just now it was Marion's turn to occupy the bath, with Christina working on her back with the loofah. They were enjoying the sensation of cleanliness as never before, and perhaps it was the effect of this make-shift hydrotherapy that caused Marion suddenly to cry out, 'Oh, you blithering idiot!'

Christina stopped scrubbing. 'Did I hurt?'

'No, not you – *me*. The servants!'

'What servants?'

'Clifford!'

'Marion, I don't understand . . .'

'After I left our house for the ship, Clifford was still there. He could have said something to the servants about whether he was planning to get away, and where to. Anything. And here I've been thinking that I wouldn't go to the house until I'd had some news about him, because

177

I once had a dream in camp that I went and he wasn't there, and I woke up crying because it made me so miserable.'

'You're going to go, then?'

'Of course. Tomorrow. Meanwhile, kindly lay on with that loofah. I'm starting to feel something like human.'

15 Jake

Stephen Wentworth was very tall, very thin, and so desiccated-looking after three years in Singapore's Changi jail that he might have been aged anything from eighty to ninety-five. In fact, he was not quite seventy. With his old shantung suit, whose trousers were held up by a striped old school tie knotted round his skinny waist, and a battered panama hat, he had become almost a caricature of an old Eastern hand.

He had come from his native Essex many years before the war to take a temporary post teaching English that would support him while he worked steadily at the novel intended to win him acclaim and the full-time role of literary gentleman. The novel had progressed little further than the few first chapters he had brought out with him, the temporary job had turned into a permanent one, and when the Japanese had invaded he had been scooped up with other male European civilians and locked away in Changi, where so many had died.

Stephen was tough in that stringy way associated with old poultry, and had survived. When the Japanese surrendered Singapore they advised Changi's inmates to remain in the hated surroundings for their own safety until the Allies came. One of those who had no intention of staying a minute longer was Stephen Wentworth. He had made straight for the native quarter, where his school had been. It had been bombed, but Buddhists who had admired his peacetime work among deprived children had offered him the hospitality of their temple and the means of starting up a mission for caring for the homeless and returning refugees, who, as he put it, tended to get the runt end of official concern.

When the women internees began arriving he made a point of a regular afternoon visit to Raffles, hoping to find, or hear news of, an old friend named Monica Radcliffe.

He did not find her, because she was dead. Instead, he found Joss, whose best friend and comrade in arms Monica had also been. They had met at Cambridge and later shared a flat in Bloomsbury. Together they had joined the Suffragette movement, opposed the Mosley gangs and marched with poor whites in America. Joss had looked hopefully for Monica at each new camp, until she heard at last of her death. She told all this to Stephen in Raffles' foyer, adding, for what it was worth, that Monica had always spoken affectionately of him.

'So you're the Joss she used to talk about.'

'What's left of me.'

'Look here,' Stephen said, glancing round the crowded foyer, 'we can't have a decent chat in this place. I've a passable brandy at my place. I was saving it for Monica, actually, hoping to split it with her in memory of old times. Why don't we do that together, as a sort of mutual farewell to her?'

'I think she'd like that,' Joss agreed readily.

'Better warn you, I'm camping out at my centre. It's a pretty ropey spot.'

'What sort of spots d'you think I've been used to all these years?'

He got up. 'Then there's no time like the present, as they say.'

'And clichés deserve respecting; apart from which, I'd be glad to escape from the attentions of our schoolmistress.' Joss indicated Phyllis Bristow, hurrying about with her clipboard and lists. 'She means well, and she's working her socks off to help us, but I just want to get out of her clutches for an hour.'

He gave her his arm, and they walked out and down the

steps past the sentry, exchanging the chatter and relative cool of the hotel foyer for the clamour and steambath humidity of the thronging streets of Singapore.

Stephen's place consisted of a large room in which his native charges sat and lay talking or sleeping, with a smaller one adjoining, which he had made his bedsitter-cum-office. The windowpanes were cracked or missing, and almost everything was makeshift, including his small bed, on which he and Joss sat side by side; but there was nothing make-shift about the bottle of brandy on the floor at their feet and that part of its contents which they drank from tumblers in toast to their absent friend.

'My sainted aunt, where did you get this?' gasped Joss, marvelling at the velvety bouquet and taste.

'Compliments of the manager of Raffles just before the Japs moved in. Crying like a baby, he was. Had to destroy the entire contents of his cellar to prevent them getting at it and going berserk like they'd done at Hong Kong. Literally thousands and thousands of bottles being smashed. You could have got drunk on the smell. I managed to bury this in the courtyard before I was slammed into Changi.'

'So, what happens now?'

'You may well ask. No time to organise teaching, of course. I'm just doing what I can to help these people. Me, who can't even tie a shoelace and was never any use with anything but a textbook. It isn't on, is it? I'm fooling myself that there's anything I can really do for them. Their physical condition alone . . . But I try. We Europeans insisted we knew what was best for them in the old days, so my theory is that it's up to us to put our actions where our mouths were. What the hell. Game to kill this bottle with me?'

'I was rather hoping you'd ask.'

Tough old things as both were, a whole bottle of finest brandy had its effect on their impaired constitutions, and it was an extremely tottery pair, depending on one another's linked arms and Stephen's stick to keep them upright, who

181

wove their way back towards Raffles Hotel much later. They were spotted, with some amusement, by the driver of a big American saloon car – a rare commodity in Singapore then – shining with polish and unmarked chrome on the outside and in almost pristine state within.

It pulled up alongside the wavering couple and the driver jumped out. Stephen, who recognised him, automatically raised his battered panama. The driver made a good-natured little bow and gestured with one hand. Without a word – and it would have been a very slurred word indeed had one been essayed – Stephen and Joss tumbled into the back seat. The driver returned to his and drove them to the obvious destination – Raffles.

Leaving Stephen in the car, he escorted Joss inside, ascertained her room, and deposited her at the door, where she summoned up enough resource to thank him and say she would be quite all right now. He left her, lingering just long enough to see her fumble the door open and pitch into the room, to be greeted with the laughter and rallying cries of unseen women already in there.

Jake Haulter's car had been the secret up his sleeve throughout the Japanese occupation. It had been hidden under sacking and other things in a locked shed behind his extensive garage and car showroom premises, where no one had troubled to search. Jake was *persona grata* with the Japanese, but that was held against him by no one; his status as a Swiss/British national had enabled him to be attached to the neutral Swiss Embassy and perform many intermediary duties, which was helpful all round and obviated many a misunderstanding and dispute between the occupiers and the civil authorities still responsible for administering the city.

Jake had other secrets beside the car, though. He was able to listen to BBC broadcasts and passed on their content to those he knew they would encourage and comfort, not least the prisoners at Changi, to whom he smuggled bulletins through his tradesmen contacts. It was not wholly altruistic on his part. He had a keen eye for the main chance and knew how to ensure that he would be rewarded for his services, both to the occupied and the Japanese, either in cash, or kind, or secured promises for the future.

He was in his early forties now. His father had been French-Swiss and his mother a native of the country in which he had been born, India. He had been expelled from his English public school for sleeping with a chambermaid. In the aftermath of the First World War he had made his way to Paris, to educate himself in the more interesting school of life. Another of its pupils had been a rich American girl, who drank too much before Jake married her and even more afterwards, so that she became a liability. He escaped by getting a job with the P & O shipping line as entertainments officer for its cruise ships, work for which his adaptability, infectious good humour, ability to smooth difficult situations, and natural attributes as a wangler and a womaniser made him an ideal employee; that was until an unfortunate situation involving both a woman and a wangle caused the company to offer him the alternative of resigning or taking a desk job in Singapore.

He chose the latter, recognising that it would offer his material ambitions enhanced scope. From making onshore arrangements for P & O visitors and organising excursions, he naturally extended to hiring them cars and accommodation, which he himself at first hired from others, then came to own. He got the sales franchise for several leading American makes of car and contracts for conveying goods to and from the docks. The P & O days were well behind him by then and the future seemed set very fair, when the Japanese came. Jake Haulter put all his wangling ability into coming to terms with them, and thus enjoyed an easygoing and profitable war.

He was no villain; just a smart operator, helpful and likeable, and it was typical of him that he should call at Raffles the following morning to inquire after Joss's health, having first visited Stephen Wentworth and found him in as good shape as could be expected. The two men had been on casual acquaintance for some years.

Joss was pale under her deep-tanned skin, and confessed to a 'bit of a head'; otherwise she was in fine fettle and not a little flattered to be visited in the foyer by this personable man in his expensive tropical outfit.

'Tell me,' she asked in an instinctively lowered voice, 'were we stinking?'

'Mellow,' he replied. 'Deliciously mellow.'

'Flatterer! It was most decent of you, though. Like to meet some of my more sober room-mates?' She had espied Dorothy and Maggie looking on with curiosity and perhaps a touch of envy. They came eagerly when she beckoned them for introductions.

'Why don't I order us all some coffee – or a prairie oyster?' he said wickedly to Joss.

'Thanks,' Dorothy said, 'but Miss says we're allowed out now. We're going to look for my bungalow in the Telok Blangah Road. Any idea how much a taxi will sting us there and back?'

'It's more a question of can you get one to take you that far. They're restricted for petrol, and they can make more from short runs.'

'What about a rickshaw?' Maggie suggested.

'Too far,' Dorothy said, and Jake nodded and said, 'Why don't I give you a lift? My car's outside.'

'Thanks, but aren't you short of petrol too?'

'Not me,' he grinned slyly. 'Never – even less so when the company's female.'

The offer was accepted without demur, as much for Jake's company as for his transportation, leaving Joss to settle down to a studiedly unhectic morning. Outside the hotel Dorothy and Maggie encountered Marion. She was trying in vain to attract any of the battered taxis, all of which seemed crammed with people in uniform.

'Having trouble?' said Dorothy.

'I've been trying to get a taxi for ages.'

Jake Haulter said, 'Excuse me, but I'm just about to give a lift to your friends. If I could help at all? Jake Haulter.'

He offered his hand, which Marion shook.

'Marion Jefferson. I'm trying to get to Alexandra Park.'

'Nothing simpler. It's on our way.'

He led them to the car, and all three marvelled at its size and condition and comfort. Jake drove them easily out of the crowded thoroughfares and up into the leafy suburbs. It seemed only minutes to Alexandra Park, compared with Marion's dream, which had seemed so real and had lingered more vividly than her last actual memory of the house.

'Crikey!' Maggie said, when Marion asked him to stop. From their viewpoint on the road the house looked in immaculate shape, tall and imposing, the front lawn smooth and close-cut.

'Would you like me to pick you up again?' Jake offered. 'About an hour, OK?'

'It . . . it would be most kind. Thank you.' Marion's reply was uttered almost absently as she got out and closed the door. She only vaguely waved the others off, her attention impelled towards the house.

For some moments she stood there on the footpath, as she had in the dream, staring at her home. The broad gate was shut, as she had dreamed it, and the raked gravel looked as if no car had disturbed it for some time. The window shutters were drawn shut, too, and there was no sign of movement: no Dolah, no Ali. For a moment, panic gripped Marion. The house was not as she recalled it in reality, but in the dream. She feared that if she opened the gate and went in she would find vegetables growing where flowers should have been – and then the *Tenko*! clatter would wake her, and she would find herself sobbing in that awful, stifling, stinking hut again . . .

The unwelcome spell was broken by a fifteen hundred-weight army truck speeding past her and a loud wolf-whistle from one of the soldiers in the back. She turned

185

and saw him and his mates waving cheerfully. She waved back, turned again, unlatched the gate, and walked resolutely up the drive. To her infinite relief, there were flowers in the front beds, as neatly set out and tended as they had always been.

She hesitated about approaching the door, feeling rather foolish at having no key to her own house. Then she heard someone singing in a low, preoccupied tone. Marion almost ran round the side to the back verandah behind the kitchen door, and on the verandah saw Dolah, kneeling down to some seed boxes.

'Dolah!' Marion cried.

He looked up, and then stood. She was surprised that he did not smile or come forward to greet her. She had to climb the verandah steps to him.

'Oh, Dolah, it's so wonderful to see you. You don't know how wonderful. Your family . . . are they all right?'

'We have survived,' he answered drily. 'I am pleased to see that you have, Mrs Jefferson.'

There was an odd stiffness about him, the way he spoke to her and looked at her. She didn't resent that he failed to address her as mem or madam, but she could have hoped for at least a warmer tone and some more enthusiastic expression of welcome and relief at seeing her again.

'You've . . . you've looked after everything beautifully,' she complimented him, striving to break the ice.

He shook his head seriously. 'That was the Japanese. The house was taken by their officers and they arranged for its care.'

'That's a relief. I see you're raising seedlings.'

'For vegetables.' He indicated the beds at the back, once a mass of blooms, and she saw at last that, as in her dream, vegetables had replaced them.

'For my family,' Dolah said. 'Food, where there was once only flowers.' It was said disparagingly.

'Of course,' Marion said brightly. 'Very sensible.'

'And you, Mrs Jefferson. Are you returning?'

186

'I don't know yet. It depends on the *tuan* . . .'

'Ah, Colonel Jefferson.'

'Of course,' she said, a trifle needled. 'That's why I came today, to find out if you or anyone knows if he . . . got away. I haven't heard of him since I left.'

'He went also. One day he came in a great hurry and locked the house and left in army lorry.'

'And?'

Dolah shrugged. 'Who knows? He said he was leaving by boat.'

'And that's all? You haven't asked about him?'

The gardener shrugged. 'The Japanese came. I am busy. It was not good to ask questions. I must feed my family.'

'I understand,' Marion said, though she had the distinct impression by now that he resented seeing her there again, wanting nothing more than to go on feeding his family from her garden instead of having to go back to growing useless flowers again.

'Is the house open?'

He indicated the back door. It was boarded up. 'The Japanese take the key away. They do not say where.'

Marion suddenly felt depressed. This house no longer seemed hers. The island itself seemed an alien place. She felt isolated, unwanted, abandoned. Surely Clifford, if he were alive, would have sent some message through RAPWI, guessing she would have been brought back to Singapore if she had survived.

After a little more unsatisfactory conversation with Dolah, she left him and went to sit on the front verandah to await the car's return. Even if Dolah were suddenly to produce the house key after all she thought she wouldn't want to use it; there would only be some further disappointment awaiting her inside.

Dorothy Bennett's disillusionment on setting eyes on her own far humbler abode was much more immediate: it was a wreck.

Jake had dropped her and Maggie off near by and driven

away to do some business of his own. They walked the short distance past other bungalows in what had been a modest European suburb. Seeing the deserted, unkempt state of the houses and 'Liberty' and 'British Go Home' daubed on the walls should perhaps have prepared Maggie for the shock.

'Oh, my Gawd!' she exclaimed, when at last they stood before the half-derelict little bungalow. The front door hung from its hinges. The window frames, complete with their anti-mosquito wire, had been ripped out. Debris was piled in the porch. The garden, which had never been much, was a mass of weeds and dumped garbage.

'You want to go in?' Maggie said uncertainly.

Dorothy didn't answer – she didn't appear to care – but went on, pushing the hanging door to one side to gain access to the front room. It was hot and gloomy; it smelt of human excreta; it buzzed with insects. There was nothing in it except a broken chair and some scraps of paper.

'You wait here, while I see what the bastards have done to the rest,' Maggie said gently. She went from room to room in the small place, commenting on the damage and the mess. Dorothy was not listening. She was trying to remember what it had been like when it had been home for Dennis and her and the baby, but found she couldn't. Perhaps it was as well.

'We can't stay here, that's for sure,' Maggie said when she returned.

Dorothy roused herself. 'Why not? Bare boards are what we're used to. A thorough clean-up and some repairs, and it'll be all right.'

'You'll get something, won't you? Compensation and that?'

'Huh! I can imagine how much, and how long it'll take to drag it out of them.'

The prospect was certainly a disheartening one. They were still contemplating it, seeing little that could be done

188

about it, when Jake came back to collect them. He surveyed the mess without expressing dismay.

'I've seen worse,' he said.

'You're joking.'

'I kid you not. It was pretty tough here under the Japs, for all they're supposed to be so clean at home.'

'We've lived in worse than this ourselves,' Dorothy agreed. 'Cleaning up would be no problem. Repairs could wait. We need a bit of furniture, though, and some cooking things.'

'That's no problem.'

'What *is* a problem is that we've no money.'

'That's nothing, either. The godowns downtown are jampacked with stuff picked up by the army from the Japanese. Things they'd looted from private houses for their own use, not to mention all the stuff taken into safekeeping until the owners surface to claim it back – if they ever do.'

'You mean I might be able to find my things?'

'Needle in a haystack department. No, you just go take your pick, sign a receipt for what you get, and move it in. If anyone later traces something to you that they particularly want back then you have to hand it over. It isn't likely.'

'What are we waiting for then?' Maggie enthused.

'For me to drive you to the main godown, I'd guess. Mustn't forget to pick Mrs Jefferson up on the way. She'll be feeling stranded.'

Stranded was exactly what Marion was feeling, in more than one sense. She was relieved to see the car returning and glad to be among friends again. Dorothy and Maggie listened with sympathy to her gloomy report, then returned to their own exciting plans; their optimism caused Marion's growing gloom to deepen. She could imagine how it was going to be. Day by day the sisterhood which had endured so much together and become so interdependent would break up as its members went off in their respective directions. She pictured herself as a last survivor, left as unwanted as she had sensed she was back at the house. When was Clifford going to come and claim her and make it all right? Why didn't he get in touch?

She declined the girls' invitation to come with them and Jake, and got him to drop her off at Raffles. She had been occupying the car seat next to him. Now Jake invited one of the others to come up front and keep him company in her place. Maggie had taken him up on it before he'd finished speaking, and their eyes met as she placed herself as close to him as she could.

The warehouse to which he took them was packed with every household object imaginable, from rolls of carpet and suites of furniture to polo sticks, framed pictures and photographs, and crockery and kitchenware by the ton. Coolies were bringing in more things from army trucks, while others were carrying out those that had been claimed or borrowed in the way Jake had proposed.

'So what's your taste?' he grinned, expansively waving an arm at it all.

'Who cares, so long as we can live off it.'

Jake clicked his tongue reprovingly. 'That, if you'll take my suggestion, isn't the shrewdest of attitudes. Allowing for the fact that what you take might never be reclaimed, you'd be better going for Hepplewhite and that sort of thing with a value. Never know, you might want to sell it some day, and it's sure to have gained in value.'

'I get it,' Dorothy said. She gazed about. 'Er . . .' Then she surrendered all pretence, and with a rare laugh admitted, 'What's Hepplewhite look like?'

Jake knew. Jake knew antique furniture as he knew many other things of intrinsic value. Under his guidance they dug out a complete set of Regency chairs for starters, and a couple more hours' delving secured enough things to furnish and equip the bungalow more than adequately. Everything had a number or a name attached to it, but as she signed the final list Dorothy felt little emotion about the fate of the owners.

Others were also searching, among them a uniformed Salvation Army couple who were rummaging among trunks belonging to people known to be dead in search of clothes and other things suitable to issue to returning refugees. The woman saw Maggie look at her hold up and then immediately discard a cocktail dress and jacket in sequins.

'Lovely, isn't it?' she smiled at Maggie.

'I'll say.'

'Hardly practical for our poor refugees, though. I suppose you wouldn't care to have it?'

'Me?'

'We really can't use it. It won't improve lying here, and the poor dear lady who owned it was drowned in one of the ships. Do have it.'

Maggie held it against her. 'It's the most beautiful dress I've ever seen,' she gasped.

'And it suits you to a T. God bless!'

Maggie ran to the others with her prize. Dorothy was grubby but smiling and excited. Jake looked at them both. 'You're like a couple of happy kids,' he told them. 'Pretty, with it,' he added and winked at Maggie.

It called for a celebration. Jake suggested a club, the China Seas Bar, where anyone could become a temporary member. He invited them to bring some of their friends along and the proposal went down well. The constraints so far imposed on them by Phyllis Bristow and other welfare administrators, understandable though they were, had inhibited them from properly celebrating their return to freedom. Money was another problem, especially, it seemed, to Mrs Van Meyer. Her boasts about her wealth had irked them throughout their captivity. She declined to come to the party, on the excuse that she did not frequent bars.

Beatrice Mason had her own reason for feeling like a celebration. A Sikh doctor had fixed her up with a pair of spectacles compatible with her eyesight, literally and figuratively transforming her outlook. Marion, whose face was blotchy from tears when Dorothy sought her out to invite her, surprised her by accepting eagerly. The reason became apparent when they got to the bar: Marion could not wait to get her hands on a drink, and had polished it off before Jake could propose the toast to Dorothy's and Maggie's success with the bungalow. He sent for a refill for her for the purpose. Beatrice gave her a look of doctorly concern, which Marion caught and returned with an uncharacteristic scowl.

There was dancing with the army and navy officers in the bar, and more drinks, mostly paid for by Jake, who was especially attentive to Beatrice, who discovered that she liked the rare experience of flattery. When he slipped in a casual mention that he would be grateful to know if she should happen to hear through medical contacts of any new shipment of penicillin, as he might want to buy some of it to supply to a friend running a local private clinic, she thought what a considerate man he was on behalf of others.

The evening wore on, and reached the point where Dorothy, beginning to feel the drink affecting her, remarked to Maggie that she thought she had better be getting back to the hotel. At that point there was a commotion near the entrance, and they saw Mrs Van Meyer forcing her way past a doorman, who was trying to explain that she must pay the nominal club fee and sign the book before she could be allowed in.

'You must let me through,' she insisted. 'It is a matter of life or death. I have come all this way especially to bring her back to the hotel.'

'Bring who back?' asked Joss, who was nearest.

'Marion. Phyllis says it is urgent, and I said I thought I knew where to find her.'

Joss looked at the dancing throng. 'Marion!' she called. 'Marion!'

The crowd rippled apart and Marion emerged, followed by the naval officer who had been her partner.

'There you are,' Mrs Van Meyer greeted her with relief. 'Phyllis wants you urgently.'

'What is it?'

'Your husband. You are to come at once.'

16 Clifford

He was waiting for her in the converted sitting-room that she shared as a bedroom with the others. His blond hair had more flecks of white, which became him well, and he wore the insignia of a brigadier on his jungle-green tunic. Otherwise, he had scarcely changed since Marion had last seen him at their enforced and hectic parting in 1942. He was well set up and as fit as she had ever remembered him.

With nothing more coherent than a cry she ran into his arms. For some moments they rocked together in a tight embrace, their cheeks pressed together, before moving into a long kiss.

Marion didn't cry, but speaking was difficult.

'I thought you . . . they couldn't trace you . . .'

'Bungling idiots thought I was some other Jefferson. I'm not with the regiment now. Intelligence at Kandy.'

'And you're all *right*?'

They stood back at last to regard each other. She saw his frown of concern at her appearance.

'Yes, I'm fine. What about you, though?'

'I'll pass, I hope. Any news of Ben?'

'Flourishing. Your parents, too.'

Only then did the tears of relief flow. He held her close again, rocking her patiently till she recovered. Then they subsided onto the edge of her bed, and with his arm about her he told her how he had left Singapore only two days after she had, with important documents to get out. Like hers, his ship had been sunk, but a junk had rescued him and taken him to Java.

'And I got home from there,' he concluded.

'Home? *England*?'

'Yes. Far East Planning wanted chaps with knowledge of Malaya, so I was seconded.'

'All the time you were in England!' she said incredulously. 'Then . . . you *saw* Ben.'

'A good deal. He's doing splendidly at Wellington.'

He fished out his wallet and produced a photograph. As Marion marvelled at the young man she had left behind as a teenage boy, Clifford talked on. 'That was taken last summer. End of last year I was posted out to India – in on the planning of the recapture of Rangoon. Then on to Ceylon . . .'

He checked himself, realising that through all the time of which he was speaking so blithely she had been cooped up in jungle prison camps.

'My poor sweet, you've been through so much.'

'It must show.'

He shook his head. 'You're just the same to me. I heard your ship had sunk. I told myself you'd make it all right, but after a year with no word . . .'

'They wouldn't let us write letters. Not even Red Cross cards.'

'Bastards!'

He held her tight again, then said, 'By the way, that RAPWI woman told me a batch left this afternoon, so there are some rooms vacant until tomorrow. She's arranged for us to have one.'

She got up. 'Then I'd better gather my things before the others come back, or they'll keep us talking half the night. D'you know, it'll be the first time in three and a half years that I'll have slept in a room on my own.'

'Only, you won't *be* on your own,' he reminded her gently.

In fact, the love they tried to make after so long was a total failure. When patience finally ran out they turned on their backs, side by side, just holding hands.

'It's ridiculous,' Clifford growled.

'Just out of practice,' Marion comforted him good-humouredly. 'It'll be all right in time.'

'In our own bed, for one thing.'

'You mean at the house? We're staying in Singapore?'

'Hang it, I haven't even got round to telling you. This isn't just a visit. I'm posted here.' His tone changed to anxiety. 'Can you bear the place?'

'I think so. I've been to look at the house. From the outside it looks habitable. Only . . .'

'The thought of Japs living there, you mean?'

'No, not that. It's . . . nothing.'

She could not have put into words what it was. She didn't even know. There was only vague instinct to tell her how much she was going to miss the comrades who had been with her in the long struggle to survive and triumph.

The introductions to them were made next morning in the dining-room. Already Marion was finding it strange to breakfast alone with Clifford at a small table some distance from the big one shared by her friends. Their glances were unconcealed, and she could guess what innuendo was flying about. When they had finished eating she took him over to them.

'We've met before,' Beatrice Mason reminded him, and Marion felt for her when she saw Clifford's brows furrow showing his inability to remember.

'At the hospital,' she prompted. 'Back in '42. Beatrice was doctor in charge.'

'Of course!' Clifford strove tactfully. 'Didn't recognise you without your white coat.'

'Are you leaving us, then?' Beatrice said, recognising the kindly effort.

'Course she is,' Maggie answered for Marion. 'Wouldn't you, if you had a place like that to go to?'

'You must all come and visit us,' Marion said, and meant it more sincerely than such general invitations are usually meant.

196

'Of course,' Clifford agreed. 'Excuse me while I go and check about the car and one or two other things.'

He went, followed by admiring looks. Marion said, 'I must go up and get my things. No goodbyes, please.'

Beatrice went up with her. 'Not surprising he didn't know me,' she remarked. 'It was nice of him to pretend.'

'It's a wonder he knew *me*,' Marion reassured her.

'Well, you're the first to go, then. Next Maggie and Dorothy'll be off to their bungalow. Then they'll start shipping the rest of us out.'

'What have you decided, Bea?'

'I'll go home first. Might as well take advantage of the free passage. Then I'll come back and take up my old job. There's nothing to stop me, now I've got these.' She tapped her spectacles.

'You haven't considered staying on in England?'

'No point. I've specialised in tropical medicine, and I've no ties – nothing in common with my sisters. Perhaps if they'd been stuck in a prison camp with me we'd be different. You're more a sister than they are, Marion.'

'Oh, Beatrice . . . !' They hugged one another on the landing, near to tears.

While Clifford was at the reception desk he suddenly found a Eurasian girl at his side. He realised she was the one he'd been introduced to at the breakfast table, though he hadn't taken in her name. He begged Christina's pardon for it.

'Excuse my troubling you,' she said, 'but I used to know someone in your regiment. Simon Treves. I wondered if . . .'

'Treves – oh yes. Nice boy. I saw him quite recently. He's in India now.'

Christina's eyes sparkled. 'I didn't even know he was alive.'

'Very much so. He was wounded a couple of years back. Nothing too serious. Turned out a blessing in disguise, in fact. He married one of the nurses. Excuse me . . .'

The clerk had come back with the information he had been awaiting. When he turned round again the girl had gone. He mentioned the encounter to Marion when he remembered it much later. She grimaced, and then he recognised his gaffe.

'Never imagined,' he said. 'Still, she's probably well out of it. Doesn't work out, mixed marriages, you know.'

Marion didn't trouble to argue the point. There had been a time, something over three years ago, when she would have automatically agreed and given it no more thought.

Incredibly, the house and its contents were just as they had left them. Nothing appeared to have been stolen or damaged, though Marion had braced herself to expect scenes of spiteful destruction wrought by the departing Japanese occupants. There was no sign of the servants.

'Dolah was still here the other day,' she told him again. 'Though hardly the old Dolah.'

'I suppose they'd worked on him. They've left quite a legacy of anti-British feeling among the natives. The others are probably goners. You heard about the massacres? Twenty thousand Chinese slaughtered in the first few days. We'll get the bastards responsible – for that and what you and the rest went through. That's what I shall be doing now, co-ordinating war crime investigations. Your commandant will be top of my list, I promise you.'

Marion was surprised at what sounded almost like fanaticism in his tone. Their conversation was interrupted by a faint sound from the hall. There was a tentative tap at the open sitting room door, and an elderly Chinese woman showed herself on the threshold. With a broad smile she said, 'Welcome home, *Tuan*.'

'Minah!' cried Marion, running forward to embrace her. 'How *are* you?'

'I survive.'

'Your sons?'

The smile remained, though without its radiance – the

Oriental smile which covers any display of heartfelt emotion.

'Both are dead. They are killed by Japanese soldiers. Now God send bomb to punish them. Master Ben is safe?'

'Yes, in England. The *Tuan* has seen him. I . . . I've been in one of the camps.'

'Then you have suffer much, mem. I see what happen in Changi.'

Clifford intervened. 'You've been coming here, Minah – since the Japs left?'

'Every day.'

'That explains why the place is immaculate,' Marion said. 'Thank you.'

'Yes,' Clifford added crisply, 'and the first thing I want you to do is organise some more servants.'

'Yes, *Tuan*.'

'No, Clifford,' Marion countermanded. 'I'd rather . . . I can manage, with just Minah.'

'Nonsense.'

'It isn't as if we'll be entertaining on any scale.'

'There'll still be the cooking and the laundry and . . .'

'Good lord, I've been doing a darn sight more than that.'

'You're not in a camp any more. We're not having her lift a finger, are we, Minah?'

'No, *Tuan*.' The smile was warm again.

'From now on you're going to be thoroughly spoilt.'

Again she didn't argue. Although she knew herself to be no longer the archetypal European mistress of a household in a colonial dependency – the brigadier's lady now – Marion sensed the changes within herself. She knew, though, that it was too soon to define and rationalise them. Some things were bound to have gone for good, others perhaps only temporarily. She had to wait and let time and recovery and new circumstances sort them out for her.

The truth of this was reinforced by the failure of their own bed to have any magical influence on their love-making that night. After a while they lay back again and simply talked, with the muted glow of the bedside lamps lighting up their old familiar surroundings and objects.

Clifford was inclined to blame himself. 'You seem so fragile . . . I'm afraid of hurting you.'

'I'm not that fragile. Don't worry, darling.'

'Did they ever . . . in the camps. . . ?'

'No. Never. Not me.'

'Others?'

'There was an incident in our first camp. The men concerned were punished. There was never any other attempt to force us.'

'Though some didn't need forcing, I dare say. Were there many?'

'There were a few who made sort of friends with the guards. They'd only one thing they could trade for a few little favours and what must have passed for tenderness of a kind. They never let their friendships betray the rest of us.'

'Were there any other sort of betrayals?'

'Only one that I knew of. Lillian Cartland, in fact.'

'Johnny Cartland's wife! The one you were at school with?'

'She did what she did to get extra food for Bobby. They moved her away smartly when she was found out, and she and Bobby got bundled onto one of the first ships away from here. The RAPWI girl told me Lillian died on the voyage home. Poor Bobby. He knew she was starving herself for him, and he didn't need it, but she wouldn't listen.'

'What she did – tell me about it.'

Marion said, 'No, please. I'd rather not. I want to forget all that now.'

The first night's sleep in their own bed did wonders for Marion's strength. Against her husband's protests she was up for breakfast with him. But when he had gone off in the staff car for another busy day among the returning hundreds of ex-prisoners she found that Minah had been left

200

with strict orders not to let her do a hand's turn about the house. To spare the loyal Chinese servant's feelings Marion acquiesced and settled down on the drawing-room sofa with the Singapore edition of South-East Asia Command's newspaper. It could not hold her attention. She switched on the wireless and listened to Bing Crosby crooning, the bland sound contrasting with her restless mood. It was a considerable relief, after hearing the doorbell's ring, when Minah came in and said that a Mr Jake Haulter had called.

'Hello again,' he greeted her, invited in at once. 'I was out this way and thought I'd look by. I heard about your husband. Wanted to say how glad I am for you.'

'Thank you, Jake.'

'You certainly look brighter. Hope I'm not disturbing you, though.'

'Not a bit. I was feeling at a loose end. Clifford's had to start work in the thick of it.'

'Tell him if I can be of any help – transport problems, labour difficulties . . .'

'I'm sure he'd be grateful.'

'Meanwhile, perhaps I can be of use to you, as I'm going into town. How about a lift to Raffles?'

She accepted without hesitation. That evening, she had no hesitation, either, about telling Clifford about her enjoyable day's reunion with her friends when she shared their luncheon with an appetite as yet undiminished for the limited official fare available. She told him about Jake and conveyed his offer to help. Her news was not graciously received.

'I may not have seen you for some time,' she teased, 'but I know that frozen-faced look of yours. I was bored and I wanted to see the others.'

'I could have dropped you there, if you really *had* to go.'

'I hadn't thought of it till Jake called.'

'If your Jake is the type I picture, I don't care for it.'

'What "type"?'

'Finger in every pie. Feathered his nest during the occupation. Very convenient being half Swiss.'

'Everyone says how invaluable he was as an intermediary – on the quiet as well as semi-official.'

'I bet he turned a pedigree like his to profitable use.'

'Pedigree? He was educated at Radley, that's all.'

'Mother Indian, did you say?'

'What if she was?'

'Nothing. Nothing.' Clifford reverted to the old smile which could change him instantly from the senior officer back to the young subaltern she had first loved. 'Don't let's spoil our evening getting het up about Mr Jake Haulter. I've something far better to tell you. I had a chat with a fellow in RAPWI who thinks he could wangle you an early passage home. Possibly next week.'

It was something for which Marion was so totally unprepared that he saw he had been too abrupt with the news.

'I know, darling,' he hastened to add. 'It's the last thing I want, too. But I'll be up to my eyes over the next few months. You'll be best off recuperating with your parents, and you'll want to see Ben as soon as possible . . .'

His look changed to surprise when Marion interrupted, 'It's too much of a rush. I'd prefer not to leave until the others have settled their plans.'

'They're looked after,' he protested. 'That RAPWI woman . . .'

'Phyllis doesn't know them as I do. I can't just ditch them, Clifford. Several of them have problems that need sorting out.'

'Darling, you're not their leader now.'

'I feel responsible, all the same. Wouldn't you, if they were your men?'

'It's hardly the same.'

'Oh yes it is,' she answered, and surprised him by her intensity.

She had not exaggerated: there *were* problems to be sorted

out among her friends. A couple of major ones were about to erupt.

A new draft of arrivals had come off a ship, some of them to Raffles.

'Anyone we know?' Joss asked Beatrice Mason, who had seen them in the foyer.

'A couple from the second camp. Agnes Laidlaw.'

'Sour-looking creature? Always complaining?'

'That's the one. Phyllis was going to put her in here, but I heard her asking if she could stay with her own crowd.'

'Thank God. She never did approve of me. Who's the other?'

'Enid Trotter. Lost a child. She looks half-demented. If only we'd been allowed that quinine the kid might have made it.'

Joss grunted. 'Like now. Stephen's desperate for penicillin for his people, but can he get any through official channels? Oh no. Brits first, and bugger the natives.'

'Jake Haulter was asking too,' the doctor remembered.

'Seems it's like gold-dust, which is no doubt what that fly young man'll turn it into, whereas Stephen . . . Bea, maybe with your contacts. . .'

'What contacts? Be different if I were back in harness.'

'Any news on that front?'

'I'm seeing the administrative bod at the hospital tomorrow. Talk about nervous – you'd think I was up for my first interview, not arranging to get my old job back.'

'Big B' some had called Beatrice Mason in the camps, referring solely to her strength of will and the confidence they instinctively retained in her as a doctor; even though she had only makeshift materials and instruments, and suffered her share of their illnesses, she always came back to carry on in often nauseating conditions. To her previous knowledge had been added over three years' experience of the worst ravages of tropical diseases and conditions. With one trained nurse, Kate Norris, and the various unskilled helpers whom they had taught to do the simplest nursing,

Bea had dragged women back from death's clutches, insanity and despair; they had bullied others into practising such hygiene as had been possible, so that their constitutions had kept fundamentally sound enough to recover.

The hospital administrator, a civilian wearing army major's rank, complimented her on her work and on the valuable knowledge gained through it. Everyone was grateful to her and others like her and proud of them, he concluded.

'Thank you,' she acknowledged. 'But to come to the question of my future . . .'

Her file was open before him. 'Ah yes. No doubt you've had time to think about your plans.'

'More than enough.'

'You'll be going home, I imagine?'

'For two or three months. I'd like to resume my post in the new year, if it will be a convenient time. I realise the Colonial Office is responsible for organisation, but a word from this end . . .'

He interrupted her, frowning. 'You mean you wish to return here to work, Dr Mason?'

'If I'm wanted, that is.'

'It's not a matter of being wanted. God knows we need all the European staff we can find, particularly people of your calibre. But do you really think it would be worth it?'

'How do you mean?'

'Well, it would only be for a limited period.'

Beatrice was able to smile. 'I may look decrepit but I'm nowhere near due for retirement yet, if that's what you're thinking.'

The administrator was being strictly serious. 'I wasn't thinking of your official retirement, Doctor; rather of your enforced one.'

Her smile faded. 'I don't understand.'

'I'll be frank. How long would you be able to go on working? Under the circumstances, wouldn't it be better to stay on at home, get some part-time welfare work until . . .'

204

'Under what circumstances?' she asked sharply. 'Until what?'

The man stared at her across his desk. It was beginning to dawn on him that she knew less than he thought – had perhaps not even been told . . . As she caught his look, Beatrice misread it as giving away that he was covering something up.

'If there's something wrong that I haven't been told, I think I have the right to know about it here and now,' she said.

'I really don't think it's my place to . . .'

'Good God, man, I'm a doctor. I don't need cushioning. Is it my eyes? Tell me the worst.'

The unhappy man handed her a piece of paper from the top of the file, murmuring apologetically that he'd understood that she had already been informed.

Beatrice read the document, once swiftly and then again carefully. She handed it back and got up. The administrator rose too, genuinely distressed.

'I can't tell you how sorry . . . ,' he was saying, but she cut across him brusquely.

'I imagine they thought it better to wait until I was – what's their jargon? – "psychologically equipped" to cope with the blow. Obviously, I shall need to reconsider my plans. Good morning.'

Beatrice walked with stiff-backed dignity to the door.

She kept on walking from the hospital, not caring that there were taxis and rickshaws waiting there for hire. She saw nothing of the streets and the people crowding them as she kept going, trance-like, not even noticing a file of dejected Japanese prisoners, whose escort halted them to one side to let a staff car get by. The car stopped a little further along, and after calling in vain from the lowered passenger window Clifford Jefferson got out and came up to her, making her stop and raise her eyes to his face.

'Oh . . . Brigadier!'

'I thought it was you, Dr Mason. Bit off the beaten track, aren't you?'

'I . . . was taking a walk.'

'Not very wise. Not on your own. Let me give you a lift back to Raffles.'

She was set to refuse, but he insisted, getting into the back of the car with her.

'Actually, I'd be glad of a word with you,' he said when they were moving. 'Officially, I mean. About the conditions in your camps – the way the Japs treated the women.'

Beatrice tried to give him her attention, but her mind was mostly on her present troubles.

'Surely Marion's your best informant,' she tried.

'She seems reluctant to talk about it. Major Smithers tells me he found the same.'

Beatrice roused herself. 'Well, we were in three different camps, our group.'

'Under the same commandant, though, I believe.'

'Yamauchi. Yes.'

'What was he like?'

Beatrice's resentment of the man under whose command she had seen her charges suffer and die, and had herself grown prematurely old, half-blind and, it was clear, of no more use to her profession, welled up in her bitter yet precise answer.

'I hold Yamauchi directly responsible for the deaths of over a hundred women and children and the permanent disablement of many more. When they finally surrendered he opened up the store cupboards. They were full of drugs, medicines, vitamins; all the things we'd been crying out for. Most of them need never have died.'

There was a moment's silence between them. Then Clifford asked, 'Dr Mason, would you if necessary be prepared to stand as a witness against him?'

Beatrice nodded emphatically.

When he had dropped her off at Raffles she immediately

encountered Kate in the foyer. She was talking with Christina Campbell.

'Hello!' she was greeted. 'How'd the interview go?'

'Fine, fine.'

Kate looked at her curiously.

'Everything's fixed up, then?'

'Certain amount of . . . red tape to be unravelled. How was your day?'

'Don't ask.'

'Tom's not worse, I hope.'

'No thanks to some people. That Major Smithers came creeping round the ward collecting evidence against Japs, no matter what state anyone was in. He even tried to question Tom, but I put paid to that.'

To Kate's surprise Beatrice replied unsympathetically, 'If it helps to put people like Yamauchi behind bars . . .'

'There's a time and place. Even he had the grace to apologise. Said he was acting under Clifford-bloody-Jefferson's orders.'

'I don't think you should criticise Brigadier Jefferson for trying to bring a criminal like that to justice.'

Christina butted in with an objection. 'Aren't you prejudging Yamauchi, Beatrice?'

'What d'you mean?'

'Calling him a criminal before he's even been tried.'

'Oh, come on, Christina. We know what he did . . .'

'He was acting under orders from their High Command. He often showed kindness.'

'To you, perhaps. Not to the dying, the sick.'

'That's true,' Kate agreed.

'Some of us will bear the scars of his inhumanity for the rest of our lives,' Beatrice said, speaking more bitterly than Kate ever remembered.

'He was a sick man himself,' Christina persisted.

'That doesn't excuse his giving Sato a free hand.'

'I agree. All I'm saying is . . .'

'Calm down you two,' Kate warned them, as heads turned their way.

Beatrice advanced her face a little towards Christina's and said, in a lowered voice that quivered with her emotion, 'When Yamauchi goes on trial I shall stand up and give evidence against him. I've told Clifford Jefferson I'm prepared to. And what's more, I hope my evidence will help them hang him.'

The other impending upset concerned Dorothy Bennett. She and Maggie Thorpe had gone out early in the day to Dorothy's bungalow, prepared to work hard at getting it habitable. To their surprise the missing window frames and mosquito mesh had already been replaced with new.

'Jake doesn't waste time, does he?' Maggie observed.

'I wonder why he's going to this trouble over us?'

'Fast worker in more ways than one. I wouldn't mind obliging him. Just think, Dot, once we've got this place fit to sleep in, and the furniture comes, we'll be free. Really free.'

'I know. I felt freer in the camp than in Raffles, with that Phyllis breathing down our necks.'

Dorothy got down to scrubbing, and for the first time the task was a pleasure. Maggie washed the walls with rags.

'What are you planning to do with the place?' she asked at one stage. 'Sell it and go home?'

'I don't know,' Dorothy replied. 'Can't decide.'

Under the rough veneer acquired in the camps, and was still maintained to make Maggie feel at ease with her, there was the young woman who had never worked for a living, who had married Dennis while he was in leave in England and who had been brought out to what had promised to be a better standard of living than she could have expected at home.

'Thought of staying on?' Maggie asked.

'I don't know what I'd do.'

'Get wed again sooner or later. There's always something meanwhile.'

'I'm off men. I wish I had their sort of know-how, though – Jake's kind. Wheeling and dealing, that's what I'd like to do. Something exciting.'

'Bit risky. Me, I'd sooner be more settled.'

'We'd have the bungalow,' Dorothy said. Maggie was surprised. She'd thought of the arrangement as purely temporary where she was concerned.

There was a surprise for them both in the afternoon. A small open truck drew up outside and a grinning Malay driver unloaded two ladies' bicycles, by no means new but in perfectly good order. They came with Jake's compliments. He had suggested they take up cycling to save on transport, but they hadn't expected he would go this far.

Scrubbing in the steamy heat had left them longing for the cool of Raffles and a soak in the bath. The arrival of the bicycles could not have been better timed, and soon they were freewheeling down the long hill, exulting in the breeze in their hair. Freedom seemed even closer to being complete.

The first threat to their new-found happiness reared itself in Raffles foyer as they chatted with Kate, whom they found there. The women of the new intake were milling about. One of them, recognising Dorothy, came over and deliberately spat at her. She walked away quickly. Expecting Dorothy to start after her Maggie seized her arm, but Dorothy made no move.

'Filthy cow,' Maggie said. 'Know her?'

'Enid Trotter. From the camp before last. She was always going on about me and Shinya, the guard who got killed.'

'Jealous, maybe.'

'She'd lost her kid. Turned a bit. She wasn't the only who lost someone,' Dorothy added.

There was worse later. They had had their baths and afternoon tea, during which Dorothy had told Maggie her decision to stay on and see what life offered. She invited

Maggie to share the bungalow with her, which was accepted with gladness. As they were returning to the room where they still had beds they chatted with excited anticipation about the house-warming party they would give, but turning a passage corner found themselves facing a group of women, with Enid Trotter to the fore. A growl of abuse went up at sight of them.

'What's this, then?' Maggie demanded.

'It's not you we want,' answered another woman, pointing to Dorothy. 'It's her. The Jap-lover.'

Dorothy recognised her accuser as the sour Agnes Laidlaw, also from the second camp.

'Come on, Dot,' Maggie urged. 'Take no notice of them.'

'Oh no you don't!'

The little mob surged forward. Dorothy recognised the intensity of hatred in their eyes and turned to try to run, but they surrounded her, reaching out to snatch at her clothes and hair. Dorothy fought back with fists and nails, while Maggie, whose bar-keeping days had taught her lessons about brawls which she hadn't forgotten, went to work with elbows flailing and feet kicking. Shrieks of 'Collaborator!' 'Whore!' 'Bitch!' topped the general clamour of anger and pain. It brought Kate and Mrs Van Meyer hurrying out of their nearby room, unable to see precisely what was going on but calling in vain for peace. It took a loud command of unmistakable authority to cause the attacker to hesitate and stare at the remarkable sight of Joss, wrapped only in the big towel into which she had just stepped from the bath, her white hair standing up in grotesque spikes.

'Stop that at once!' she commanded. 'At once, do you hear?'

Before the avengers could recover themselves, Dorothy had slipped from among them and run off down the corridor. She went down the broad staircase at a speed that would have bowled over anyone unlucky enough to meet her, a figure of terror with tears streaming down her face.

She ran past a staring Phyllis Bristow, across the foyer full of astonished onlookers, and out of the front door, almost full tilt into an approaching nun before whom she managed to pull up without colliding.

Even in her panic to get away, Dorothy paused and stared.

'Ulrica!' she gasped.

Without heed of onlookers, they fell into each other's arms.

17 Maggie

For part of her time in the camps Marion had kept a diary. It had been hard to do. Scraps of paper had to be salvaged from the Japanese waste, and a sliver of charred wood used for writing when no stub of pencil was left. Even then, there was precious little worth writing about. Day piled upon day with such monotony that the only happenings to record tended to be melancholy ones such as another death, a funeral, an admission to hospital, or a particularly noteworthy punishment.

Nevertheless, keeping any sort of journal helped her remain orientated with life, real and imagined: a dream of treacle pudding was a pleasant enough escape to get recorded in the tiny script which she used to economise on space.

It was a dangerous occupation, but she had persevered, and brought her later chronicles to freedom with her. Part of them were in a little notebook, which Christina had got for her from Headquarters, and this she flipped through one afternoon, in the quiet comfort of her drawing-room. She sat in a soft chair, surrounded by ornaments and flowers, feeling somehow guilty because she could not make herself constantly appreciative of being free. It was absurd, but something positive seemed to have been left behind in the past that she felt deprived of in the present.

She got out of the chair to answer the telephone, and did not return to it. Clifford sat in it when he came home dog-tired late that evening and sank down, thankfully, with a nightcap. It was then that he came across the diary, which had slipped between the chair arm and the seat cushion, and as he sipped his whisky he flipped through the pages with growing interest.

Marion, who had gone up to prepare for bed, was furious when he remarked innocently that he had been looking at her camp diary and recognised what vital evidence it contained for his prosecutions.

'You had no right to read *my* diary,' Marion insisted.

'Sorry, and all that. I happened on it by sheer chance, and by the time I'd realised what it was . . . Anyway, it's a most valuable document. It gives dates and other details – Rose Millar's shooting and death, for instance – that could be devilish hard to pin down otherwise. There's nothing *personal*.'

'Not to me, maybe, but to some of the others. You just said it's become obvious to you that Dorothy was nothing but a tart for the Japs, and Maggie the next best thing. I call that personal.'

He replied stiffly, 'As far as my department is concerned, whatever they got up to is too petty to be interesting. If the Japs had forced them, on the other hand . . .'

'But they didn't.'

'So that's an end of it. Look, Marion, isn't it time you left off seeing them? I mean to say, if it gets out that you and they are . . .'

'Friends? We are, so it's a risk I'll just have to take.'

'You're making things very difficult for me.'

'The war did that. Are you determined to use my diary?'

'I'm afraid I have no choice – now that I know what's in it.'

'So I presume it will go the rounds of the department, if only for the juicier plums to be picked out.'

'Have a heart,' he protested.

'I think my trouble may be that I do have one,' she riposted, and turned from him. As an afterthought she added, 'I'll be grateful if you'll drop me at Raffles in the morning, please. I want to alert Dorothy and Maggie about the diary.'

213

'Is that absolutely necessary?'

'To me it is. I feel I owe them an apology for any embarrassment that might come their way through my carelessness.'

It did not need Marion's diary to bring troubles home to Dorothy. She was called to the RAPWI office in Raffles Hotel next morning to face an embarrassed Phyllis Bristow, who asked her to close the door before addressing her.

'One of the new internees, who was with you in the second camp, has made a complaint about your behaviour with the guards. Collaboration, she called it.'

'So?'

'She . . . it could prove troublesome for you. I'd like to suggest it might be better for all concerned if you changed your mind about staying on here, and went home. I'm suggesting it for your own good, Dorothy.'

Dorothy exploded. 'My own good! Other people's convenience, more like. Let me tell you I'm not shifting from my bungalow for the sake of any tell-tale bitch. If I could take the Japs, a few little bitches aren't going to make me turn tail and run home to mother. As for you do-gooders . . . get stuffed!'

She stormed from the office, pausing only when the receptionist called her over to collect a letter. Without glancing at it Dorothy thrust it into her jacket pocket and went to get her bicycle. She pedalled furiously all the way to her bungalow.

Maggie was there already, whistling as she happily painted a kitchen cupboard door. Dorothy told her what had happened. Maggie was predictably sympathetic and indignant, but she did suggest tentatively, 'You sure you wouldn't sooner go home anyway, Dot? I mean, you've not to think of me. This place is yours to do what you like with. I can easily get somewhere else.'

'Back to Edgware?' Dorothy groaned. 'Back to Mother, and her antimacassars and pot plants. She'd have me under her thumb again in five mintues.'

'I reckon it'd take more'n a thumb now,' Maggie laughed. She went on painting, oblivious to Dorothy, who had remembered the letter in her pocket and opened it. What made Maggie turn round to look at her again was a loud sob.

'What is it, love?' she asked, putting her brush down. 'Got some news?'

'Two years back, and I never knew,' Dorothy cried. 'Mother copped it. A bomb on the shop where she'd just gone down for the paper. She used to buy me comics there when I was a kid.'

'Two years ago!' Maggie echoed. 'Makes you wonder what else has been going on.'

Dorothy blew her nose. 'Can't pretend we were that close, and at least it was a quick way to go. Saved her ever hearing she'd lost her grandchild, too.'

'Your house wasn't hit, then?' Maggie said.

'Nor it was,' Dorothy mused.

'Is it yours, then?'

'Must be – if nothing else happened to it. I'd no sisters or brothers. Not half a bad place, either. Quite a size. Hey – I could turn it into a boarding-house. Make a living off it. See what this place'll fetch, and . . .'

She broke off and looked at Maggie, who was regarding her wistfully. Maggie read her thought and moved to put an arm around Dorothy's shoulders.

'Don't care about me,' she assured her. 'There's plenty other places I can fit meself in. So come on – let's get cracking.'

'What doing?'

'This place. Finishing it off. Want to get the best price for it, don't you?'

They worked all day, improving the home they would never share. Marion, having missed them at Raffles, came out by taxi to warn them about her husband's discovery of the diary, and her own carelessness, and was surprised how little they cared. And back at Raffles that evening Dorothy

215

took a weight off Phyllis Bristow's mind by telling her that she would accept a homebound flight after all. It was allocated immediately; her plane would be leaving within the week.

Jake Haulter offered to sell the bungalow on Dorothy's behalf, refusing to take a commission. (He knew that the purchaser he had in mind would leap at the restored little property and reward Jake handsomely for the opportunity.) It was his idea, too, that there should be an eve-of-sailing party for Dorothy at the bungalow itself. He laid on the drinks and eats and a Chinese waiter and brought out his own gramophone and a pile of dance music records.

All Dorothy's friends from the camps were there including Sister Ulrica, who was staying at a nearby convent to recover her strength. She had been a great support to Dorothy since she had run – literally – into the nun outside the foyer of Raffles. Joss brought Stephen Wentworth, and even Clifford Jefferson came with Marion as a gesture of contrition. A noisy, happy time was had by all.

'Well,' Jake said to Maggie at the height of it, 'where are you fetching up? Staying on at good old Raffles?'

'The girls' boarding-school, complete with prefects? Screw that!'

He regarded her. 'I've got a spare room at my place. You're more than welcome.'

'You really mean it?'

'If it'll help.'

'Help! I'll say!'

Dorothy got a quiet word with Clifford Jefferson.

'That diary Marion says you just happened to read . . .'

'I'm sorry. Please believe me, it'll only be used against the Japs.'

She nodded. 'But take a tip from one who knows, Brigadier. Not all Nips are bastards.'

*

Next morning Jake and Maggie sat up side by side in bed, eating bread and Marmite and drinking champagne.

'You don't do things by halves, do you?' she said admiringly. He was a good-looking feller, she thought, but he hadn't hustled her into bed; she had had to drop the hint.

He grinned at her, though his eyes were guarded as he said, 'Just so long as . . .'

'I know, I know. We keep our freedom. No ties. So you can tell me all your wicked past, and I won't hold it up against you.'

'Kicked out of school. Got hitched to a rich and older alcoholic. Joined a shipping line as an entertainments officer. Picked up the right contacts – and here I am, with a very nice little contact indeed.'

'And the war?'

'Told you. Swiss passport. Everyone's friend. What about you? Not worrying about your future, are you? Plenty of things I can fix you up in. You can stay here as long as it suits you.'

'Thanks. No. I'm not worrying.'

But she was. She had made up her mind to have a quiet word with Dr Beatrice Mason.

Of them all, Beatrice was finding it hardest to come to terms with freedom. The shock of being told that her career was as good as finished and that all she had to look forward to was worsening eyesight, very likely culminating in total blindness, had depressed her utterly. There was nowhere forward to go. She had excused herself from the jollity of Dorothy's farewell party, just as she had excused herself from attending the funeral of Kate's Tom, who had succumbed at last in hospital. She felt no incentive to leave the hotel; she merely sat about, preoccupied with her thoughts, waiting for something unlikely to turn up.

Maggie went to her in the sitting-room used as a dormitory. No one else was there. Beatrice was staring out of the window.

'You weren't at the party, then,' Maggie observed superfluously.

'I wouldn't have been much use,' Beatrice replied in the flat tone she had adopted of late.

'Lord love us, what they've been saying about you's true, then. You have got the glooms.'

'Yes, I have, so they can say what they like.'

'Well, I dunno about not being any use, but you can be to me. I want some advice, please.'

'What sort?'

'Professional.'

'I no longer have a profession.'

'Oh aye? Been struck off, have you?'

Beatrice turned angrily, but Maggie went on, wagging a finger at her.

'I'll tell you something. When I first came to the camp I didn't take to you much. A right bossy cow, I thought. But I did start to admire your guts. You wouldn't throw your hand in then, nor you wouldn't let anybody else throw theirs in, either.'

Taken aback, Beatrice had no retort. She said, 'What did you want to ask me about?'

Maggie's assuredness had left her suddenly. She faltered, 'Well . . . the thing is . . . I've been feeling a bit off colour . . . Oh, heck. I think I've got a bun in the oven.'

Beatrice stared. 'But surely . . . We've been in Singapore less than a month . . .'

'Didn't happen here. It was two months back – in the camp. No, not a Nip. Kate and I broke out one afternoon to try to get to the men's camp, and we met one of 'em on the road. He and me made up for lost time. Go on – look at me like Kate did, as if I was a trollop.'

'I've given up casting judgements, Maggie. How many times did you see this man?'

'Only the once. Mind you, it was quite a once.'

Beatrice asked her to sit down and after a number of questions gave her a superficial examination. At last she

218

said, 'Well, it looks as if you're right, so far as one can be certain at this stage. We'll have to arrange some proper tests up at the hospital. If they are positive . . . what will you do?'

'Not go looking for the father, that's for sure. I didn't even ask his name. I'll have to make me mind up quick some way, though, shan't I?'

It was that universal fixer Jake Haulter who offered to make it up for her. Her leaving his bed hastily to be sick in the bathroom was no surprise on the morning after a boozy party with champagne, Marmite and other pleasures. But when she was sick again next morning, following no such excesses, he quickly put two and two together.

'You're pregnant, aren't you,' he said, making it sound casual.

'You guessed?'

'Call it intuition. Wasn't I going to be told?'

'I dunno. I only knew for definite yesterday.' She told him about her visit to Beatrice, and how the whole thing had come about. He couldn't help grinning – it seemed so typical of her – but he added seriously, 'If you want help I've got a contact who's got a few other girls I've known out of a similar spot. She's medically qualified, so there'd be no risk . . .'

To his surprise she snapped back, 'You can stuff your contacts! You think you can fix anything, don't you? A word in the right ear, and Bob's your uncle. Well, it just so happens I don't want fixing up.'

'Take it easy. I'm sorry. I shouldn't have jumped to conclusions. Are you Catholic or something?'

'You don't have to be Catholic to care about an unborn kid.'

'Well, if it's a question of finding someone to adopt it . . . You know your room here's yours as long as you want it, and if you need money to tide you over . . .'

Her anger gone, she kissed him and said, 'Thanks, Jake. Sorry I went for you like that.'

'It's OK. We could get hitched, if that'd help. No strings, of course,' he hastened to add, 'but it'd give the baby a name.'

'I can never make you out,' she said, moved to tears. 'Blast you! Now you've ruined my bloody mascara.'

'I mean it,' he persisted.

'I know, love. Thanks, but you don't want to be lumbered with a wife, even without no ties to it. I suppose I'll go back to England with the others – if there's still room on the ship.'

'Don't let that worry you. I used to work for the P & O, remember. I've kept up some contacts.'

'Trust you!'

'We might have made a go of it, you and me.'

'Not a hope in hell. When your time comes it'll be some nice rich widow. Hey, there's one in our lot at Raffles, Dutchie, Mrs Van Meyer. Nice armful when she's back to normal, I reckon, and loaded the other way, according to her.'

'If I can't have you, Maggie, I'll play the field a while longer, thanks.'

'Bless you, love.'

When Maggie told Beatrice her decision she got a concerned look in response.

'You realise it'll mean a home for unmarried mothers.'

'Well, I 'spose there's a lot of us about. Can't be all that bad.'

'From what I hear, Maggie, it's still pretty grim. I worked in one once. Girls forced to scrub floors right up to going into labour, and then no painkillers, as a punishment, Oh dear, there must be something better than that for you. I'd take you home with me, only I'll be going to an old father and . . .'

'It's all right. No need to spell it out, but thanks.'

'What about Dorothy and her place? What a pity she flew out yesterday before this came up.'

'I wouldn't have asked her. Me with a baby, and her having lost hers, you know.'

'Still, knowing what an unpredictable girl our Dorothy is, who knows?'

'Don't bother. Unmarried Mums, here I come.'

But it was not to be. When she told him, Jake Haulter's reaction was the same as Beatrice's.

'Not good enough,' he said firmly. 'Dot's the answer.' When Maggie wheeled out her reply to that he shook his head. 'A new life, a new place, and a new Dot, you'll see. Besides, she'll have to get used to kids sometime.'

'Not through me she won't.'

He gripped her shoulders and looked hard into her eyes.

'Know what you are, my girl? Perfect martyr material. Rotten childhood, tatty jobs, prison camp, pregnant by the first chap you chance to clap eyes on. Isn't it time you broke the habit?'

'Not at Dot's expense.'

We'll see about that, he thought, and went to find the nearest telephone. He spoke to Dorothy in London and explained at length Maggie's position and its implications; she responded to the situation immediately – she would be waiting for Maggie at the house in Edgware. Dorothy had not said it, but Jake tactfully added, in relating their conversation to a flabbergasted Maggie, that Dot had realised she would need help to run her house as lodgings and had already regretted not having asked Maggie if she would go in with her.

'You sure she won't mind the nipper?' Maggie asked when she had stopped indignantly protesting that she wasn't having Jake or anyone else running her life for her.

'Said she's looking forward to being its godmother,' he lied. 'By the way, I got you a little something for it.' He handed her a bulky envelope.

'What's this?'

'Occupation postage stamps. Know how we were told to burn the Nip occupation currency? Well, I didn't. I gathered up all I could get and took it straight down to the Post Office and bought up every Jap stamp I could lay hands on before they could get round to burning them. The stamp dealers in London will pay through the nose for them. Make sure you hold out for the best price, though. Wish I could be there to deal for you.'

'Wish you could, you jammy so-and-so,' Maggie replied, and meant it sincerely.

18 Yamauchi

Maggie had chaffed that Jake could do worse than take up with that wealthy widow Mrs Van Meyer. What she did not know was that the Dutchwoman was at present going through the throes of not knowing whether she was either wealthy or a widow.

She had gone to the bank where her personal shopping account was established and found, extending far along the street, a queue of former internees, like herself seeking to find out on what footing their finances stood. With growing impatience she waited for her turn at the counter to come, and then it was only to be told, after much searching through the files, that the cheques she had issued in the heady abandon of freedom had already taken her to the overdraft limit authorised years earlier. She demanded to see the manager forthwith.

'If you would be good enough to join the queue, madam,' invited the overworked teller, indicating another line of glum-looking customers whose slumped demeanour seemed to indicate that they had been waiting days rather than hours.

'Young man,' she fumed, 'I have just spent over three years queueing, in order to find nothing at the end of it. Given the bank's ridiculous meanness, I see no likelihood of getting any better results from waiting further.'

Whatever relief it gave to express her dissatisfaction, the fact remained that she had to leave the building empty-handed, without the fresh chequebook she had demanded. She needed money. In another street she saw another queue, and recognised the nature of the premises at the head of it. Keeping her face averted from passers-by she joined it, ashamed at being the only European in it behind a lot of native men and women carrying bundles; but at least when she got to the partitioned counter some money – though it was less than she had confidently anticipated – was forthcoming in exchange for the jewelled ring that she had removed from a finger once so white and plump and perfectly manicured.

'You must understand that it is not for myself,' she explained loudly to the laconic Eurasian clerk as he scrutinised the jewel through an eyeglass. 'I am merely doing a kindness for a poor woman who is too ill to leave her bed.'

The clerk didn't trouble to comment. He had heard everything since the formerly wealthy ones of Singapore had come flocking back to their changed lifestyle.

Later she bewailed her situation to Christina, who had decided that, despite her pride in her half-British blood, she would be staying in Malaya.

'You are fortunate to have a choice,' Mrs Van Meyer told her. 'For me there is no prospect. My husband dead, my beautiful house in Sumatra destroyed.'

'You don't know that,' Christina reminded her.

'I am sure of it. Every day more Dutch arrive from there and Java with stories of what those native upstarts are doing. As for my poor Jan, I need no stupid piece of paper to tell me that he is dead. Better I had died in the camps, as I so nearly did.'

'Haven't you any relatives in Holland? What about your husband's family you've always talked so much about?'

'Of course, they would welcome me with open arms. But I have lived in the East since I was a girl. I am too old to start again.'

'You're not old at all. You're in your prime. And look how people who were thought to be dead are turning up all the time.'

'No, no. It is too bad of Jan. If he cannot be alive, then

he might at least be properly dead and the bank can settle his estate in my favour.'

The effect of this cynical pronouncement was spoiled almost immediately by the approach of Phyllis Bristow.

'Mrs Van Meyer, we've just had a call from the Dutch RAPWI. Perhaps you'd better sit down.'

Mrs Van Meyer remained standing.

'It is news of my Jan?'

'Yes. Some refugees arrived yesterday from your part of the island.'

'And they bring proof that he is dead?'

'On the contrary. It seems he is very much alive.'

Only at that point did Mrs Van Meyer collapse into a chair, stunned.

'Poor old Dominica,' Marion said to Clifford in the bar that evening. 'She told me she's dreading having to go back to her husband and the island. Actually opened her heart to me. He's fifteen years older than she, and they hadn't got on well for years.'

'Glad enough to have his money to spend, I dare say,' Clifford grunted.

'Oh yes. Marrying a Van Meyer was a great catch for her. Her family hadn't much at all. Apparently he doted on her when she was young and pretty, but she couldn't give him a son and everything fell apart between them. Just went on being married to keep up appearances. I feel sorry for her.'

'Sad none of you could stand much of her in the camps.'

Marion grimaced and made no reply. She knew that was another inference he had drawn more from reading her diary than from anything she had told him. That intrusion into her privacy still rankled.

'By the way,' he told her, 'your friend Yamauchi's been brought here. He's under lock and key. That ought to cheer all of you.'

In fact, the news, when she passed it on, got a varied

225

reception. Beatrice was delighted to hear that their head gaoler for all those years was now in Changi gaol himself.

'Under the ground would be even better,' she added.

Generally, the reaction was less embittered. Retribution was more a preoccupation of those in charge of organising it than of the ones for whom they were partly acting. It had become their new job, and they meant to do it well. The erstwhile victims, for the most part, simply wanted to get on putting their own lives together, not taking others' apart.

Marion lost no time in getting in touch with Jake Haulter. He arrived at the house in his car next morning after Clifford had gone off to work.

'Maggie had told me you were working out at Changi,' Marion said.

'That's right. A nice demolition contract for some rat-ridden huts and things. What can I do for you, Mrs Jefferson?'

'Marion, please. To tell you the truth, I'm hoping to visit our old commandant, Major Yamauchi. They've got him locked up there.'

'Want to punch him in the eye?'

'Not at all. We don't have to treat them as they treated us.'

'A very Christian sentiment.'

'Whether I'll be allowed to see him I don't know.'

'There should be no problem, I'd think. Did you know that Christina Campbell's been already?'

'She told me. But there was a sergeant breathing down their necks all the time. I'd like to see him on his own.'

'Say who you are.'

'Caesar's wife being above suspicion, you mean?'

'Quite. Or could it be that Caesar doesn't know about the proposed visit?'

'I wouldn't be going as Clifford's wife.'

'In that case I recommend a leaf from my own rulebook. Bypass red tape.'

'How?'

'Ignore it. Ask permission to do something and you lay yourself open to being refused.'

'I can't just walk in.'

'You could – with the right person. Someone who knows his way around. Someone who's owed a favour by the chap in charge of Yamauchi's block.'

'How do you know what block he's in?' asked Marion, astonished.

Jake tapped his nose. 'I make it my business to know things. How did you know I might be able to help?'

Marion smiled.

By late that morning she was being shown into a small cell in the gaol whose memory would haunt its European survivors for the rest of their days and disturb their nights with horrors. Yamauchi was sitting on the small bed with his back to her, writing a letter. He had taken no notice of the door opening, but when he heard Marion's voice he turned, then struggled to his feet and made a low bow with an indrawn hiss of respect.

'Mrs Jefferson.'

'Hello, Major.'

It was not all that long since she had last seen him but he looked much older and greyer. His skin was blotched and raw with sores. His face, which had been chubby when she had first known him, was a film of skin over protruding cheekbones.

'I have not expect to see you again,' he said.

'I thought I'd better find out how you were. Are they treating you well?'

'Yes, thank you. But for Japanese soldier death is better than imprisonment. You sit down, please?'

He indicated the bed and she sat. He remained standing.

'I am writing letter to my daughter,' he said.

'They allow you paper, then?'

'Christine Campbell brought it for me. I write letter, but I do not know if my daughter receive it.'

'Oh, I'm sure it will be sent,' she said, not forgetting how deliberately neglectful the Japanese had been of their prisoners' mail.

'I mean I do not know if she is alive. She or my grandson. They live in Nagasaki.'

'I see. Would you like me to make some enquiries?'

'No, please. Not to trouble.'

'I could get on to the Red Cross.'

'I am most grateful.' He bowed. 'You are looking more well, Mrs Jefferson.'

'I'm feeling much better, thank you.'

'I have met your husband. He has interrogate me. He is good soldier.'

Marion hesitated before saying, 'Major, there's something I want to tell you. I kept a diary in the camp. A second one, I mean, after the first was destroyed.'

'Ah, so. But I know. I know that Christina Campbell steal paper from my office.'

'You overlooked it?'

'It was not much.'

'All the same, they are going to use it in evidence against you. I'd like you to know that I tried to prevent it.'

'Why? If you write truth.'

'One puts things in a diary that . . . at the time . . . Well, it's never simple, is it?'

'No,' he said. 'But they will hang me. If only I had committed honourable death, like Captain Sato.'

'We must all meet our God sooner or later, Major Yamauchi. We can only hope He will be merciful.'

He bowed again.

'Goodbye,' Marion said, and left abruptly, before emotion should choke her.

When Clifford came home that evening she could sense that he knew. He made some light conversation, to which she replied in kind, and then she came out with it abruptly.

'I went up to Changi today.'

'With Jake Haulter, I gather. You might have told me before the event, you know.'

'I didn't tell you because I knew you'd stop me. I went to visit Yamauchi.'

'Darling, how d'you think that must have looked? Brigadier's wife visiting one of . . .'

'I didn't go as your wife. I went as ex-leader.'

'You really think they'd have let you in if you hadn't been my wife? I don't know if you're being naïve or if you're doing this deliberately. That man is going to be tried as a war criminal. There's enough evidence in your diary alone to hang him.'

'That's why I went. He probably lost his daughter and grandchild in Nagasaki. I wanted him to know that one can still feel humanity.'

'He didn't show you much when he held back those drugs and cut your rations to virtually nil.'

'We dropped those bombs on them. Wasn't that enough tit-for-tat?'

'I just don't understand you, Marion.'

'No, you don't,' she burst out. 'You don't understand that I'm not the person I used to be, a well-groomed line-toeing reflection of yourself, without a mind of my own.'

'Rubbish! I never expected that before, and I don't now. What I do think I'm entitled to is a certain awareness of my position. I know you've been through a lot, and I've tried to make allowances . . .'

'And, my God, it's been a strain, hasn't it? You don't like my attitudes. You resent my friends . . .'

She crossed abruptly to where the bottles and glasses stood and poured herself a savage gin.

'I don't resent your friends,' Clifford was saying, his voice raised. 'What I do resent is playing second fiddle to them. Half the time you're over at Raffles with them. You're more concerned with their problems than with mine.'

'They *have* more problems than you, Clifford. So have I. If you can't come round to seeing that, then . . .'

'Then what?'

'. . . Then I don't think there's much future for us together.'

He stared at her. Fortunately at that moment the door opened and May entered to ask if they would be ready to dine soon. The domestic interruption served to cool the mutual hostility, and they ate without making further reference to the subject. It had to return, though, and did when they were alone. Clifford made the first move, to which Marion riposted with the classic response, 'There's nothing more to be said. We'll only end up bickering.'

'Oh yes there is,' he told her firmly. 'You may be content to throw twenty years of marriage down the drain, but I'm not.'

'You think it's what *I* want?' she rounded on him. 'Don't you think I'd give anything to turn the clock back?'

'Then for Christ's sake why not?'

'Because I've changed. My feelings, attitudes, everything's different. For the last three years I've been *someone*, a person in my own right, not just the colonel's lady.'

'You were never just that, Marion. Oh, blast that bloody camp!'

She said more reasonably, 'It wasn't just the camp. It started before that. I was all set to go back home in '41 . . .'

'Only because of Ben.'

'Not only that. I was fed up with life out East. I felt totally redundant.'

'You weren't redundant to me, darling.' He took her unresisting hand. 'I'm sure we can still make a go of it. Look, I've been thinking. Why don't you go home? See Ben, get it all out of your system, then come back in the summer. By then it'll all be less hectic for me. The trials will be well under way. The military will have handed over most things to the civil authorities. We'd be able to spend as much time together as we can't now, which is all my fault.'

'It's not your fault at all, darling,' she objected. 'It's your job. You have to do it.'

'Yes, well . . .'

'You know, I'd be happier doing a job, too.'

'Out here?'

'Something worthwhile. I can't go back to sitting at home watching the servants doing everything, with a bit of shopping and cosy teas at Raffles thrown in.'

'There is an alternative,' he said, looking at her seriously in the eyes.

'What's that?'

'We could have another baby.'

Marion's mouth almost dropped open. Clifford pressed on.

'You've always said your happiest time was when Ben was little.'

She found her voice again. 'Can you honestly see it happening? We've not exactly been getting anywhere in that line these last few weeks, and I'm not in my first flush any more.'

'But worth the try. If it came off it'd make up for missing so much of Ben's childhood. If it didn't, well, I'm sure there'll be jobs going . . .'

'Not just a time-filler . . .'

'I doubt if the old days of *tuans'* wives lolling about under parasols will come back. That's not the future I see for Singapore, or anywhere else. Surely we've learnt that lesson?' He paused and then added, 'I do understand, you know – your resenting the fact that *I* was able to be with Ben. You think I wouldn't gladly have changed places with you? The thought of your going through all that, while I sat on my backside in an office . . .'

Marion asked, 'Is that why you feel yourself personally responsible for getting Yamauchi?'

'I'll never understand why you defend him.'

'Because of all the things I *didn't* put in my diary. The things that would have explained him as a person, a Japanese acting according to his lights, his upbringing, his nationality. Duty first, instant obedience. But I think Yamauchi was one who did question whether it was the right way. In different circumstances you might have respected him.'

The telephone rang. With a sigh Clifford got up to lift the receiver. After a moment he beckoned Marion to take the call. When she had hung up, her expression was one of concern. She came back and told him, 'Phyllis Bristow. She thought I should know Joss has been attacked in the street by some thug.'

'How bad is it?'

'Bad enough for hospital – and at her age . . .'

'I'll drive you over,' Clifford said. And in the car she agreed to his plan for their future; and before getting out at the hospital she leaned over and kissed him on the lips.

19 The Foundation

The door of the relief centre being run by Stephen Wentworth and Joss bore a notice in English, Malay and Chinese: 'Open 11 am – 4 pm: Please leave urgent messages in box outside.'

Beside the door was a board on which were pinned or stuck photographs, scraps of description and other pathetic details and pleas for news of the whereabouts of people of all ages, many of them doubtless now dead or certainly no longer recognisable from the prewar studio portraits, wedding photographs and blurred snapshots.

Joss and Stephen were there every day and often long into the evening, bickering as they worked, abusing one another every so often. Yet they were providing a service that officialdom had not got around to matching on behalf of those too ignorant, or bewildered or foolish to go through 'the proper channels' to seek medical help, food and cast-off clothing. The finance came from Joss's funds in London; the provisions were largely supplied from Jake Haulter's under-the-counter sources and his contacts in the hospitals.

The work carried its risks, not least from the authorities. A particularly nasty occurrence involved Joss and Christina Campbell – she also lent an occasional hand – who were picked up by a police patrol suspicious of the contents of a hold-all they were carrying between them. A search revealed black-market goods and naturally led to accusations of trafficking for personal profit. A search of the centre uncovered the truth, so that there were no charges, but the place was left in chaos and Joss, who clung to her opinion of the police, forged during her Suffragette days, and let them know it, was reported to RAPWI as an undesirable influence.

Phyllis Bristow pleaded with her to accept the berth available on the liner due to take her friends home next week. She talked it over with Stephen at the centre later.

'I told her I'll go, but only for as long as I think fit, and that's that. How about you, by the way?'

'What?'

'Going back to England, you old fool. Shall you?'

'Oh no. I've decided not.'

'Not even for a visit?'

'What to? A younger sister I didn't even like and can hardly remember? A London I shan't recognise. I believe even my club's gone.'

'I've been thinking,' Joss said. 'We could do with some skilled medical help.'

'Fatuous sort of remark.'

'Not when there's the best bloody doctor who ever laid hands on me mooching about Raffles because her eyes are going and they won't employ her.'

'Beatrice Whatsername?'

'Mason. Thinks she's finished. Lost all sense of purpose. Even her crusade to get Yamauchi the chop seems to have burnt itself out. Think what she could be doing here.'

'For a pigheaded old woman you do have the odd bright notion. D'you think she'd come?'

'It'd be my pighead against hers. I'll talk her into it.'

Stephen chuckled. 'I'm glad you turned up in spite of everything. Saved my life.'

'Saved my own, too. I was in danger of slipping into graceful old age.'

'Graceful? Not a chance.'

She did manage to persuade Beatrice to come and help, at least until the ship sailed. A week was better than nothing, and it lifted Beatrice's morale correspondingly, even if the two ancients did exist in a perpetual muddle and resisted all her efforts to sort them out. She fell quite enough into their ways to return their thoughtless insults in kind, and all three worked well together.

'Considered coming back?' Joss asked her without preliminary one day. Stephen was away fetching supplies.

'Back?'

'Here. This centre. From England. God, do I have to spell every word?'

'You mean . . .'

Joss groaned as if trying to get through to an idiot.

'*Yes*! Stephen's staying on. I'm only going home to say goodbye to a few relatives I don't much like and who can't stand me. Suffragette in family, doncher know. Let the tone down. Then I'm coming back to work on with the old fool for these poor sods. Think of anything better to do with yourself?'

'Actually, no.'

'Actually, neither can I. You've no ties there, have you?'

'None that I wouldn't rather sever.'

'Done, then?'

'Well . . .'

'Good girl. We need a doctor. Doctor needs a practice. Hey presto!'

Beatrice felt her whole being suddenly transformed. She almost regretted the interruption of having to go to England and back, but it was all arranged now. There were only a few days to go. Excitement was beginning to mount, in spite of the sensation of impending separation among the women.

Kate was going back to Australia, to study for a medical degree. Mrs Van Meyer was returning to the dubious pleasure of restoration to her husband and his large estates, more especially of the latter. She felt consoled that at least she would be rich again, and harboured an inner feeling, gained from her camp experience, that she might just be able to gain ascendancy over him and win his haughty family's acceptance with some ready tales of her war heroism, which she was rapidly beginning to believe herself.

Christina Campbell was staying in Singapore, to live with a friend of her mother's in the Chinese quarter. There was clearly no shortage of good jobs in prospect for her. Sister Ulrica having gone through a long and spiritually traumatic period of doubt had reconsidered her passive role and had got permission to work in a leper settlement.

Maggie itched to be back in harness with Dot, two of a kind who later that year would be three. As for Marion and Clifford, the brief explosion, the frank appraisal of one another in a new light, and their plan for the future would soon ease their tensions and wipe away the feeling of being strangers obligated to one another by old bonds. They were on the threshold of a new love, under Nature's approving guidance.

And then came this telephone call from Phyllis Bristow. Marion and Clifford sped to the hospital but met Stephen coming away from it, looking bad-tempered and sorry for himself.

'Won't let me in to see the old trout,' he grumbled. 'She's resting and I've got this damned cold they don't want her to catch. No, no, you mustn't risk any damned germs, either.'

But they insisted on driving him back to his centre, and he told them on the way what had happened.

He and Joss had been walking away from the centre that evening when there had been a rush from a side alley and a youth had snatched Joss's capacious handbag. She had had the presence of mind to hold on, so he had pushed her violently, throwing her to the ground. Stephen was not nearly good enough on his feet to hope to cope with him, and he had got away with the bag.

'Little gangsters all over the place these days,' he grumbled. 'Not like prewar.'

'But what about Joss?' was Marion's concern.

'Well, she was lying there. I tried to help her up, but for all that she's so frail she was too much for me, and I could

236

see her arm and side were hurt. I didn't want to make it worse.'

'How do they say she is?'

'Cracked ribs and a fracture. Her bad arm, at that. Thank God she's in a proper hospital this time – with all due respects to Bea Mason.'

When they had dropped Stephen they drove on to Raffles to join the others for a drink, over which there was no other topic than Joss.

'She's broken more bones than I've had hot dinners and bounced back, despite her age and camp conditions,' Beatrice reassured them.

'All the same,' Phyllis said dubiously, 'I doubt she's going to be on that boat.'

'Want a bet?' said Kate.

They all planned to go to the hospital next day, but it was agreed at length that Beatrice should go alone, as the one best fitted to find out Joss's true condition. As she pointed out, there might be shock symptoms which would make it undesirable for them all to go crowding in.

She found Joss in a corner of a small ward, in a bed next to a window. Rather than ask for the blind to be drawn to keep the strong sun out of her eyes she had put on her old broad-rimmed straw hat at a rakish angle. Her ribs were strapped and her arm in plaster. Her eyes were bright, but even Beatrice's defective vision showed her that Joss was weaker than she wished to appear. Her breathing was painful.

'My dear Bea, this is good of you,' she wheezed.

'Don't talk if it hurts. I just came to check up on you. Looks as though you'll do.'

'Course I'll do! How's the centre?'

'I'm going on there now. The authorities have come across with a load of medicines.'

'Tophole!'

The ward sister approached. 'Lady Josslyn. There's a Mr Ling to see you. I told him you've had your one visitor for the morning, but he says you've sent an urgent message.'

'That's right. Must see Ling. D'you mind, Bea?'

'Not a bit. May I come this afternoon, Sister?'

'Course she may. Let 'em all come.'

'No. Just Dr Mason today. We'll see how we are in the morning.'

'Bloody martinet,' Joss returned. Sister Pickering grinned at Beatrice, who leant over to kiss the withered cheek and leave.

A smartly dressed Chinese in a European tropical suit was sitting on the chair in the passage. He had a shabby briefcase on his knees. 'Mr Ling,' Sister Pickering invited, and he went in.

Beatrice returned in the late afternoon. 'How is she?' she asked outside the ward.

'Not the easiest of patients. A law unto herself.'

'You're telling me!'

'She must have been developing a cold. It's come out with a rush. Poor old thing must be in agony when she sneezes. Don't you catch it.'

Beatrice went in, knowing where to find Joss this time. The straw hat was lying on the floor beside the bed. The plastered arm was stretched down along the sheet. Joss was dozing, undisturbed by the chatter of visiting time.

'Only me, lazybones,' Beatrice said. 'Come on. Tenko!'

Something about Joss's complete stillness alerted her medical instinct. She reached gently for the other arm and put her fingers on the inner wrist. There was no pulse.

'Oh, Joss!' Beatrice choked. 'Don't go. Don't leave us now.'

But she had.

There was nothing of unseemly haste about holding the funeral next afternoon. The ship was being prepared for them to board first thing the morning after. They were all at the graveside: Beatrice, Maggie, Kate, Mrs Van Meyer,

238

Christina, Sister Ulrica, Stephen, Jake, Phyllis, and Marion and Clifford. Each of them scattered earth when the words had been said and finally Stephen stepped forward and after a moment's hesitation let something flutter down on to the coffin. It was Joss's old straw hat.

They gathered at the Jeffersons' for the combination of wake and farewell party. Mr Ling, who had attended the funeral but had stood discreetly at a distance from the grave, had approached them as they turned to leave and said that he had something to say to them all on Lady Josslyn's behalf, so he had been invited to go along with them.

They were determined that it should not be a gloomy gathering, and drinks flowed and plates of food circulated as Joss would have wished had she been there. Mr Ling chose his moment and asked in a raised voice if he might have their attention.

'A moment only, ladies and gentlemen, if you please. Apart from having the honour of Lady Holbrook's friendship since many years, I am a solicitor. She sent for me to the hospital in order to make a will, not knowing what had become of her former one – most probably destroyed.'

He drew it from his inner pocket and unfolded it.

'Aside from bequests to certain family and friends in England, she has left to her good friends Mrs Marion Jefferson, Sister Ulrica, Miss Kate Norris, Miss Christina Campbell, Mrs Dominica Van Meyer, Miss Margaret Thorpe and Mrs Dorothy Bennett the sum of one thousand pounds each . . .' He glanced at the paper and read with a slight smile, ' "to be spent on enjoying themselves and *not* paying any bills".'

It brought a little titter, following on the gasp of initial surprise. The little man read again: ' "To Doctor Beatrice Mason and Mr Stephen Wentworth I leave the sum of five hundred pounds per annum each, on the understanding that they will be joint trustees of the centre as a charitable foundation. *However*, they must oversee the building and running of the Foundation personally, otherwise the fifty-two and a half thousand pounds will be donated to the Fawcett Society."

'I believe, ladies and gentlemen, that that society has something to do with Suffragettes.' Mr Ling bowed, and stepped back out of the limelight.